THE CURSE OF BECTON MANOR

Patricia Ayling

Burning Chair Limited, Trading as Burning Chair Publishing
61 Bridge Street, Kington HR5 3DJ

www.burningchairpublishing.com

By Patricia Ayling
Edited by Simon Finnie and Peter Oxley
Book cover design by Burning Chair Publishing

First published by Burning Chair Publishing, 2021

ISBN: 978-1-912946-15-0

'Thou shalt not suffer a witch to live'

Exodus 22-18

Chapter One

1957

I knew nothing of the original family who had lived in the old Tudor manor house on the edge of Derbyshire. Except that, according to my Uncle Charlie, the house was said to be haunted.

I didn't believe in ghosts. The house and whoever lived in it was of no interest to me; in fact it sounded like a monstrosity. At nearly sixteen, and in a school where I was perfectly happy, I wanted to stay where I was. I didn't want to move house; and definitely not to a run-down pile in the middle of nowhere.

As we approached the small village of Becton in my dad's battered old Morris Minor, the exhaust labouring as it fought its way up the hill, I noticed only a few small houses, a couple of little shops and some old cottages; a village long gone to sleep.

'This must be it.' announced my dad, suddenly driving even more slowly. We entered a narrow track, rather like ones usually saved just for tractors, and came to a stop. 'Oh my God,' he half muttered as part of a large dark building came into view.

After getting out of the car, I stepped out into the sultry still heat of that day in July 1957.

My younger sister by two years, Annabel, was eager to keep up as we walked to a rusty iron gate just a couple of yards from where we had parked. The dirt track was lined with laurel hedging, but the gate stood in the centre of a clearing wide enough for a vehicle but extensively overgrown. Annabel ran ahead and pushed at the gate, which creaked before almost falling off its hinge. The remaining walk, about forty or so yards down a gentle slope, was through tall willowy grass. Spiky weeds partially hid an upturned pram, with only three rusty wheel rims.

There it was, dismal and derelict. A manor house, built in 1593, for God's sake. We just stood and stared.

The rotten front door had some weather-worn initials above it; maybe a letter "H". It was hard to tell.

Filthy windows, three sticking out from the roof, were framed with sheets of grey silk-like cobwebs; thick in each corner, years of spider work. I brushed away troublesome flies while feeling not the heat of the day, but the heat of sheer anger and frustration.

Mum and Dad were waiting for the solicitor who was coming to give us the keys for our first viewing.

Becton Manor had been empty for years, but my Uncle Charlie, a war correspondent, had bought it in 1940. Although he survived the war, he fell ill while working in the Far East: some kind of dysentery. He had lived in it for a short while but was concerned about strange 'goings-on'. My mother of course, chose to disregard that knowledge. She, the new owner of an Elizabethan manor house, would be the envy of all her friends.

I loved our old house. *This can't be happening,* I remember thinking.

Twisting her index finger around her long dark curly hair, Annabel twitched her nose before announcing, 'Gran says old houses give you an aura.'

'An aura?' I teased her. 'What, you mean ghosts and ghoulies and stuff?'

'I don't know.'

I remember thinking it might mean bleak and dark, or a disappointing feeling. The result of those strangling weeds, ugly nettles, and thorny shrubs failing to hide that upturned pram. As we walked towards the side of the house, empty tin cans emerged among mysterious bags of rubbish.

I kicked one of the old tin cans—hard—away from the edge of the overgrown path. Mickey, our old but active Golden Labrador, took chase. No. An aura was something special. Becton Manor was not.

Annabel tutted. 'It's no good, Tom, being miserable. You'll soon be sixteen. You could get a job. Down the coalmine or the steelworks. Not bad money either. That Janet James's dad works down the pit and she has loads of posh clothes and they bought a telly not long back.'

A good idea: get a job with a wage. Get away from all the jibes about not doing homework, not washing properly, picking my spots and growing too quickly out of trousers costing a fortune. Oh, and taking too much notice of girls. That last one always surprised me because, in my opinion, I simply avoided them. They didn't seem to like looking at me either.

Anyway, money would come in handy; although it might take a while to save up and get away from this monstrosity.

The click-clacking sound of my mother's black patent shoes broke my train of thought. I watched her excitedly peering through windows while adjusting her little blue hat.

'Come on, Albert,' she demanded. 'Mr Easton isn't due for another five minutes. Let's have a quick look round. Oh, this is wonderful, so old. All ours eh? Oh you can see from the style that it's definitely Elizabethan. We can do so much to it: just look at all the potential. I can't wait to get the keys. Oh, Albert, I've always loved history and now this is mine... Ours.'

Dad surveyed the weeds with disgust and his expression got worse as he spotted the eaten-away masonry and rotten window frames, battered by centuries of relentless winds and rain. I could tell that he certainly didn't agree with Mum.

'Oh, of course. Yes dear, lots of potential.'

I laugh now, when I think of all the times Dad agreed with Mum just to keep the peace. It exasperated me then, but it was at that point that I realised his long time limp, caused apparently by trapped shrapnel in the Second World War, was exaggerated in times of stress.

Becton Manor was a big project and probably after his long shifts working at the local lead mine, far too much work for him, but he would do anything for Mum.

Just then we heard a car pull up on the track. 'Oh, that'll be Mr Easton now. Shall we go back, Albert and meet him?' Mum reminded me of an excitable little girl.

'Yes dear.'

Mr Easton was a short stocky man, aged about fortyish, who gave us funny looks as he walked over. We were introduced by my effervescent Mum.

'Oh hello, children.' His smile wasn't genuine and I didn't like him. 'You have a lot to do here.' He sort of smirked, his eyes briefly scanning my parents up and down as though he was judging their ability to tackle such a large project.

'This place has not been inhabited since…well before the war,' he continued. 'You need to check that financially it is an affordable project for you. It will need some heating, but I'm afraid the electricity won't yet be connected. This is a very rural area, you must understand. Anyway, I have the keys but you must expect the door to be warped. I think it was replaced at the back half of the last century, as were the windows. They're not original lead, of course.'

As he fumbled with the keys, I saw his face transform, rather like a plump tomato and his chest was heaving up and down with frustration.

I heard Dad whisper to Mum: 'That man sees himself as superior. Insinuating we have no money to put things right… Bloody cheek…'

'Shh…'

Mr Easton found the correct key and pushed hard on the door with his broad shoulder until, with a creak, it opened a couple of feet before it got stuck again. He was beginning to sweat and stank of alcohol mixed with body odour.

We entered a large hall. A damp fustiness hit us as we walked in and around the space. The lino on the floor was cracked, and wide stairs led to a galleried landing off to the right.

'We can't go upstairs yet,' Mr Easton said. 'Too dangerous I'm afraid.'

I looked up the stairs and could see lots of holes and splintered wood. I reached out to grab the bannister but it shook with the slightest touch. Mr Easton glared at me and I remember thinking he looked like Joker in my Batman comic.

There seemed to be so many doors. The one on the left led to some sort of sitting room and the bigger room on the right was perhaps used for dining. Both had huge, dirty fireplaces. The dining room one was an inglenook. Annabel went to stand in it and we giggled, much to the solicitor's annoyance.

There was a small passageway the other side of the staircase which led to a large room, and Mr Easton hurried on, like a little kid needing to be in the lead. He stood in the doorway. 'This room was the scullery.' Another false smile.

It was a long room, the full length of the house with a dining area on the left and kitchen on the right. Old French windows opened out to…well…a jungle.

I tried to open them but the glass frames rattled, they were so loose.

'Don't touch those, sonny.' God, he was so pompous.

We then entered a storeroom on the left, adjoining the dining area, before he led us to a back yard. Here is when Mr Pompous fell from grace. While showing us the outside loo, which was a few paces along the yard, he marched into the thickest cobweb I have ever seen.

What followed was a slapstick comedy performance far exceeding that of Charlie Chaplin. Watching this superior being throwing his arms about and shrieking like a banshee brought a howl of laughter from Dad, who, when noticing the glare of Mr Pompous, promptly cleared his throat and apologised, looking down to hide his grin with his hand.

The solicitor regained his composure. 'One other thing for which you will be pleased: it's summer. You have the outside lavatory, but there is no bathroom.'

He looked at us with arched eyebrows to gauge our reactions. 'That will be another expense for you. There is a cesspit towards the bottom of the garden. We'll walk to it. This will need to be pumped out quite frequently... You don't want rats, after all.'

I knew those last words would be by far the most irritating for Dad. He hated rats.

'Huh'. By this time, his limp was massively exaggerated, his right hip was sagging to one side.

'Don't limp, Albert. Everything will be fine,' snapped Mum, but she was looking at me. 'And don't you look so glum either. Come on.'

Just like my mother when she wants her own way. Her voice crisp, everybody gets it in the neck. Dad of course was limping on purpose to attract attention and I purposely made glum faces just to annoy her. Thrusting my hands in my pockets I slouched, cursing the thorny sticky brambles, bees, willowy weeds, and most of all that snob showing us around this monstrosity. I was suddenly bored.

'Bloody hell!' Puffing, I stood still and let them all carry on to the bottom of the jungle. The air was humid.

I turned to see the back of the house. It looked huge.

So many bulky chimneys. A very solid, wide stone wall at the left side of the house looked strangely out of place, the rest of the house being mainly brick. It took up almost the whole of the wall until it tapered towards the eaves, becoming a majestic chimney.

Then a shadowy flicker of a movement in an upstairs window caught my attention. A face—a small face, I was sure of it—disappeared as quickly as it came. A trick of the falling light?

Motionless, I concentrated on the window, willing it to return. The whole house turned a soft purple colour as the evening dusk began to drop. It was all so eerily quiet. Maybe it was an aura. I willed the experience to happen again, just once more. I was totally mesmerised; I couldn't look away from the window. Could someone actually be inside, upstairs? Perhaps squatters?

The magical silence abruptly ended. The biggest black bird, a raven, stretched its wings directly above me and glided smoothly till it landed on a garden post. A glossy creature with piercing blackcurrant eyes, it looked straight at me.

I stared back. It didn't feel like an ordinary bird; it didn't flinch or even begin to look away, even as I tried to approach it. Then Annabel's shouting disturbed him. He sprang from the post with a loud sort of 'prok' sound. Annabel covered her ears but, instead of flying away, it circled in the air and then came back to swoop aggressively towards us. I ducked hard. 'What the bloody hell?'

'Hey, less of that!' Dad shouted back at me. They were all too consumed with the manor house to have noticed the bird, which had settled again on the post to survey us. I got the distinct impression it didn't want visitors.

As Dad shook hands with Mr Easton, I interrupted:

'Mr Easton, I think someone may be inside. Upstairs. I saw a face at the window.'

'There's no one in that house lad, I can assure you. The evening light plays tricks, that's all.' He chuckled and shook his head, mumbling as he walked away, 'Kids' imaginations, huh.'

Dad checked everyone was safely in the old Morris estate car. After a few attempts, it managed to choke a sluggish start. 'Well, a new car is definitely not on the list for a long time. It will take years, and a lot of money, to get this place straight—and that's just the outside. God knows what the upstairs is like!'

'Stop moaning, Albert,' said Mum. 'You were starting to sound positive a few minutes ago. We're very lucky anyway to have a car at all.'

Annabel and I sat cramped in the back seat. She shook her head as if to say, *Here we go again.* I looked into the rear view mirror and saw Dad's frown. If it's the car he was worrying about keeping, he would be upset, especially out here in the middle of nowhere. He would like to keep the car on the road, especially if we were to live here, in isolation.

He didn't continue the discussion. There was enough to think about as it was, I suppose. My thoughts were on the shadowy movement in the upstairs window and on that evil-looking raven. The thought of living there suddenly became even more horrendous.

As the car chugged away I looked back and saw the raven circling over the house.

Chapter Two

1597

The Earl of Becton, William Harrison, was a tall man, elegantly dressed in the style best befitting his status: starched white linen shirts, padded and jewelled doublets and silk hose. His duties today had prompted him to wear his broad-brimmed hat and long slim leather boots. It was not going to be pleasant.

By his side was his squire, John, who had been in his service for a good few years. John was a more robust man, still tall but stocky; dressed smartly in similar attire to his master, just without the jewels or embroidered cuffs on his shirt sleeves. Both favoured the thick beards and moustaches which were in fashion.

They had come to understand one another, to appreciate their differences, respect each other's position in life, and laugh at each other's jokes and quips. Yet the matters of the times were dangerous. Their conversations were often accompanied by discreet and cursory glances. Spies could be anyone, anywhere.

Both men fidgeted with their hats as they removed them from their heads, grimacing as they faced the scene before them. John's usual ever-present grin had changed to a pursing of his lips and a squinting of his eyes. The earl felt his lofty forehead start to dip to one side, but today he knew he needed to be strong and so he straightened his back and smoothed back his hair.

The dark and wretched cell was filled with the rank stench of blood, sweat, excrement, stale air, and the thick smoke rising from the brazier in the corner of the room. The only light came from the embers, a couple of wall torches, and a dim lantern over the rack.

The torturer glanced at them before smiling an evil smile as he turned the handle on the rack, increasing the levels of pain for the skeletal figure of an old man spread and shackled. The chains rattled and the man lifted his head while his spine arched; wispy white hair tumbling backwards, catching the light. His mouth opened to release a feeble shriek, just as his angular bones cracked.

The torturer, now grunting, secured the tension of the ratchets. Latin utterances of merciful prayer did not distract him from his duties. Again, the old man's mouth opened wide like a fledgling, his spirit wanting to protest, but his strength had deserted him and his tiny sunken eyes screwed shut. His red belly, bulbous veins and paper-thin flesh swelled, like a woman about to give child. His oppressor grinned and nodded with satisfaction, greasy hair like rat's tails, slithering into his mouth.

The earl felt a sudden heat and battled the urge to vomit given that the beast was staring at him, but it was a brief encounter. There was still pain to inflict; still a confession to be made.

The torturer's bulky nose twitched as mucus dropped onto the old man's chest. Perhaps it was the sensation of the moist drops or a dogged determination, but the old man opened his eyes and turned his face towards the earl, who looked at him closely.

The frailty of this figure had disguised him, but now recognition dawned. This was a priest: a companion of his son's tutor, Father Robert. Together they helped to plan the construction of the secret hiding places at Becton Manor, his new home. The earl was jolted into decisive action.

'This man has endured enough. You will release him immediately and wait for further orders.'

The beast squinted, before grunting and turning to wipe his tools.

'Have you forgotten how to address a servant of the Queen of

England? You do not turn your back on me. Do you perhaps want to know what it is like to feel your bones leave your skin, sir. It can no doubt be arranged… Well?'

The torturer, his bandy legs bowed, swaggered as if proud. He slowly wiped the blood from his hands as if contemplating the earl's next reaction. Yielding was clearly not something he liked to do, but he eventually relented and managed a more humble demeanour.

'Forgive me, my Lord. I will send the old man back to his quarters. I act on orders from my own Master, who is more than satisfied with my work.'

The earl said nothing but nodded in the direction of the old priest, whose eyes suddenly became lively with fresh hope. He beckoned John to follow him up the stone steps and out into fresh air. He hungered for air he could breathe. Mounting the steps with legs that felt soft and unsupportive, he realised that the foul and ungodly episode had rendered him weak. He discreetly crossed himself as they reached the street. No doubt his reluctance to help the torturer gain a confession would soon be relayed back to the court.

As John gathered the horses, the earl reflected on the Queen's insecurities.

In truth, she was unnerved by the many plots to dethrone her, but his mission to oversee the questioning of Catholics suspected of plotting against her gave him an uncomfortable guilt. Yes, he was well aware of the growing number of Jesuits infiltrating the country using various disguises. These men—of his own faith—were captured, jailed, tortured, hanged, drawn and quartered—or gibbeted on London Bridge—yet, while the Queen of England trusted him, she was vulnerable.

During their last meeting, the earl had been struck by her sad, shrunken, red-rimmed eyes, set deep in a gaunt and sombre face; her white face paint cracked and dry, a woman with her spirit withering. It betrayed the façade of a ruling Queen in bright silks and heavy jewellery; it revealed her sense of loss.

In the last few years, he had watched her closely when at court. All her trusted and long-serving advisors had died. New blood at court was new arrogance. She was irritated by the extravagance and pretentious nature of the squabbling courtiers. More often than not, arguments focused on the power struggle between Catholics and Protestants but the irony was, she had been tolerant of the differences; until now. The glory of the defeat of the Spanish Armada was long gone and the execution of her cousin, Mary, Queen of Scots, had left her morose; intensely tired of conflict and suspicions. She was persuaded, however, to remain mindful of the many plots to dethrone her. Now he could see more than ever before; the peace she yearned for in her old age was not even a dim light.

In her state of mind, she could easily be persuaded to accuse the Earl of Becton of treason.

Chapter Three

1957

By August, Becton Manor was declared safe to live in. The roof was complete; repair work to the staircase meant it was no longer dangerous and the rooms had been cleared of debris. Now there was the smell of new wood and it was less damp.

Annabel and I were the first to dash upstairs and see the bedrooms. At the top of the stairs there was a small landing leading to two bedrooms on the left, one at the front and a larger one at the back containing a small fireplace. Now I could see why I thought the front bedroom windows were in the roof: the ceiling sloped so the alcove housed the window. It was the same in the front bedroom of the far end of the galleried landing on the right of the house. Another three bedrooms faced the rear garden, all with fireplaces. The third room along was the room where I had seen the face at the window.

The last bedroom faced the front of the house with a window in a recess. An odd thing was a sealed cupboard, or a doorway just to the side of this room. Constructed over a step, I assumed it was once the entrance to the attic.

'Good God, all this lot to decorate.' Dad was on the landing. I didn't think at the time, but now I understand the anguish he must have felt at the prospect of maintaining this very large property.

The constant moaning about the lack of electricity was, I believe, fear. He couldn't possibly afford to keep this house, a house his dear wife had fallen in love with, and he tried to find as much fault as possible.

'Remember what that damn solicitor said?' He proceeded to imitate Mr Easton, the pompous solicitor's voice: *'You have a lot to do here: this place has not been inhabited since before the war. You should really have enough funds to put things right, but I'm afraid the electricity won't yet be connected. This is a very rural area, you must understand.'* He sighed. 'That man was of the opinion that we were just common ragbags with no future or ability to turn this house around.'

'Don't let that man bother you, Albert.' said Mum. 'Let's go downstairs and I'll put a pan of water on that old range and get some tea brewing, eh? I brought a box of matches... somewhere... and we have boxes to sit on until the removal men come.'

The positive thing about Mr Easton was that his attitude had presented a challenge to Dad: *We will damn well make a go of it.*

We didn't get the tea. Almost as soon as we had sat down, the sound of a big lorry on the track made us all leap up and hurry to the door, dad limping and complaining about the door still sticking. 'This needs a good plane at the bottom if we want to open it properly, bloody thing.' It made an awful scraping noise.

'At least we haven't had a new floor put in yet, Albert.'

'Huh? Oh hmm... Another expense.'

Mickey started barking furiously at the arrival of the three burly removal men. They hurriedly began to unload our furniture.

'Mr and Mrs Winchett? We have a lot to shift here, missus. Damn hot day and all. Better tell us where to put it, eh?'

Mickey circled the men, eyeing them suspiciously, responding with low grunts and the occasional irritated bark. Mum, looking harassed, removed him to the kitchen where he slumped and then groaned as he slid under the table.

'Now stay there and be a good dog.'

He groaned as only dogs can do.

I don't recall many 'aura' moments on moving day; but I still didn't fully understand the concept. Perhaps seeing the face when it was so eerily quiet was my first perception of anything slightly spiritual in nature. The shifting of all that furniture and noise was definitely not spiritual.

Allowing Mum to attend to the removal men, Dad said he would see to the tea.

Before long, the geyser started hissing loudly. Poor Dad, I could hear him moaning while we were carrying things from the van: 'This bloody thing is about to explode,' but nobody was really listening to him or caring very much. He grumbled about no electricity. He didn't want to cope with oil lamps, candles, flint and kindling for the fire. Even though I felt pity, his moans were getting on my nerves and reinforcing that life here was going to be pretty bloody miserable.

Happily occupied, Mum's arms were waving about all over the place, directing orders to the removal men.

'Oh, not there, no...oh, oh dear, there's so many places.' She giggled like a girl with a big new toy. The sweating men, holding heavy items, glared at her.

*

After we finally got a drink of tea, Annabel and I had orders to unpack the smaller items such as crockery and pans.

I made an excuse that I needed the outside loo. Once there, I wandered down the garden, which was more a jungle than anything else.

Walking a few yards further, I spotted the old shed, standing back a bit from the path running down the side of the loo. The old shed intrigued me. Broken windows peeped through tall occluding shrubs. As I got nearer I could see it was quite a big building, obviously not used for years. The rotten door, covered in cobwebs, faced the bottom of the garden and, try as I could, it wouldn't open.

I looked back at the house, to that window. The memory of the pale face surfaced again. I went back inside the house, making my way to the galleried landing. The air here remained damp and musty, even though new wood had been used to repair the stairs. Mum would come to curse all this cleaning. Cobwebs lingered where spiders soon returned after being disturbed by the builders.

I turned right at the top of the stairs and made my way to that third room on the left. I looked at the fireplace at the right hand outer wall. It was a dark wooden one in a deep recess, flanked by dark wood panels, interrupted horizontally by a crooked beam, once painted in a lighter colour: green, I think.

The linoleum, so cracked and black in places with hard-to-shift mould, resembled a mosaic from an ancient monument. I walked towards the window, taking cautious, quiet steps, although I wasn't sure why. The garden seemed much longer viewed from above and even more jungle-like.

I was studying the long shed again when a sensation of cold air swept across my neck. My skin tingled and my legs went jelly-like; the way they do when you are stood at a perilous height, at risk of falling. Bloody Annabel, what was she up to?

'Annabel, stop that!' I said sharply, but before I had time to turn round I spotted her in the garden, playing with Mickey. I turned slowly, to face…no-one. *That* wasn't a trick of the light. My hands delved deep into my pockets and the rustling sound of the bag of rock sweets in my pocket normalised the moment. As I took one out the bag ripped apart, spilling the contents all over the floor. One caught my eye as it rolled towards the back of the fireplace, but then it disappeared with a clunk somewhere under the floor.

Avoiding a dilatory woodlice, I discovered a small misshapen hole right in the corner of the fireplace. Pushing my finger into this hole, I was surprised to discover a metal lever which, when pushed to the side, caused a grating sound next to the fireplace. By repeating the action, the grating happened again, until I saw the wooden panel shifting slightly. Using my shoulder to push the panel, it gave way with a scraping sound to open inwards to a very tiny space.

'Tom, are you up there?' Dad shouted, making me jump so badly that I banged my head on the panel. 'I need your help, son, to shift a chest. Can't expect those blokes to do everything.'

I pretended I couldn't hear him and climbed inside the tiny chamber-like space.

*

It was full of grit and debris. About four foot up was a ledge to the right, big enough to climb onto.

'Tom, where the hell are you?' Dad was now on the landing.

Why can't I bloody do what I want?

I quickly climbed back into the bedroom, in time to face him in the doorway.

'About time. I can't manage these heavy things without help. God, we've just bloody moved in case you haven't noticed. You have to do your bit, Tom, come on lad. Help me with this chest, on the landing.'

'Dad, I've just found a secret cupboard.'

Dad shook his head. 'Don't be daft, lad. Shut up and lift.'

Bent almost double, we struggled with three more chests until all of them were placed on the landing. Then the bombshell. We started to lift mine when Dad announced my room would be the third on the left.

'What? Not that one, Dad. Please. Annabel can sleep there.'

'Why don't you want it?'

'It's eerie.'

'They're all bloody eerie. All right: it's damp, dingy and huge, but some people would give their eye teeth for this, you know. It's a rare opportunity…according to your mother at any rate.'

'Huh, it's rare all right. I saw a face at the window of that bedroom when we came last time and now I've just found this secret panel.'

'A what?'

'A secret panel by the fireplace. I just told you. I'm not being daft. I found it by accident. I dropped a sweet and it disappeared down this hole, but the hole conceals a little lever. Come and look.'

'Faces and secret panels. Ha! You've been reading too many scary stories, Tom. You're letting your imagination run away with you. Some of these rooms are far too damp but this one is not so bad. You can swap when they dry out a little.' Dad opened the window, then turned towards the fireplace to watch me open the panel.

He examined the narrow chamber. 'It stinks foul. There's nothing in it anyway. What did you do exactly to open it?'

'There's a little metal clasp, inside this hole: look.' He watched me twiddling in the hole until the panel opened sufficiently for me to push it inwards. 'My sweet must have dropped below somewhere.'

Dad appeared intrigued for just a few seconds, glanced quickly inside, looked upwards and all around, then screwed up his face in disgust. 'It's just an old cubby hole, badly constructed at that. Didn't know how to do things properly in those days.' Exasperated, he sighed deeply, shook his head and threw up his arms in frustration. 'Don't get saying anything to your mother about faces, panels and missing sweets, eh? I'll have to seal that up.'

'I won't say anything, but don't seal it yet.'

He shook his head again, tut-tutting as he left to get more boxes…and he was limping. Oh God, he'd got enough on his plate.

*

Our evening meal made me feel like Robin Hood: chunks of bread, large piece of cheese, ham, pickles and spuds. Mum's turn to complain about the lack of heat from the old stove.

'It took blooming ages to boil them potatoes!' But as she sat down at the table, her broad smile was infectious. The old table was adorned with lots of tall candles and, I have to say, the memory of it is delightful. To step back in time and feel you are experiencing a part of history, of the way our ancestors lived, gives us a sense of appreciation.

'We'll just have to manage without electricity; after all, they did it before the war, except posh folk any road, but hey, it looks like it should do in a house like this, all these candles, eh? Very romantic. It smells better too. I feel like I should be wearing a long gown, Albert: one of them with a hula hoop inside.'

'A farthingale, dear.'

'Yes, that's it Albert: a fathering gale. Funny name.'

'I suppose you'd want me in breeches and wearing a hat with feathers in it, ha.'

I didn't think it was funny, but I ate my cold meat and spuds, then waited until they all went back into the kitchen.

At the sound of dishes clattering, Dad groaning at the lack of hot water, and Mum complaining again about the oven being too slow and old, I took myself off to explore. Just as I rose from the table, I heard Dad exploding: 'All right, all right, we'll get a new oven! I told you, this place will cost us an arm and leg.' It was a good time to get away; Annabel had already excused herself.

It may have been the vibration of their yelling, but the gold and cream light from the flickering candles, calm while we were dining, now cast the shadows of agitated fire flames all over the walls. I sensed eyes watching me enter the hall. The only light was from a solitary majestic candle set in a slender but heavy candlestick on a small round table at the bottom of the stairs. To see the staircase, your eyes had to become accustomed to the darkness. The only sound was the ticking of the Westminster clock on the hall dresser. This moment of eerily quiet stunned me. Another 'aura'. The eyes of many spiders watched me, but why did I think there were other eyes?

I picked up the candlestick, shielding the flame with my hand, which immediately blackened my vision. I stood still and shifted the candle until I could see a blend of dark patches: the dresser and the spindles of the staircase... and many shadows.

Then, as if all the doors and windows had been opened, there was a surge of arctic air. It was freezing cold. I couldn't breathe properly. I heard whispered voices: '*San...pater...san...pater... pater.*'

They echoed with increasing urgency.

It was cold. I shivered, but I still somehow mounted the stairs to the landing, feeling each heartbeat as a thud on my chest.

'Who are you?' My voice trembled. No response. 'Who *are* you?' I took a few more steps but the brightness of my candlelight obliterated my vision. Yet again I looked into utter blackness.

'Who are you talking to?'

I almost dropped the candle as the loud voice cut through the spell. Annabel, another candle in her hand, was looking up from the hallway, squinting.

'Go back and get more light, will you? I thought I heard someone.'

She turned quickly towards the kitchen, raising her voice, 'Mum, we might have a burglar! Tom's heard someone upstairs, come quick!'

With all the shouting, Mickey rose from his bed in the kitchen and started barking furiously as my irritated mother followed him to the staircase.

'Quiet, Mickey!' she scolded, but he took no notice and ran up the stairs, passing me along the landing. The whispering had ceased.

'Don't be silly, Annabel,' Mum sighed. 'It's just the creaking sounds of a very old house. You'll both have to get used to it. For God's sake, put that candle down before you set us all ablaze; there's too much bloody wood in here! Mickey, come here!'

We could no longer see him on the landing but heard him whining.

Chapter Four

August 1597

The earl, his tall slender frame now bent over his steed, felt a new energy as he broke into a gallop. As he neared his beloved Derbyshire he was eager to see his family but also to rid himself of the vision of the tortured priest.

His men had trouble keeping up with him, especially the one with the provision packs either side of his saddle. The earl saw him but was irritated. The man had willingly loaded the packs and now they were not going to stop. The galloping, after all, meant that they were nearly there: at the new home, the place where his wife Charlotte, son Oliver and daughter Mary were eagerly waiting for him. It had been six weary days and nights, staying in inns and waiting for the horses to be rested, but the hot parched weather had caused the already deep ruts in the rough road to become rock-hard. Riding had been difficult.

*

The earl wiped his face with his kerchief as he surveyed his new home. The soaked cloth had absorbed days of rancid sweat and, although he could taste the residue on his lips, he was smiling at the sight of the new home and the large, shining windows.

How they reflected the sunlight! His wife had wanted even larger windows like those of her friend Bess of Hardwick, but in this smaller manor house, the current ones looked fine.

Crowning the heavy front door was the beautifully carved coat of arms; his initials, *WH*. The sound of his children's laughter was near. They were not at their lessons today as his letter had said he'd be home by Friday. He felt a rush of excitement at the thought of the looks on his children's faces when he would greet them at long last.

He hastily dismounted just as the stable boy, Henry, was running up to lead the horses to the stables and Father Peters was walking around the side of the house. Close behind him were his charges: Oliver, the earl's son, and Jack, the whipping boy.

Oliver ran to his father.

'Welcome home, sir.' Both were laughing as they embraced, the earl picking his son up and swiftly spinning him round.

'How have you been, my son?'

'Well, sir.'

Oliver smiled. Father and son, both slim and tall, shared the same dark dancing eyes and thick dark shoulder length hair. hair which curled on their shoulders.

Jack stood watching until the earl greeted him.

'Well, lad, you are taller.'

Jack grinned and nodded. The earl patted the boy's back as he recalled the day the idea of having a whipping boy was put to him. *'It will challenge your son's spirit to ensure he remains the superior of the two,'* Father Peters had said. *'Keep him on his guard. The beating of a subordinate will indicate his own failure.'* He hadn't particularly liked the sound of it but, as it turned out, he had been pleasantly surprised by the mutual affection between the two boys, their trust in one another and their progress.

Jack was the son of the local herb woman, Kathleen Melton. The earl also offered lessons to Jack's younger sister, Ruth, who had become a close companion to his daughter, Mary. It was a beneficial arrangement but, sadly, his wife Charlotte did not share his views. She rarely smiled at the presence of *'low births'* in the house.

*

As the two boys ran away, the earl greeted Father Peters. The earl noted the priest's wide grin as he watched the boys laughing and running. He was a trusted friend and confidante, but there was an important issue at stake, that must be discussed with him. Sadly, he feared the happiness, clear in that wide grin, would no longer exist, following the words that needed to be spoken.

The pair embraced tightly, each patting the other on his back. Father Peters spoke first.

'Welcome home, brother,' the label, a token of their shared faith. A strong bond had formed over the years.

'I am indeed relieved to return to my new abode, Robert. It is good to see you…and you look well, brother.' The earl wanted to say more but he disguised his concerns…for now.

The image of the priest in the torture room continually tormented him; the scrawny arms and swollen red belly would be imprinted on his mind for the rest of his life. It could easily have been Father Peters on that rack. That must never happen.

They went indoors. The earl was about to fling his hat onto the hall dresser when another child shouted with glee. His daughter, Mary, was running towards him, her companion and fellow student Ruth—Jack's sister—holding back to allow the two to greet one another.

'Father!' the young girl with a pretty round face, ran towards him, her reddish brown hair bouncing and her large blue eyes wide with joy. Slight of frame, her red velvet dress proved too heavy for her to be running in, despite her holding it high with both hands. Unlike her brother, she wasn't expected to address her father as 'sir'.

He hugged her, then noticed her lips. They were almost the same colour as her dress: bright red with cinnabar. Her doll-like face was a pallid white, painted with a lead powder and vinegar mixture, just like the noble ladies at court. The Queen, perhaps afraid of her advancing years, seemed to apply hers more thickly each new day.

He regretted the time he had told her of the women at court and their desire not to look brown and weathered as villagers and workers in the field do; such faces were only seen on those of a low birth. Now he couldn't determine if her face or her ruff was the whitest.

He imagined his daughter growing old with a cracked white face and shuddered. He no longer cared if she never became a lady-in-waiting. It was always going to be dangerous for Mary to be at court. Just then, the raucous laughter of the two boys disturbed them and the earl noticed his daughter's frown.

Father Peters interrupted his thoughts.

'I will take the boys to the courtyard, my lord. The Lady Mary has much to discuss with you.' He smiled and nodded towards the earl's daughter, but Oliver must have been listening. He leapt forward, seemingly from the open door.

'Yes please, Father Peters. That will indeed be welcome, will it not, Jack? It must be so boring to spend such time caring about how you look at court.' He glared at his sister.

'You still have to learn, brother, how to present yourself,' an irritated Mary responded.

'That's enough!' said the earl but he was amused, by the healthy banter between siblings. Mary had been a sickly infant but now she was a high-spirited nine year old. Far too eager to get to court, however.

'Have you decided yet, father, when I shall be presented at Court? You promised me it would be soon.'

'Yes, I am fully aware.' His smile was forced. The desire to endlessly fuss over the Queen and vie for her favours, he found tiresome.

'How do you like this new gown?' She spun around, the full red velvet revealing little clusters of pearls. She tossed her long red tresses behind her. 'I must be dressed as becomes a lady of the

Court, or the Queen may dismiss me.'

'You look beautiful, Mary.' *But she must not go to court.*

Mary nodded, pleased with the compliment, before turning to her nervous companion. 'Come, Ruth, don't be afraid of Father, he will never hurt you.'

'No, indeed!' The earl confirmed as he threw his head back and laughed heartily. The shy girl came closer to him and coyly curtseyed.

He thought she would never relax the way that her brother had done, but he was of the opinion that Charlotte had once upset her and, ever since that day, she had shown a sense of inferiority.

The earl remembered the occasion. He and his wife were in the parlour, the door was open.

The girls were in the hall. His wife, he knew, was well aware of this and he was both surprised and disappointed at her words, spoken loudly, bitter words of contempt:

'She smells incessantly of her mother's herbs and hedgerow plants! They are very lucky children to be taught alongside our own son and daughter, William. Who else gives such charity to a whipping boy and his sister, offspring to a mere herb woman?'

Lord Becton recalled the scorn in her voice as he had chastised his wife, but he knew the words would resonate with Ruth for a long time to come. She did at least enjoy her lessons with Mary and the governess, Anne Sawyer.

Ruth sighed with relief when the earl turned his attention to his daughter.

'Mary, I need to speak with your mother. Where is she?'

Mary knew not to ask the reason why, noting the suddenly serious expression on his face. 'I will fetch her, Father.'

*

As was often the case, Lady Charlotte was found in the garden, pruning and weeding. There she could attain a quietness and contentment; unlike at court, which she hated. She found large groups of people mortifying.

She was often observed speaking to her plants; so much so that some visitors thought she was bewitched. The garden had come to be her pride and joy. She turned swiftly on the gravel path as she heard running and smiled at the sight of her daughter. Here was a young lady whom she hoped, one day, would be wedded to a suitable rich suitor, to consolidate their status and wealth.

'Mary, don't run so. When you get to court you must not be so exuberant. It is not becoming.'

'Sorry, madam. Father wishes to speak with you.'

In the parlour, the earl had been gazing out of the window and, on hearing his wife enter, he turned to face her. His expression was stern, his index finger and thumb rubbing his chin. Charlotte nervously fiddled with her kirtle. 'What is it, husband?'

'There are many whisperings at court, Charlotte, of Jesuit priests disguised as teachers and meetings addressed in code. You know recusants are guilty of high treason and the punishment is by hanging?'

'Yes, but what matter is that of ours? We should not heed the punishments of others…'

The earl shook his head at her dismissal of the torment of others: innocent others.

'*Hanged* is what I said, woman. It could be the fate of Father Peters. All you understand is your plants.' As soon as the words were spoken, he cursed his impetuous outburst.

Lady Charlotte raised her voice.

'I am aware of other things, sir. You are away so much, what else am I to do? The children love you to come home because you never discipline them as I do; my domain is not the troubles at court. Father Peters is safe with us, here in Derbyshire.'

There was a silence as Lord Becton sought the words to make his wife understand the dangers they needed to be aware of, and that living in Derbyshire was no safe haven. She was staring at him and he knew that she would rather be dismissed to return to her garden, but instead she drew closer to him.

'Look at all the silver and gold he attained from the old King's ruination of the monasteries,' she said. 'We must have treasures hidden everywhere. He is too clever to die, William.'

There was another short silence before the earl spoke with deep emotion. 'You remember the priest: Henry Walpole? His death was long and tragic, by God: hanging for hours, but still alive when his body was drawn and quartered. A short while ago, I had to witness a torture on the rack. He was a friend of Father Peters. The old man was here in this house to discuss the construction of hiding places. They spoke at length. I remember his dignified manner, his knowledge and enthusiasm. I can hear him laughing, both of them, but I was mindful of their commitment to the Sacraments.'

The earl gazed out of the window, sadness etched on his face. 'He was so frail, Charlotte.' Then his demeanour changed as anger swept over him. 'Only following his faith, for Christ's sake!' He yelled now, arching his neck backwards, looking towards the high ceiling as if seeking retribution from God, but his vision, once again, was filled with that of the priest on the rack and the torturer laughing. 'In the name of the Lord, I could do nothing. Nothing!' His eyes glistened with pooled tears.

There was a loud bang as his fist struck the table.

'Executions do not overlook titles or wealth, or give privileges according to where you reside, Charlotte. Even our own daughter, if she was at court, would pose a threat to us. Our faith has become a burden.'

Lady Charlotte was startled at her husband's words. She had not seen him so full of anger, and even fear, before. He was studying her, wanting a response. It was not what he wanted to hear.

'You are aware of how bad tidings bring on my melancholy sir and force me to my chamber for days,' she said. 'Frances will have to find my soothing balm. I am not sure I am able...'

'In heaven's name, madam!' the earl shouted. 'You must learn control; your balm will not change things. Father Peters is in danger. We as a family are at risk. Our faith is the old faith and punishable by death. So...do not deem thyself, madam. I have taken the decision to dismiss Father Peters and will seek a new tutor: a Protestant.

Charlotte simply asked to be dismissed. Lord Becton nodded but, as she opened the door, Oliver and Jack were close by. Her eyes glistening with pooled tears prevented her from speaking but their faces showed they had heard some, if not all, of the quarrel.

Chapter Five

1597

Father Robert Peters was born in 1564. As a child he had shown great academic ability and his parents had secured a tutor for him in the house of some wealthy friends. He had triumphed in Greek, Latin, theology, and philosophy; even medicine. Eventually following in the footsteps of his elder brothers, he entered the Catholic Church. After many placements teaching, he was ordained as a priest.

Some time around 1588 he was studying late into the night in a small upstairs room at the home of a family friend when he heard strange knockings. He extinguished the solitary candlelight by his side and crept along a passageway in the dark towards the sound. At the end of the narrow passageway he was astonished to observe a man busy with what seemed to be repair work in a cupboard.

The young man, short of stature and of similar age to Robert, caught sight of him watching and laughed as he climbed up and out, not from a cupboard but a distinct hole. He immediately held out his hand to shake Robert's. Realising this man was of little threat he grinned, but curiosity was overwhelming him.

'What in God's name are you doing here?'

The man, still smiling, replied without hesitation. 'I could ask the same question of thee young sir.'

The young man was called Nicholas Owen. He was a priest supporting the work of the Jesuit Superior, Henry Garnett, but his disguise was that of a travelling carpenter and his task was the construction of hiding places for priests. After hearing accounts of ferocious persecution for followers of their faith, Father Owen inspired Robert, who had heard of such persecutions. The conversation did not take long before Robert felt compelled to join his new companion in support of the Jesuits.

Shortly after this event, Father Peters was offered a job as a family priest and eventual tutor for the young son of the wealthy Earl of Becton. Realising the family wished to retain their faith, Robert requested the services of Father Owen to construct a place where they could hold Mass and hide priests if necessary.

Now in his mid-thirties, he felt settled and content, teaching and attending to duties in his religious life.

*

The addition of Jack as a whipping boy had made a strong difference to Oliver. Father Peters had met his mother, Kathleen when she attended the sick in the village where he used to teach and give sermons. The boy was keen to learn and Kathleen eager for him to do well in life. The earl had agreed to the suggestion for Jack to be Lord Oliver's whipping boy.

Both boys were competitive, and Oliver's perception of Jack as inferior inspired him to achieve according to his status. Jack, however, was a good match with a keen mind.

Father Peters watched their progress and demeanour very carefully and chastised Oliver if he became too headstrong and pompous. He liked Jack and encouraged the boy to learn as an equal and not a subservient student. The boys knew that Father Peters had their best interests at heart and they worked well for him.

Mass was performed in the hidden chambers behind the manor house, cleverly constructed behind a secret panel at the back of the stables.

As he was preparing to meet with Lord Becton, he pondered the dire changes in the church. Under the early reign of the old King Henry, his mentor—the priest, Father Murphy—was adorned in elaborate and jewelled robes. There was a sense of importance of his role as a priest. Now priests were in disguise for most of the time, their intentions wrongly interpreted as political and suspicious. He was glad he was able to tutor.

Although monasteries were stripped of their ornate wealth, during the dissolution Father Murphy had been quick-witted and shrewd, anticipating the grab of this wealth by the country's aristocracy. He managed to hide his vestments, alongside gold and silver belts, robes threaded with gold, and many other artefacts and jewels. Towards the end of his life, he had passed these on to the younger priest. They were now safely hidden in Becton Manor. Only the earl knew of their exact whereabouts.

At the end of the school session in the twilight of the day, the earl placed a large lantern on the table, next to a flagon of mulled wine and two goblets. While he prepared for the arrival of Father Peters he was considering the potential loss of not only Oliver's education but also a dear friend. There was too much at stake, though, to keep him.

Father Peters knocked twice and entered when beckoned, noting the serious expression etched on the earl's face as he did so. Chairs scraped the cold stone floor as they sat, face to face, in the dim light.

'You serve my son well, Father, and his learning is progressing more than I could have hoped for.'

Father Peters sipped the warm liquid, then nodded while smiling at the earl as if to reassure him he would accept the words to come. When the earl paused and faltered, he responded:

'I understand your concerns, my Lord. My compatriots also hear whispers. The Jesuits are increasing their number, some not as discreet as others, I hear. You remember, Father Owen was captured?'

'Yes… But he was released, was he not?'

'Only following torture and when a hefty fine was paid, my Lord. Alas, I consider it my duty not to cause you a similar concern, or threaten your reputation by exposing my allegiance.'

The earl nodded but his smile did not linger. He rubbed together the tips of his fingers with his thumb, a mannerism the priest had noticed before when the earl was troubled. Father Peters felt a sudden sadness that the boys' progress may never be discussed again; on the other hand, he felt a deep hatred for those persecuting recusants. It was against his ethos, but he raged inside for what had happened to his good friend, Father Owen.

He understood the plight of the Jesuits, the horror of torture and foul prisons, the indignation of the burning of papal documents and images; the absolute denial of the Catholic faith.

His thoughts were broken by Lord Becton's question, 'What will you do, Father?'

'That, my lord, must be kept secret. I will reside perhaps with Kathleen and assist her in her work, gathering the herbs and producing good medicine…and of course, the white powders for the Lady Mary. She uses such a lot of the stuff, eager to be pleasing to the eye and be accepted at the court of Elizabeth. If you do not mind me saying so, my lord?'

They laughed and the air was lighter. For a moment Father Peters thought it was like old times.

The earl seemed happy to be distracted. 'She will need a strong suitor, that one. But how she has grown strong herself, from such a frail child. Do you remember, Father? That frail sparrow of an infant? We almost performed the last rites, did we not?'

'We did indeed, my lord, but aye…she is a determined spirit.'

A poignant silence. The earl hesitated, as though he was finding it difficult to send Father Peters away. The priest rested a hand on the earl's arm and raised his head to nod gently in silent resignation.

'Do not fear for me, brother. I understand your decisions.'

They both rose, but then the earl was startled by the priest's raucous laughter.

'I have to admit, my lord; being rather stouter than Father Owen, the thought of me trying to breathe within those tight spaces he devised was filling me with dread. So you may have done me a service.'

'I will make sure you have money, Robert, to sustain you whilst you seek further duties.'

'No need my lord, I will fare well. I have always been of a resilient nature. If I was a pauper, I trust you would assist me, but my treasures within these walls is our holy secret, our *sanctus occultus*. If you are in agreement, they can stay here.'

There followed a slight pause, before the priest looked quizzically at him. 'I do have a question.'

'Ask it.'

'Who will instruct the boys? They are doing so well in their studies. And I was right, my Lord: Jack's presence yields much from young Oliver, mind and heart.'

'Yes, I almost forgot. I heard of a young man, new to the village. His name is Master Edward Griffin.' He has good references; being of the new faith, we will need to be discreet, but he will not reside here. I would appreciate it if you could meet with him to discuss your lessons with the boys. He will come in the morning at ten, after he has met the boys.'

'As you wish. We will remain good friends, brother. You cannot get rid of me completely.'

The spontaneous laughter and intimate hug that followed was a testimony of the trust between them.

Father Peters opened the door, turning back slowly, to face the earl. '*Sanctus Occultus*, my lord.'

The earl forced a smile, before the door was closed. He felt uneasy but more than that, despised himself for his dishonesty. Father Peters was an honest and loyal man.

He frowned. Nothing had been said of the priest on the rack.

The immense guilt he felt choked him, but he couldn't admit to his inability to save the old man or give Father Peters any more sadness

*

Master Griffin was indeed young and of very smart attire, which seemed in tune with his air of superiority. His dark squinting eyes belonged to one who enjoyed devising schemes, Father Peters thought, as they eyed each other on that first meeting, the air thick with mutual suspicion.

Griffin held his shoulders back and his chin seemed permanently lifted, as if to unnerve all those who dared to face him. Father Peters, believing that first impressions were very important, was disappointed with the meeting.

Introductions were congenial enough but Master Griffin immediately took charge, beginning to inform the priest how the boys were to be educated by him.

Squarely facing Father Peters, he raised his chin further.

'I am of the opinion, sir, that each boy has received too much leniency. Good manners is one thing, but their learning and character I find to be somewhat weak. With respect, perhaps your approach has lacked robustness. So far, I found their knowledge of the subjects they need for university rather piecemeal, I have to say. Of course it doesn't matter about the whipping boy, but with regard to Oliver, whose years have passed ten, I have much to do. No matter…with rigour, this can be achieved and he will excel, I am sure. You have no call to look disappointed sir: the basics are there and I have after all only seen them for a few hours.'

Father Peters gave him a cold stare.

'With respect sir, young boys need peace of mind to study effectively. Without this, they may not hold information for very long or be interested in their learning. They learn from each other. Jack has never needed the birch.'

Master Griffin was quick to respond. 'Hmm…I find discipline to be an essential tool: strong discipline and commitment. I pray it is not too late to instil these virtues!'

Father Peters chose to hide his disgust of this arrogant, despicable man. He calmly decided to say nothing further regarding the boys. 'I am late for another appointment, sir. I will bid you farewell… please try to heed my words.'

Father Peters left the room with a heaviness he had not expected. He looked up towards the schoolroom, not daring to say goodbye. Another time perhaps. He was afraid for Jack. This new man's heart was a cold rock.

*

The schoolroom was at the end of a small corridor at the top of the stairs. The corridor branched left, leading to the front of the house where there was a guest bedroom and a small library. The family bedrooms were situated on the left side of the galleried landing and they all faced the back garden.

Frances the housekeeper, Anne the governess for Mary and Ruth, Margaret the cook, and Father Peters had rooms in the attic; Frances, had her own small sitting room downstairs. The old gardener Ged and the stable boy Henry came in on a daily basis, along with two other scullery maids. All lived in the village.

Frances and Margaret watched Father Peters as he walked along the quiet village path away from the house, his paltry belongings slung over his shoulder. His head was hung low as if he were deep in thought. They looked at one another and shook their heads. Neither had taken a liking to the boys' new tutor.

Chapter Six

1957

I well remember my first night's sleep at the manor house—or should I say, *attempt* to sleep. I couldn't get the scenes out of my head: the shadowy face at the window, the anxious whispers on the galleried landing, incessantly resonating, *'San Pater, San Pater.'* *'San Pater, San Pater…'*

What did they mean? Who had spoken them? Ghosts did not exist, so was it the wind? But then again, it wasn't a windy night at all; and anyway, even wind can't whisper like that.

Mickey had growled on the landing, but then he was whining just before I saw him backing off. He only did that when he was afraid or anxious. So what exactly had he seen? When he reached the bottom of the stairs, he ran immediately to hide under the table. I'd heard that dogs have a kind of sixth sense: they see, hear and feel things that humans never do. Perhaps Mickey could sleep up here in my room. I stared at the panel, worried it might suddenly open and, looking at the window, I remembered the cold breeze on the back of my neck. Every time I closed my eyes there was a sense of someone approaching me so I quickly opened them again. God, I hated that house.

A whole week passed with no further strange events.

Life for us all had taken on new routines.

I would soon be starting a new school, for just one more year, although it hardly seemed worth the effort. I could get a job now, without sitting exams and enduring boring lessons. Mum and Dad wouldn't hear of it, though.

My old school was too far away and Dad insisted this new one was even better. The thought of new people made me nervous; kids always look suspiciously at new arrivals. I'd seen it at my old school and was ashamed to admit that I had been a bit of a bully myself to one of the bright sparks.

I wouldn't be seen as a bright spark or swot, as my mum would say. I would more than likely get teased for my spotty skin.

Gradually I slept without constantly opening my eyes to check who might be in the room but I did demand that the rocking chair in the corner of the room was moved. I could not look at it without imagining an old woman sat in it.

'Tom, I'm not doubting what you think you see lad, but old houses do sort of change the way we dream, I reckon.' Dad was unconvincing.

Mum shook her head. 'All right, all right, I'll put it back in the cellar, where I found it, and get you a lamp. Tomorrow we'll have electricity.'

Dad grinned. 'Don't you want the chair, Alice? Shall we put it in our bedroom?'

Mum looked embarrassed, 'Err... No, there's no room.'

Dad smiled and winked at me.

The lamp was comforting. At least I could see what might be going on. The flame threw eerie shadows but the light was welcome. No one would come in the room if it was light, would they?

*

The following day was Saturday, and I slept late. I was woken by the sounds of digging. Looking out of the window I saw Dad, spade in hand, busy digging by that shed. He hated messy gardens and had decided to clear all the overgrown shrubs hiding the shed.

I watched him for a while until I got distracted by the sound of men's voices in the hallway. They were from the electricity board.

I heard clomping on the stairs, before someone knocked on my door, opening it and peering in.

'Hello there, you can finally have some lighting in your room eh? Name's Harry; you're Tom, right?'

I nodded. After the quick introduction, he started to pull up the floorboards, before looking positively disgusted.

'Cor blimey, a weird smell under these floorboards. A very old house, though. Some people say this house has buried treasure, y'know.' He laughed. 'Haven't you found any yet?'

At that moment, Dad shouted from the hallway.

'Tom, will you come down please? I have something to show you.'

I looked at Harry.

'Don't worry about me, lad. I have work to do.' Out in the garden, Dad showed me a few horseshoes and parts of bits and stirrups that he had dug up.

'Perhaps the shed was built on the site of an old stable, eh? I've been digging for hours; why don't you have a go and see what you can find? I need something to eat and just to check on the electrician. Mind that damn cesspit though. There's no lid on it yet.'

So that was the plan. Get me to carry on digging, or maybe he didn't want the electrician distracted. Well, might as well make an effort, I supposed.

I dug deep, in search of any more clues to this house, until my spade hit something hard but shiny. A cylindrical piece of metal glinted in the sunlight. I cleared away the soil from around it to discover it was more like a goblet. Rubbing it, I noted inscriptions around the top but, as I stood up, that damn raven swooped out of nowhere, squawking. It actually swiped it up in his beak, like a demented magpie. A few yards on, he dropped it.

Mickey was running across the garden, chasing a ball that Annabel had thrown in the same direction, as the bird dropped the goblet.

'What are you looking for? Mickey's got his ball.' Annabel was watching me.

'No, I wasn't looking for Mickey's ball.'

I was disappointed not to find the goblet—the bird had definitely dropped it—so I went back to my room in frustration. Harry was still busy wiring but looked up when I entered:

'There's a big garden out there, Tom. I was just asking your dad if he wants any help with tidying and all. I'm a bit of an amateur but willing and able.'

I became suspicious. Maybe Harry's interest wasn't in the garden, but buried treasure.

*

Everybody was getting on my nerves. I needed some air and so I strolled down to the village shop to buy stationery for school. It might please Mum to know I was being constructive. It turned out to be quite a walk, but I needed it to do some thinking.

The shop assistant was a tall thin man, probably in his early sixties.

'Not seen you around these parts. Do you live round here?'

He had a friendly smile, so I told him about Becton Manor and that I'd never wanted to live there. He was all ears, so I carried on with my account of the eerie goings-on. He didn't laugh, or tell me I had a wild imagination. He believed me. After I finished, I thought he'd think me quite daft but he leaned over the counter closer to me.

'I know exactly where you live... I had a friend who lived there, when I was a kid. Born and bred in this village, as I am. Then... his folks couldn't stand it anymore. He used to say there was a ghost there, walking about in the garden, maybe a priest. Anyway, some apparition always in black.' He grinned. 'Funny thing is... whenever he appeared, so did a big black bird; you're right, a raven it is. Did a lot of squawking and local folks say the bird is evil. It was worse when the priest and the raven were seen together; not sure why. So don't go near him if you see him, just in case. Don't want to frighten you, but some say he can peck your eyes out easy, if he so wished. People say something very tragic happened.'

'What?'

'It was hundreds of years ago, of course. Every year, there's some kind of rumpus in the early hours of Midsummer's Day. Something to do with that raven hating the priest. So bad it was, the family used to move away for a week. They thought they could put up with all the other stuff—whisperings mainly, but nothing that bad—the rest of the year. Nothing ever hurt them: it was just all a nuisance, they got used to it. Laughed at it. And anyway, they believed there was some hidden treasures there: you know, from the times when Henry the Eighth sold off all the wealth of the monasteries. Legend has it there's a stash at up there but nobody's been able to find it.

'Anyway, my mate's family had enough and made plans to leave. Not many stay in that place. It's been boarded up more times than it's been lived in, I can tell you. They call it the old legend of Corvus. That's Latin for raven. They say he protects the place, like the ravens at the Tower of London. Always there, flying around protecting the place from God knows what. In fact, for several years the house has been called 'Corvus Manor' because that raven owns it really'. He chuckled. 'What's your name by the way? Mine's Mr Haslam. John Haslam.'

'Tom.' We shook hands.

I thought about what he'd said and how conceivable it was that the bird thought he owned the house.

He continued. 'There's a challenge for you in that house o' yours. My friend thought if he could lift the sadness by solving the mystery, all would be well again. Troubled souls, that's all: just troubled tormented souls. A legend, an old legend.'

The man's words echoed in my head.

*

What exactly happened? Was it true that no family could live in the house? Why was that raven always hovering? Could it be true that there was the spirit of a priest and he and the raven disliked each other? And what was all that about Midsummer's Day and a stash of hidden treasure? Mr Haslam was certainly interested in that.

As I neared the house, Harry was driving away. He waved to me. I really wasn't sure about him. His permanent grin was too sly and, just like the bloke in the newsagents, he seemed too interested in the house.

'Is that you, Tom?' Mum shouted. I hurried excitedly to the kitchen to tell her what I'd found out.

'The shopkeeper in the newsagents used to be friends with a boy who lived here. He said there's a ghost here and that frightening things happen right here on Midsummer's Day. So scary, the boy's family moved away!'

'Tom, enough! You're talking so quickly you're making me dizzy. There are no such things as ghosts and I don't want to hear anymore, is that understood? No more talk of ghosts or weird things; it's just a very old house and you're simply not used to it, letting your imagination run all over the place.'

Why couldn't she listen to me for once? No wonder I was always being accused of being sullen. No one ever listened to me. Why couldn't adults listen to kids properly, for God's sake? This 'challenge' would have to be mine and mine alone. I would explore, all by myself.

Running back up the stairs, I wanted badly to get into the secret cupboard and explore the ledge on the right. Must be getting the hang of the lever to the panel, I thought, as I was much quicker. I got a small footstool from Mum's room to help me up.

The so-called cupboard was narrow, about five feet high by two feet wide. There was no room to turn round. On the right hand side was a ledge which, without the footstool, was pretty impossible to climb onto. Once on the ledge, which was about eighteen inches in width, one could only crawl. The height was about two foot again. I scrambled up inside but it was tiny. I felt almost trapped, but I could see it was long enough to go somewhere.

The next bit was craggy, narrow, smelly and dark. I could crawl along it but, having no torch, I had to rely on touch. Small avalanches of gravel fell from my weight on the ledge. Some of that gravel fell a long way down before I heard it softly hitting a hard structure, a rock maybe. I crawled slowly, the gravel sharp on my knees, but as I jerked a knee to one side, stones, bricks and mortar suddenly gave way, cascading into the dark chasm. A few seconds later the debris splintered and shattered against the rock, but this time, it was followed by a distant splashing sound. Water. Maybe there was a well shaft somewhere close by.

The bricks on which I was precariously balanced wobbled beneath my weight. I wished I had tried to find a torch. What an idiot. It wasn't easy crawling backwards and avoiding the gaps I had made in the ledge. 'Oh God.' I couldn't shout because I was afraid that would cause another precarious bit of stone to disintegrate. I also knew that no one could hear me. I had been foolish not to say anything. My body was teetering on the very edge of a steep fragile precipice, each small manoeuvre causing further fragments to fall. Then my feet dropped into a hole behind me. My left leg slipped and dangled over the side. The fingers on my right hand grasped a jagged rocky protrusion on the closed side of the passage.

I decided the best way back was to lie flat and very gently shuffle my body along. Feeling the unbroken ledge with my outstretched right foot, I pulled my left leg back up, checking the foothold carefully before each shuffle backwards.

In a panic, I cried out, 'Help!'. 'Help' my voice echoed back.

When my feet dropped again, it was into the cupboard and I steadied them on the footstool. Relieved, but suddenly wanting to rush, I slid back with speed, grazing my belly.

Smothered in grit and dust; my left knee bleeding, I wept with sheer relief just to be alive.

I remembered what Dad had said to Mum once, after she'd

tripped on the kerb and fallen into the street: '*You're in shock, love, and you just need to take it easy and breathe deeply.*'

Whether it was fear, shock, or just sheer relief, I fell onto my bed and cried buckets. I could tell no one. No one. Was all this happening to me because I kept calling this house a monstrosity? I'd set myself a challenge but what would I do now, alone, to try and solve this 'mystery'?

When the crying stopped, I realized the ledge and the sheer drop were all part of that huge stone wall on the exterior, which ended in the majestic chimney and, wiping my eyes, I resolved to explore further.

Chapter Seven

November 1597

And so the ambitious Edward Griffin became the new tutor for Oliver and Jack. A clever man, he had studied literature, astronomy, mathematics, and chemistry at Oxford University. He was passionate about learning, particularly in the sense that to excel in all studies ventured was paramount, not only for the good of the soul, but to meet the demands of the world. He had wanted to carry on to study medicine and was fiercely ambitious, but his father, a reasonably wealthy yeoman, had died suddenly, leaving debts incurred by heavy illegal gambling.

As a result, Edward Griffin had been forced to leave university, farm his land and provide for his mother and two younger brothers. He was deeply resentful of this and grew increasingly bitter, believing his divine rights to wealth and academic excellence had been denied to him.

He wanted more than just to inherit the farm and its land. He had been cruel to his brothers and impatient with his mother and, when his younger brother obtained a place at university, he was overcome with anger and resentment. He had constantly felt the need to vent this onto others; anyone who crossed his path.

*

His brothers had wanted to study and so there had been bitterness when Griffin stated they had to take their turn at managing the land, because he was leaving.

His mother disowned him and his brothers refused to speak to him. There had been harshness from his mother who cut him from the will, and no joy in his life for years.

Smiling or laughing became alien gestures and his thin, tight lips betrayed a miserable demeanour, yet also an air of superiority. When others showed pleasure, he saw this as shallow.

The worst scorn he felt was directed to those of lesser status; it satisfied his need for empowerment. He had been with the earl for only a few short weeks when Anne—Mary and Ruth's governess—caught his eye. He was captivated by her fair hair, flawless skin and deep blue eyes. Anne appeared to be a woman of intelligence and, despite his mistrust of women, he discovered a liking for her presence: a desire, such that he had not felt before.

He had asked her about the boys and her own methods of teaching. They discussed the different ways of learning as they strolled down to the river one quiet and peaceful early evening. He agreed with her ideas of teaching but said she must remember to discipline her charges. Otherwise, he said, children simply do as they wish and run amok. She smiled at this. It was true: Mary and Ruth both liked to run.

She gave his words some consideration.

'Ah but sir, you must remember… Learning is life and as such, it is to be embraced, not something to escape from or fear.' He smiled and agreed; at that point their eyes made contact and lingered.

Standing by the window, the formidable Frances, the housekeeper who noticed most goings on in the house, watched them walking together. She frowned. Considering herself a staunch woman of character, able to judge sincerity in people, Master Griffin's charm did nothing to impress her.

*

Early in the morning, just after dawn, Margaret and Frances heard Griffin pacing up and down the schoolroom, which was just above the scullery.

'Why does he pace so?' Frances asked, head looking towards the ceiling, not really wanting an answer, but Margaret, also looking up, tutted.

'The man isn't of sound mind, Frances. I can tell folk who are troubled and the devil has dealings with him.'

They heard him shouting, but it was muffled. Frances opened the kitchen door and beckoned Margaret, wiping her hands in her apron, to listen at the bottom of the stairs.

'Oliver, you have barely answered one question today. You sir, are not listening to me or have become a mute! Come here, Jack! Hold out your hand.'

Margaret shook her head. Her face crumpled with disapproval.

*

In the schoolroom, Oliver began to uncomfortably shuffle in his seat, his mouth opening but nothing coming out. Jack did as he was asked and Oliver, startled and frightened, watched as ten strokes of the coarse birch rained down on Jack's open palm.

He saw Jack's bottom lip tremble and tears without cries trickled down his scarlet cheeks. Griffin was unmoved as he commanded him to sit down. Trickles of blood from Jack's quivering hands quickly soaked in and stained the wooden floor.

At the end of lessons, Master Griffin tightened his grip on Jack's hand during the customary handshake at the end of the day. Jack's mouth opened ready to yell but, although he suppressed it, he couldn't stop the low moan as his bottom lip quivered. Griffin's grip was unyielding, the tutor's thin lips widening into a pleasurable grin. That gesture triggered the fiercest expression on Jack's face as he faced Griffin. A glare that could only signify an intense hatred.

*

Mary came out of the lower schoolroom, with Ruth close behind. Oliver and Jack were descending the stairs.

'What ails you?' she asked the boys, looking from one to the other. Oliver began to explain to her, when Jack stopped him by shaking his head and interrupting. He had seen the watchful gazes of Frances and Margaret at the doorway to the scullery. They would tell his mother and he didn't want her to know.

'Nothing,' muttered Jack, and he quickly left the house.

Ruth started to run after him.

'Stop,' commanded Mary, as she grabbed Ruth's arms tightly. 'We're finding Father Peters' treasure, remember?'

'I beg your pardon, my lady, I must go with my brother.'

Mary's attention was turned to the tall figure at the top of the stairs. Edward Griffin was smiling at her, but not a smile that denoted sincerity. She did not trust that man. With no words spoken, he turned back to his classroom. Something had happened to upset her brother and Jack. She would discuss this with her father.

*

Frances was a housekeeper who never missed very much in the household; after all, it was her business. She'd heard the striking of the birch before, she told Margaret. Margaret confided in the housekeeper that the noise made her wince every time.

'The boys' schoolroom is a room of hatred,' she complained to the housekeeper. 'No longer do I hear laughter, just the master shouting and the birch thrashing; too many strokes, I swear. Jack is being whipped beyond all measure. The man wants perfection. I do so pity Jack; it can't possibly continue. How can Anne be smitten with this beast of a man?'

Frances shook her head. 'I told you, the devil owns that body, but Jack saw us watching him. He is a proud young fellow. I doubt that he will want Kathleen to know any of this. Did you see his eyes? They were red with tears from pain, but Lord Oliver has the paleness of death, Margaret. He too suffers. Master Griffin's shouting and anger is whipping his soul into a quivering wreck. I wish Father Peters were here.'

*

All the way home, Jack's pace was speedy and he refused to say anything to his sister, until she threatened to tell their mother everything.

'No!' He stopped abruptly and faced her. 'Don't you see? I will just get thrashed harder. It's expected of me. That's why Lord Becton has me there. The Lady Charlotte will just let us both go and you know mother wants us to be educated. That will not be possible if we have to leave.'

Ruth was quiet. She said nothing to their mother but, ten days or so later, Kathleen noticed the agony on her son's face as he sat at the table. She had seen him many times wincing and recently observed him hiding his hands from her.

'Jack, show me your hands, and your back.'

'Please mother, there is nothing wrong.'

'Show me your hands then, now!' Kathleen swiftly uncoiled his fingers and gasped. 'Take off your shirt.' She was stunned at the sight of his palms and the deep weals on his back.

Jack stared at the shock on his mother's face. The skin on his back, now open to the air, was burning. His bravery could not be sustained as he absorbed his mother's misery and he started to cry; tears, at first pooling then escaping down his cheeks. He drew in deep breaths of air to stifle the sobs that wanted to come.

His father, now well passed, had wanted him to be the strong man of the house. He had promised him on his deathbed. He would not let him down.

'I cannot be taught by Master Griffin, Mother. He is vicious and makes Lord Oliver very nervous, such that he cannot answer anything, so I get birched. It used to be a few on my hands but now if Oliver cannot answer correctly, the master turns to me.'

There was a little sob. 'Oliver is so afraid of him, his thinking becomes blocked. He knows the answers to his questions, but he cannot utter them for fear of the Master. I understand why I am there, but he is so different to Father Peters. We cannot learn from him, only how to be harsh and evil.'

Kathleen's bottom lip quivered. She knew her son wanted to learn, to do well.

'I understand your silence, son. I wanted you and Ruth to learn about the world, to do better than your father, but not like this. I am so sorry Jack. Sorry that we are so poor and sorry I have to earn our bread by steeping my herbs and grinding the lead for the ceruse… We have to depend on their money but we are worthless souls in their eyes, just worthless, and Lord Becton has been good to us.'

Sinews in her neck protruded and her face was blotchy and red. The anger and tension had mounted so much that her body stiffened, her shoulders were raised and fists held tight, showing ivory white knuckles. Jack feared that she would suddenly collapse as her breathing was laboured with the effort to contain her strong emotions.

She hastily gathered up Jack's shirt, seeing dried bloodstains She hated Master Griffin, she hated the earl for dismissing Father Peters, and she hated with a vengeance all titled people, born with immediate privileges.

'Lean over, Jack. I will bathe these wounds.' The pair of them were now quiet but thoughts of revenge were raging through Kathleen's head. At that moment, she could kill.

'Don't say anything mother, not to his lordship. Griffin will just thrash me harder.'

'You want this to carry on, son?'

Jack merely shook his head.

The next day Kathleen went to the kitchen door of Becton

Manor with Jack and Ruth.

Margaret opened the door and greeted them. Kathleen was struck by how red and sweaty she was, hair strands stuck to her skin like dead worms dangling from under her coif, the end of her nose glistening with globules of something horrible ready to drop.

'My... Kathleen, you look spurned by the Holy Spirit Himself. Jack should go with haste to Master Griffin; he is late for his lessons. He will be full of scorn if you don't hurry, lad.' Margaret always liked to keep the peace.

Kathleen sighed, 'Ruth, you can go to Mistress Anne. Jack is staying with me.' She showed Margaret the wounds on his back.

'Oh mercy, I was afraid of this.'

'You knew of this?'

'It's not my place to speak out against the new Master. Jack's place is to receive the birch. That is why the earl agreed to him coming... but then he knows nothing of this, being at court all the time.'

Kathleen looked from side to side, to check for listening ears. 'That new Master is pure evil, Margaret. If you were a mother, would you expect the payment for learning to be this, even for a commoner boy?'

Just at that moment, Master Griffin entered the room. Both women jumped as he had approached so quietly. 'Jack. Why are you late? You must get yourself into the study room at once!'

Kathleen turned to face him, took a deep breath, and lifted her chin.

'He will not attend your lessons, sir, if you insist on regular thrashings.'

'Madam!' Griffin's eyes widened as he glared at her, 'That is why your son has the privilege of being taught alongside Lord Oliver. You are disadvantaging him. Further, you are defying Lord Becton. You must see that your son will grow robust, resilient and educated. How can you deny him this?'

'My son learns when he feels comfortable with his master and that, sir, is not you! You are an evil man. I do not know what kind of revenge you seek, but you cannot punish my son for your own past shortcomings or resentments. Only weak men beat young boys because they are unable to defeat their demons. You must have an abundance of demons, sir! You are not a fit man to teach!'

Master Griffin's slit-like eyes were only just visible through his dark lashes as he took a sharp inward breath, astonished by this outburst from a mere herb woman.

Her caustic words had reminded him of his past, his weaknesses. His brothers had been given easier paths and yes, he resented it. He was entitled to better. This forthright wench could cause him a lot of grief if he lost this position. How dare she confront him?

'You are insolent, madam. How dare you insult me? You are an ignorant creature, a witch, by my understanding, and one who is poisoning a child with the face powder intended for older women. Queen Elizabeth may paint her face but she does not lick the poison. Have you been too stupid to notice? I have studied medicine, madam, and know you are meddling with poisons. You will see what will become of the young Lady Mary.' He bent closer to her face. 'You will see the harm you cause. One day, you will receive your just fruits, witch!'

Kathleen stepped back, horrified at the gall of this man. Margaret's face became more crumpled than ever, with shock and concern.

Master Griffin hastily left the room, shouting as he went. 'You will see who is right when the earl returns, madam!'

Kathleen did not let him have the last say, 'If I am a witch, sir, I curse you so nothing but ill fortune comes your way!'

'Strong words madam, which you may one day regret. You are witness to this curse, cook, are you not?' Griffin yelled over his shoulder, not waiting for a reply.

Margaret, her mouth wide open, remained aghast and speechless. Kathleen left hastily with Jack, her body shaking with a fury she had never before experienced.

*

The atmosphere at Becton Manor was subdued. Frances had told Lady Charlotte of the incident with Master Griffin, but she seemed unconcerned, as long as Lord Oliver continued to receive a strong education. She tended to share the opinion of Master Griffin— that Jack was very fortunate to be receiving an education at all— and told Frances to refrain from any more talk of his evil nature.

Frances sighed heavily. She knew that if Lady Charlotte was pleased with how things were, the earl would not make a fuss. This new tutor was a snake in the grass who had already snared Anne. The blushing of the governess whenever she saw him was sickening.

Frances briefly recalled the time she was jilted by a similar man. She felt a hatred for Griffin at that moment, but also a pang of jealousy.

She thought this may be detected by Anne. When she had tried to warn her of his nature, her words were met with a strong rebuff.

'Master Griffin simply has strong principles, which I admire. Perhaps you would do better to keep your attention on the servants. I saw young Henry from the stables steal a cake, but you are too busy being inquisitive about other people's business to notice. Or could it be that you find him attractive and perhaps covet the attention he gives me?'

At that accusation, she turned and fled the room, her kirtle sweeping the floor. Frances closed her eyes for a few seconds. She hated any reference to her romantic life; realising that a relationship was most unlikely. Although getting on in years and probably unable to conceive, there had once been a young man she had fallen in love with. He had married someone else which not only had soured her life but made her distrust men. She had decided instead to be married to her work at the manor. Anne was desperate to marry and blindly smitten. She didn't see the greed or quickness of temper.

Chapter Eight

December 1597

When the earl's father, a rich yeoman, had died some five years earlier, he had left most of his estate to William, being the eldest son. He had owned a vast amount of land bordering Yorkshire and Derbyshire and passed on the title of Earl of Becton, which he had inherited from his own father, originally earned for military duties completed during the Wars of the Roses.

Gilbert Harrison, Esq was the earl's younger brother. Although he had married a woman from a wealthy family, he coveted the land and wealth of his older brother. Gilbert, however, had invested in new lands and buildings and thus now collected rents from many tenants in nearby Barlow and Brampton.

The two brothers generally shared the same views; except that Gilbert Harrison was a willing convert to the Anglican Church. He was also a more efficient business manager than his elder brother and, over time, Gilbert had grown resentful of the debts that the earl was incurring because of poor management of his estate. His visits usually centred on finances.

One frosty morning in early December was one such visit. The earl was not at his best. The dominant Gilbert enjoyed a confrontation; the earl would rather avoid one.

On hearing the heavy knock on the front door, Frances

nervously straightened her coif. Gilbert Harrison was greeted with a small curtsey.

'Please enter, sir, the earl is waiting for you.'

The tall, flamboyant figure briskly entered, swept off his large hat and cloak to reveal a thick green studded doublet. He handed the discarded items to Frances, who always admired his elaborate clothes . He marched into the front parlour, just as the earl was rising wearily from his chair.

'Ah, William, you look tired and brow-beaten. Life is not treating you well, brother? It may be you need a rest.'

To try to establish a stronger footing, the earl straightened his back and looked directly into Gilbert's eyes. 'Not so, brother. I am well and busy.'

'I don't think busy enough, William, if your accounts are not growing. You still have not invested in your land, have you? What in God's name are you doing with the income from the Sovereign, if I might dare to ask? Has the building of this new house cost you more than you expected? You should have kept father's existing one and not listened to the wants of your wife. You should be comfortable, brother, with no debts.'

'Enough!' As always, the earl felt intimidated when his brother lectured him and now the anger he felt triggered an irritating pacing up and down. His brother was clearly of a mood to wear him down: not really seeking answers to his questions, merely wanting to vilify him. And now here he was, smugly watching him with a stern gaze, waiting for a reaction.

'Well, brother, to which question do you want a reply?' asked the earl. 'In truth, it was such an onslaught, that I can barely recall the detail in each one. But I will endeavour to explain, yet again. My share of the land, as you well know, is only fit for pastoral purposes and farmland.' He raised his chin 'I have fewer tenants than you and they manage their own smallholdings. You know we have suffered greatly from more than one year's bad weather and poor crops. It is easy for you to be smug, with your unfair rents, even from the poorest who can hardly feed themselves after you have had your greedy share!'

Gilbert had not expected this, but he relished a fight. He stood and raised his voice so much he was heard in the scullery by all. The servants were not the only ones listening in doorways, suitably ajar; Master Griffin, lurking nearby, noted every word, some already resonating in his head:

'You have never been a great overseer of your finances, William. Father affirmed this to me on his deathbed. Your agent is obviously not astute. You need someone to have the foresight to further increase your yield! Why are you so unable to see this? If your land had been given to me, I could have made it profitable, but you, YOU...have no perception to move forward. Furthermore, another matter, there are those who suspect you still adhere to the Old Religion. You are seen to some, brother, as a Papist. The whisperings of the locals have come to my ears. It is a good thing at least that I hear you have rid yourself of that priest!'

Lord Becton had started to pace again. Why would his father discuss him on his death bed? That was a lie; and who actually suspected that he maintained his old faith?

Suddenly the frosty cold wind blew in through the scullery window and a door slammed shut with a loud bang, which stunned the two brothers into silence. The earl was the first to break it. 'I must ask you to leave my house, talking in this manner.' Both glared at one another before the earl continued: 'You can rest assured that my accounts are not in as bad a state as you think they are.'

'Very well, I will leave, but heed my words, William: Charlotte and the children as well as this house will suffer unless you gather your wits.'

Master Griffin, his ear turned towards the closed parlour door, raised his eyebrows at this last comment, his devious thoughts running wild. This fantasy of acquiring wealth and position for himself possessed him, and he was rooted to the spot. He was slow to slink away when Gilbert Harrison's rapid strides and the swift opening of the door caught him unawares.

'Who are you?' Gilbert demanded. 'Are you eavesdropping, sir, on private meetings?'

'I beg your forgiveness, sir, but I was on my way to meet with the earl myself and about to knock on the door. I am Master Griffin, the boys' tutor.'

'Ah yes, I have heard of you. I trust you are not a Papist, sir?' He glared at Griffin suspiciously as he waited for the reply.

'Indeed not, sir. My aim in its entirety, is for the young Oliver to excel and to be ready for university, as my position dictates. I myself am an excellent mathematician.'

Gilbert Harrison looked surprised and wondered how much of the discussion with his brother had been overheard.

'Indeed…perhaps you should discuss your talents with the earl, Master Griffin.' At that, he gathered his hat and left the house.

Imaginings of taking over Becton Manor ran wild in Master Griffin's head: *Yes, I can manage the household accounts and gain a higher status, even the house itself, perhaps.*

He had already started to plan his next moves and knew he must do so while the earl felt threatened and vulnerable by his brother. He must not hesitate.

Lord Becton however, was in no mood for another meeting. He looked up as his brother left and saw Griffin in the doorway.

'Oh, can it wait, Master Griffin? I have much to attend to.'

'Of course, my lord.' Griffin sighed and walked away, disappointed but not beaten.

*

That evening, unaware of the incident with her brother-in-law, Lady Charlotte asked to speak with her husband concerning Master Griffin and the report from Frances. She had decided to act upon this when she realised it might be affecting her son. When the evening meal was over, the earl was still not in a good frame of mind, the recollections of his brother's confrontation going round and round in circles. He could not shake off the nausea of intimidation, but now Charlotte disturbed his reflection.

'I have heard from Frances and also Mary that Master Griffin is a hard taskmaster and has given Jack the birch many times. Mary is pleading with me to request that you dismiss him.'

Wanting to be strong, but feeling irritated by another issue of concern, he quickly responded, 'Madam, that is what Jack is here for. Griffin can treat the boys as he thinks fit, as long as my son obtains a sound education.'

Lady Charlotte was taken aback. It was not a good time; her husband was in no mood to discuss Jack.

She tried once more. 'Forgive me, husband, if you wish the schooling to go on…'

The earl raised his hand to silence her, but she was insistent.

'You must listen, husband. Master Griffin has to limit the number of lashings Jack receives. I have thought about it. It is not a good thing that our son is witness to such harshness. Frances has told me the schoolroom floor is often stained with blood and Oliver is seldom in high spirits but pining as a boy should not do. He will not tell me what upsets him but Mary has noted this too. This will not make him strong.'

The earl sighed. 'Yes, yes, very well. I do not want to hear any more of that matter, is that understood? I will speak to him in due course. You can tell him that I will meet with him.'

Charlotte said no more as she left the parlour. Something else was troubling him, she knew, and she always feared conflict within the household.

The next day, she sent for Master Griffin before lessons commenced and told him her husband wanted to discuss a matter of great importance. Then, fearing that discussion may be some time off and worried about her son, she added, 'In the meantime, Master Griffin, my husband requests that you reduce the thrashings to Jack. This is causing distress to more than Jack, you must understand.'

'Of course, my lady. I apologise for any distress that I may have caused. The boys are already becoming more robust in their characters so I see this as a reasonable option at this stage.'

Lady Charlotte found his smile surprisingly beguiling and she could see why Anne might be infatuated. Realising she had been looking at him for longer than might be considered suitable and slightly embarrassed, she turned to leave. Griffin slowly stepped between her and the door.

'There is something, my lady, but perhaps I should discuss it with Lord Becton, if I may?'

'Does it concern my son's education? In which case you may speak freely with me.'

'Thank you my lady. I am concerned that Lord Oliver's learning in mathematics is not all it could be. I wish to try alternative instruction methods. I would like to discuss these with Lord Becton. I am of course, of keen interest for him to succeed in his studies.'

Charlotte very much doubted that her husband would care one way or another regarding Griffin's teaching methods.

'Very well, I will remind his lordship of the need to meet with you.'

Master Griffin bowed his head, thanking her, and hurried up the stairs to the schoolroom. The thought of not giving so many lashes of the birch irritated him; in truth, Jack irritated him. The whipping boy had only just returned to sessions since Kathleen's outburst, following reassurance that her son would not be harshly treated, but to secure his plan for wealth he must try to control his urges and bide his time.

After a subdued morning of lessons the boys appeared relieved; but not comfortable enough to run off, hiding and playing games, as they had done when Father Peters' lessons had ended.

It was seven o'clock in the evening when Master Griffin was putting away his books. The senior maid, Frances, knocked at his door.

'If you have finished for the day, sir, the earl wishes to speak with you.' It was a command, rather than a request, and Griffin found it distasteful.

He sensed she had an interest in him, even desire, and that amused him. He wondered if she had ever been with a man. She was prim, too pedantic, but he had a mind to tease her.

'Ah, indeed. But may I say, Mistress Frances, you look quite becoming this evening. It is a shame you have to hide your hair under that cap.' His eyes wandered across her face, before lowering to her full bosom. He smiled; her blush was the response he wanted.

'Tell him I will come directly.'

Frances was not used to being told what to do by Edward Griffin, but oddly, for reasons beyond her judgement, she was unable to confront him. She wanted to linger and watched him tidying the schoolroom.

'Oh sir, I would have thought you would have made the boys do all the tidying.'

Master Griffin grinned at what he perceived to be a flirtation. He strolled nearer, now very close to her. He lifted her chin high with his finger and then held it, his large thumb indenting her soft skin. She could feel his warm breath on her cheek. Why did she suddenly feel like a small insect trapped in a spider's web? Why was she afraid of him? He released his grip and continued to tidy.

'Is there anything else, Mistress Frances?' She shook her head and turned to leave.

As she walked down the stairs, she contemplated the reasons for men's behaviour. Some men could indeed be charming, intelligent and kind, but there would be an ulterior motive; the devil lurked in their thoughts and deeds, provoking them to use evil to achieve their desires. The devil lurked in Edward Griffin.

. *

The meeting with the earl went well for Griffin; his demeanour remained calm and he succeeded with what he sought to do: bewilder the earl with mathematical jargon. Griffin had presented the earl with his own accounts from his late father's estate. He chose just the right moment as the earl's eyes were glazing over.

'Forgive me, my lord, I assume you understand the keeping of my ledgers? After my father's death, I took on the farm accounts. Thereafter I showed that the farmland was making profits from which my mother benefitted until her own death. It was not an easy task but, as you can see, they are impeccable.' There was a pause. He watched the earl reading them, knowing he had little idea of the figures before him, especially those additional ones that Griffin had added to deliberately snare the earl. He waited almost impatiently for a response and was not disappointed when it came.

'If you are a good accountant, Master Griffin, I may have need for you. I have not had the time to monitor mine as carefully as I should. It has come to my attention that my agent, a rather old fellow who passed away, was rather weak. I hope you will improve upon that, Griffin. I will of course increase your pay, to support this extra duty.'

Griffin was delighted. 'I am most honoured, my Lord and I assure you: I will make you profits that mean you will not lose this house.'

The earl was a little perturbed. Since when, during their meeting, had he mentioned fear of losing his house? That was what his brother had said. So this man must have been eavesdropping that morning. But profits were, after all, what he needed; for now, he would say nothing.

'Very well, but you must keep me informed at all times.' He paused again before changing the subject. 'There is another matter; reports have come to my attention of your harshness when punishing Jack. My son's future is of the utmost importance to me, Master Griffin. He and Jack are good companions and the priest believed they learned from each other. He assured me the birch had never been necessary. 'Tis of benefit when both are free to seek counsel and speak out: do you not agree, sir?'

Griffin frowned. *How did these reports come to the attention of Lord Becton? Could it have been the precocious young Mary?* He would need to be careful of her watching him. For now, he chose a diplomatic response, keeping the emphasis on Lord Oliver's progress.

'It was only one occasion, my lord. I agree that I was rather hard on the boy, but it had the desired effect of sharpening the wits of both of them. Lord Oliver is beginning to excel in languages and literature and now we will also make good progress with the mathematics. You have no need to concern yourself, my lord.'

The earl now faced Griffin squarely. 'If my son reports any disparities, sir, I will not hesitate to dismiss you, profits or not. Is that understood?'

'You need have no further fears, my Lord.'

'Hmm… Well, I will consider all that you say, Master Griffin. I have other matters now to attend to. I will make necessary arrangements for the accounts ledger to be passed to you.' The earl stood and Griffin bowed his head before departing.

Then, as an afterthought, the earl called him back.

'Master Griffin, the help you give me is only privy to ourselves.'

'Aye, my lord. I would not have considered otherwise.'

Master Griffin smiled. The day had ended well. He did not want others to be aware that he was helping with the accounts, but more importantly, he wanted no one to learn of his future plans. He immediately thought of Mary. She didn't like him but, furthermore, he sensed she was waiting for him to do something wrong. Whenever they passed each other, she looked at him suspiciously. If she got wind of his ambitions of owning land and property, she would not hesitate to report to her beloved father.

Chapter Nine

September 1957

After nearly breaking my neck in the secret passageway I got rid of my torn trousers, shoving them right down at the bottom of the kitchen bin. They were too short now, anyway. I'd recently had new ones and with a bit of luck, she'd never notice.

On the first morning of the new school term, breakfast was a quiet event. Despite our dislike of the house, neither Annabel nor I wanted to go to school and it was to be a long bus journey before we arrived there. I wanted to tell her about my narrow escape, but a voice kept saying no, just leave it…so I did. I guess I couldn't face any more accusations of having a wild imagination and she could be so bossy. I stared out of the bus window, missing my old friends, even the teachers.

Would this new school be strict, with different rules? Would anyone actually speak to me? The bus turned into the school grounds and I was swept along with others as they eagerly chattered and marched into the school entrance. Everyone knew where to go, except us.

'We need Mrs Burnley, the school secretary. She will be in the office and the sign outside says *'Visitors'.*'

Annabel nodded nervously.

Mrs Burnley was a tall and elegant lady with a warm smile.

After greeting us, she sent for a prefect to take Annabel to her classroom, and then she turned to me.

'Right, Thomas, you can come with me.' It was a long time since anyone had called me Thomas. I raised my eyebrows and grinned at the formality.

As she opened the classroom door, registration was taking place. A swarm of new faces all turned towards me. It felt like they were all creatures from outer space. I became aware of my face growing hotter and hoped that my spots were not glowing. A girl smiled coyly as I was shown to a seat next to a small red-haired boy wearing glasses. The girl was sat directly behind him. He also smiled and nodded, but others glared at me.

Mrs Burnley had whispered something to the young, confident-looking male teacher, who then nodded and turned to the class.

'Everyone, this is Thomas Winchett, a newcomer to the school. I trust that you will all look after him and make sure he knows where he's going.' As I looked around at the strange faces studying me again, I had a good notion of who would help me and who wouldn't. While registration continued, there was a hum of low-level chatter.

'Where do you come from?' the boy with red hair asked.

'Near Sheffield,' I whispered.

'So why did you move?' He didn't whisper. Such directness.

'We inherited an Elizabethan manor house.'

'Wow, Elizabethan? Interesting.'

'Suppose so.'

He introduced himself as George, but other boys groaned. I soon understood why.

'They think I'm odd, 'cos I'm small and talk a lot. Born very early—that is, pre-mature, before my due date. My jabbering gets on my dad's nerves and people here get fed up with me. I'm used to it now, though, them walking away. They're jealous cos I have a high I.Q. Do you know what that means? It's a syndrome. I've been tested…'

Now I knew why the boys groaned. George never shut up.

The teacher was staring at us. I interrupted him and gave my final whisper.

'You might take a breath once in a while.'

The teacher now raised his voice: 'Quiet, George. You again.'

'Sorry sir.'

The smiling girl nearby was watching me closely. I wasn't used to the attention of girls, even though some of my friends had started taking an interest in them;

I'd rather go trainspotting or hiking. She was quite pretty though. She also didn't stare at my spots.

George had noticed the brief look and, nudging me, winked.

'Think you have an ally there, eh? Her name's Sally. She lives near me.'

There was a slight pause before he excitedly asked, 'Can I come and see your house on Saturday?'

I was taken aback with his directness. 'Oh yeah, suppose so.' I didn't seem to have any choice. I looked behind me and Sally was still gazing at me, smiling. Aware of my face becoming hot and bright red with embarrassment, I managed a half-smile back.

That night, I wasn't surprised that Mum and Dad were not ready for a strange boy to come over but a few hours was fine and anyway, they were eager for me to find new friends and settle down here, in this glorious museum of a house.

'We are quite remote, Tom. Do George's parents have a car? Make sure you give George the address so that he can be collected.'

*

The following days passed smoothly, and I was relieved that I could manage the schoolwork. I finally understood the timetable, where and how to get to the lessons.

George fussed over me and made sure I had the right textbooks and materials for woodwork, metalwork and P.E. For a small lad, he could be quite bossy. I noticed that, in every class, he often shot his hand up quickly to ask or answer questions. I could see he was irritating to others. Maybe that brag about a high I.Q. was accurate.

During one break, I spotted a group of boys tormenting him.

'What's the matter, Georgy Pixie? Looking for your gnomes?' The four of them laughed. George carried on walking and I strolled over to join him.

'Hey, you: new boy. Who do you think you are, eh? George's knight in shining armour? Bet you're another weirdo, sent from the same planet as Georgy boy.'

'Not as weird as you, mate. What distant planet of idiots are you from?'

'Ooh, not very friendly, are we?' One of the boys threw a stone, then the others followed suit. George increased his pace but I stopped and threw them back. One hit a boy in the face.

'Argh, he's blinded me!'

I doubted I had, but the ringleader, a boy called Mike, beckoned the others.

'C'mon let's get 'em!'

They jumped on top of me—one was pulling my hair and I felt painful kicks from another. I tried to get up and kick back but I was pinned to the ground.

I heard George shouting at them to stop, but that was quickly followed by a moan. From the corner of my eye, I saw two of them on top of him.

'Stop!' It was the headmaster, Mr Sampson.

'They always tease me.' George spurted out as the headmaster approached. 'Mike Thompson and his friends have always called me weird, sir!'

Mr. Sampson was breathless as he attempted to smooth down his billowy hair. 'Never mind the excuses, lads. In my office now, all of you.'

In the office, it was obvious he didn't really want explanations. 'Detention on Friday week, the lot of you. There are alterations to the school this weekend but, in the meantime, during every break, you are all to report to me before clearing litter from the school grounds and I will inspect them.'

*

That evening, Dad noticed grazes on my face, not the sort that I could explain away by scratching my spots.

'We had rugby dad, a tough game that one.'

Dad laughed. 'Nothing like good sport, lad.'

He helped Mum in the kitchen; I had got away with it.

*

That Saturday, George was dropped off in a hurry. I heard the car so I opened the front door. George's dad looked pretty miserable, I recall, as he neither got out of the car—a really old station wagon type—nor smiled or nodded towards me. George said his dad had to go somewhere but he would pick him up about six o'clock if that was okay. I said it should be.

I thought I would get a king-size headache to be honest and wasn't really looking forward to several hours in the company of a super clever babbling swot. As soon as he entered the hall, we were both silenced by the sound of raised voices coming from the kitchen. The door couldn't have been closed. It was Mum and Dad, and they didn't sound happy.

'Alice, I am about to lose my job and you want God knows how much stuff for this damn house.'

'I found a job in the library. You can find one as well, can't you?'

'It's not as easy as that. What skills have I got? I've been down that lead mine for years, woman. I've done nothing else! I don't want to work in a library or a bloody shop!'

I forced a loud cough and there was a moment's silence before the kitchen door was fully opened and my embarrassed-looking mother emerged.

'Oh, hello. You must be George.' She giggled nervously. 'Tom, why don't you show George around while I make some tea, eh?'

So, thinking outside first was the better option, I led George down the back garden path, apologising for the poor welcome.

He laughed. 'Mine row all the time, Tom. They all do it. Never get married, that's what I say. My dad is just a bully with me and Mum's too soft with him. He had an affair once and Mum forgave him…silly bitch. Dad says, *"Live o'er brush"* whatever that means. How would you live over a brush?'

'It means living together without getting married.'

'Well, why is it done over a brush?'

'I don't know. C'mon.'

George persisted. 'Another thing: my cousin had a shotgun wedding. Why would you want a shotgun at your wedding?'

It was obvious that George asked questions as well as rambling but didn't necessarily want them answered. We stopped as we got to the privy.

'Well…this is our outside loo.'

George looked at the steel bucket under some thick wooden bars, a hole in the middle.

'Is that bucket for the pee and the "soft stuff"?'

'Yeah, but we have a chamber pot in our rooms for night time.'

'A chamber pot? They're small aren't they? My auntie uses them for growing plants in. Said having to sit on them gave her lumbago. Hip pain, I believe.'

I chuckled. I was going to receive a lot of information from George; that was pretty obvious. 'We go outside last thing at night, then it won't be stinking under your bed all night! Think about me George, I have to collect it in a bucket and take it to the cess pit!'

'Cess pit?'

'Yeah, a hole in the ground, over there, a few yards past the lav; always mind that big stick if you walk over there 'cos there's no lid on it yet and its pretty deep.'

'You just chuck it in?'

'Yep. It's not that bad. They don't know, but I chuck it in the bushes before I get that far. Good for the garden, any road. Since we've been here, those flowers are huge; crap is a great fertiliser.'

George threw his head back and laughed so loud, it was a good sight after Mike and his bullies upset him.

'C'mon, let's go inside. They might've stopped rowing now.'

As we turned to go back inside, the raven—'Corvus', as John Haslam called it—swooped low and landed on the boundary fence to the right of us, proceeding to make strange guttural sounds..

'God, he's a big fella.'

'Just ignore him, George. Mr. Haslam at the newsagents said he can be nasty.'

'Is he here in your garden all the time?'

'Not all the time, but he seems pretty inquisitive. I agree with Mr Haslam. I believe he could get vicious.'

George kept his eye on him, only stopping when we reached the French windows.

I showed George to my room and then told him about the hole and how I'd lost my sweet.

'It must be somewhere, Tom. Those sweets don't just disintegrate, you know: full of hard sugar and all that.'

'Hmm. But put your finger in that hole, George, then twist that metal peg to the right.'

The panel creaked open.

'C'mon, we just need to shove,'

'Ah…blimey, what a find, Tom, but the stink…Well, the evidence is clear: you have priest holes in this house.'

'What holes?'

'Priest holes. Catholic priests—or more accurately, architects— would construct them for the purpose of hiding. It was kind of against the law to be a Catholic in the late sixteenth century. I read a really interesting story, a true story, of an escape by a priest from a window in the Tower of London and he took his gaoler with him. What a great bloke. I've read about it somewhere; and… you have to have heard of the Gunpowder Plot: all to do with the Catholics?' Looking up at the left hand ledge, he forgot the Tudor story. 'Does it go anywhere? It must do. We ought to investigate.'

Someone, at least, shared my curiosity. 'You're not afraid?'

'No way!'

'It's just that there might be a ghost, George. I kept seeing—well, imagining—an old woman in a chair in my room. She was dressed all funny, with a bonnet on like babies wear. Mum moved the chair out, but when we first got here, I heard whispering on the landing.'

'Whispering? Saying what?'

'I dunno, not in English, "san" something.'

'But Tom, ghosts don't mean any harm. Ghosts are sad for some reason. Maybe they really want someone to talk to them, perhaps about their sad lives on this earth; that's what I reckon. Anyway, I've read it somewhere, why dead people return...can't quite remember where...'

'Hmm. Troubled souls.' I recalled the words of Mr. Haslam in the shop. *Just troubled souls.*

'Oh, Tom, this smell is like two million rotten eggs. I can climb up here; must lead to something.'

'You can't climb in there, it's not safe. All the bricks are loose and start to fall away and, I mean, they fall a hell of a way down. The full length of the house. I nearly died, I can tell you. It was scary.'

'Hmm...' He wasn't perturbed.

'It's true, I'm telling you. I explored it and it's really dangerous. If you don't believe me, you go: clever one that you are, but you'll need a footstool.'

With no hesitation and no footstool, George clambered up to the ledge by grabbing small jagged protrusions. 'I'll be all right. I'm much smaller than you. Have you got a torch, though?'

'I'll get one.' But my heart started to thump; obviously George disregarded warnings. should stop him.

Luckily Mum wasn't around, because it took me ages to find a torch.

I hastily ran up the stairs, then worried. There was no sight or sound of him. Had he fallen into the abyss while I was in the kitchen? *Oh God, poor George. Oh no! It's my fault. I've all but killed him.* Why did I let him go? What would Mum and Dad say? He'd disappeared.

'George!' I yelled; then even louder, 'George!'

I got the footstool which I had placed under the bed. I looked up into the recess in the panelled chamber; not seeing or hearing anything. Panic started to rise. Wouldn't I have heard him if he had fallen? Unless he was unconscious. Should I go after him?' I should shout for Mum or Dad. What the hell had happened to George? I was starting to feel like an idiot, dithering yet doing nothing.

Then came the sound of running footsteps. George ran through the bedroom door.

'How the heck…?'

He was filthy.

'It took my weight, Tom, but I know what you mean. There are lots of loose bricks. Some little stones fell but I think your weight did all the damage. There's another way, though. Come and look.' He beckoned as he ran into the front bedroom. I was close behind.

'If you could have kept going, the passage drops down to the back of this cupboard in your front bedroom. There's a rusty trapdoor above the top of the cupboard. Surprised I could lift it. From there you simply drop down into the cupboard. Glad there was nothing in it. There are iron struts on the shaft you were talking about. We can climb down easily. At one time it was used as a ladder to somewhere. I reckon it's in the middle of the two chimneys and that's why the outside wall is big. It's an escape shaft. You live in a great house, Tom.'

Perhaps the house was starting to interest me, but George's suggestion of climbing down that shaft was not quite what I had in mind. George read my thoughts.

'Oh go on Tom, don't be a chicken. I'm up for it.'

I couldn't respond at that precise moment, as Mum interrupted by calling us down for lunch.

'Don't mention any of this to my parents or my sister. Understand? Look at the sight of you. Mum can't see you like that. There's a jug of cold water on that stand on the landing. Slosh some of it round your face and hands, quick. And I haven't agreed to your plan yet.'

'You will.' He grinned as he sploshed his face quickly, most of the water going on the floor.

George was introduced to my sister, who immediately started chatting and asking him lots of questions. Both could talk incessantly. Mum smiled as she dished out shepherd's pie, pleased that there was some pleasantness in the house, but even before plates had any food on them, George was bombarded with questions from both of my parents. Adults ask the daftest things, but always the same. *'What do you want to do when you leave school? 'Have you got a subject you're good at?'*

But George was loving the attention. People were actually listening to him. There was so much talking around the table that Mum almost forgot about the apple pie and custard. Dad had to remind her. As she finally sat down, she looked a bit flustered.

'Oh, I'm sorry, the custard's gone a bit thick.'

George, his cheeks bulging, couldn't care less.

'Oh, I didn't notice, Mrs. Winchett.'

What a creep. He polished it off before the rest of us hardly got started. As Mum and Dad started to discuss where to go that afternoon for a walk, George leaned over to me and whispered, 'We need another torch, Tom.'

'What do you need a torch for?' Annabel had darn keen ears.

'None of your business.' Then I had second thoughts. Annabel rarely let anything drop until she had an answer. 'If you must know, we may go slug hunting. A science project for school.'

'Don't believe you. You have to do that at night, stupid.'

Mum was watching us. George was quick to distract her. 'That apple pie and custard was delicious, Mrs Winchett.'

She beamed. A friend for life in my mother's eyes. He grinned at me.

'In fact it was a lovely dinner, Mrs Winchett. Thank you for inviting me. I'm really glad you came to live here.'

My mother was smiling at him. 'You're very welcome, George.

You can come again, anytime.'

God, George could be so bloody nauseating but his sickly sweet chatter gave me the opportunity to take some dishes through and whip another torch from the drawer.

When at last there was a lull in the conversation, Mum rose and beckoned Dad to help her. Of course he immediately got up and responded with his usual, 'Yes of course, dear.' Then they both went into the kitchen. I slid out, another torch under my sweater.

Annabel had her eyes fixed on me. 'I'll find out what you're really up to, sneak.'

'Just try.'

I pulled a face and George and I hurriedly left the table. We had lots of exploring to do, but I recall a very nervous stomach after what had happened to me earlier on the precipice.

Armed with torches, George scrambled up first.

I banged my head on the roof of the passage, probably due to nerves. It was only a couple of yards until we reached the spot where the hole was and where all the stones and bricks had previously fallen. My heart began to thump in my chest. George leaned over precariously, shining his torch downwards, looking and feeling for the first iron struts. He gasped. A deep abyss was illuminated below. I felt a bit sick. 'I can see more iron struts and bricks jutting out. They look solid enough. It'll make it easier.' He only got to the third iron when more debris started to give way.

'Whoa!'

I grabbed hold of his arm. 'Come back.'

'No, Tom, I can do it. I can get down, and so can you. It's a good ladder, but keep the torch on me.'

As he spoke, his echoing words bounced off the crumbling walls which fired a jet of more gravel into the chasm.

'It's not safe, George.'

'Shh…don't speak anymore, the sound is too vibrating.'

Then, with the agility of a chimpanzee, George descended the shaft with determination. His left leg secured a foothold before he lowered his right leg and his hands gripped the struts as his feet left them. It was so systematic; now it was my turn.

I kept the torchlight on him while he had stuffed his own down his trousers and I watched him almost reach the bottom. I saw grit and dust flying within the beam of light, some landing on the top of George's head.

'Aargh!' George suddenly cried out. He had stumbled and fallen I could just see the top of his head, but distinctly heard splashing along with three other echoed screeches, 'Aargh... aargh.....aargh......'

Then, the sound of trickling water and George disappeared. *Oh God, there's water down there. What if he's drowned? I didn't know if he could swim or not. What would happen to me? I might be accused of pushing him, enticing him to his death. I might end up in prison. For God's sake shut up!*

'George!' I yelled. *'George!'* the echo responded. I shone my light anxiously from left to right.

'Bloody shut up, Tom. I'm okay, just my ankle hurts a little.'

He appeared from the left. 'There's a tunnel down here and some water. Looks a bit like a cave but it's not deep. C'mon, I'll shine my torch upwards for you. Near the bottom is a missing brick I think. That's where I fell, so be careful.'

Every word was echoed menacingly.

'I should get help.'

'No!' he yelled and back screamed the echo, *'NO....NO.'*

'Don't do that!' Then the bloody echo, *'Don't do that...don't do that...'*

'Your dad will seal it all up... *'seal it all up, seal it all up...'*

'You can do it, c'mon... *'do it, c'mon, do it c'mon...'*

Going back will be easier... *'easier, easier...'*

I normally thought echoes very funny, but not on that occasion.

My God I was nauseous. *I'll fall, I know I'll fall. No you won't, just concentrate and make sure you get a good foothold. But you've got big feet. Those struts are for small feet and they've worn away over the years, they're too dangerous. Are you really going to chicken out? You'll never live this one down.* The voices inside my head were having a good old argument. *Right, idiot, make a move.*

The first strut was fine. I had a good hold. I lowered my hand and gripped hard onto a piece of rock that was jutting out. *Don't look down.* Slowly I found different footholds until, just like George, I got the hang of it but slipped near the bottom, scraping my back.

I landed in shallow water. It stank. We both had wet trousers and shoes that squelched.

'Let's just roll them up and see what's ahead. We can't give up now, just a bit further.'

We shone our torches into a cave-like opening to the left, only about four feet high and three feet width. Tiny really. Constructed of rock, the sides were glistening with water deposits. An amazed George was actually stunned into silence…for a couple of seconds. 'Wow, look at this.'

It was eerie, smelling stronger of damp and mould. Trickling drops of water landed on us randomly as we paddled forward, our backs hunched.

I heard something. 'Listen!'

George stopped.

There was a slight tapping noise and a movement in the water ahead. Reflected in the torchlight was a speedy ripple across the surface of the water, then a scurrying creature with whiskers emerged and ran along a slim ledge.

'Rats!'

'They won't hurt you, Tom. My cousin had white rats for pets. If you don't corner them, they won't hurt you. C'mon, keep going, it looks like quite a tunnel, but where does it go to?'

The stench became unbearable as we started to paddle on. We were looking at the walls until, unexpectedly, our bodies were sucked under the water and became submerged.

Chapter Ten

Christmas 1597

Village women, some poorly dressed in their simple kirtles of coarse cloth, trudged through snow-covered grass stiffened by silver frost, carrying as much kindling as they could.

With sacks hauled over shoulders, their hunched bodies wearily trod; all had tightly fastened their coifs to keep their ears warm. They occasionally lifted their heads to check the direction, grimacing at the biting winds which were too eager to batter their withered faces and stifle their breathing. Gathering fuel was a necessity to stave off the fiercest of winter chills throughout the coming months. As soon as they could walk, children were given just enough wood to hold onto without stumbling.

Onwards they would stagger: quiet, exhausted, and hungry.

In the early hours of the breaking dawn or towards the darkness of the evenings, the men of the village trudged the same ground, to bring back the biggest Yule log that they could find for the Christmas celebrations.

Becton Manor was elaborately decorated with as much 'evergreen' as possible. Lady Charlotte, Anne, Margaret and Frances, as well as the children all had their own jobs. The mistress was in good spirits and ensured all fireplaces contained a welcoming blaze.

It would keep out the cold. For once, she disregarded her status and invited Kathleen Melton, the herb wife, to the manor, along with her children and Henry the stable boy. Henry had told Jack he may not go inside the 'big house', as he called it, because the few clothes he possessed were only suitable around horses and for the purpose of mucking out the stables.

Jack had obviously discussed this with Oliver because, one evening before the school session, Oliver appeared in the stable and gave him some of his old but smart breeches, a doublet and a linen shirt. He reassured him that Lady Charlotte was in agreement that he should be dressed appropriately for the Christmas festivities; and anyway they were more or less the same size. There was much merriment and laughter, jokes and gossip.

Edward Griffin was not invited. He had been more lenient since his talk with Lady Charlotte, she had heard that from Kathleen but. although Jack returned to lessons, he remained wary of his tutor. For now though, she noticed Jack's unease ebb, as he took pleasure in the Christmas celebrations. He and Oliver were threading mistletoe around some hoops when Henry arrived. Frances let him in but hurriedly whispered in his ear, 'Only speak, lad, if thy are spoken to, y'hear?'

'Aye.' He nodded, suddenly uneasy. Oliver and Jack ran towards him, greeted him and invited him to help them. As Charlotte watched them, she smiled. She had been so busy this year and she realised she never really took much notice of her son and Jack in each other's company. Now she felt a sense of pride that her son was welcoming Henry and being kind to others, regardless of their status, triggering a tinge of shameful superiority in her own semblance. She smiled, her eyes glistening with tears of happy emotion at how Oliver and Jack were like brothers and how smart Henry looked today.

She watched Ruth and Mary decorating the spindles with sprigs of holly, giggling all the while and smiling again with contentment, until Mary's exclamation startled her. 'Oh, I have pricked my finger on the holly.'

'Who is so clumsy now, little sister?' Oliver teased. 'Take care not to touch your white face with the blood from your finger, but it will of course serve to paint your lips.'

Lady Charlotte shook her head but listened to Mary as she looked up indignantly. 'Master Griffin said my lips become like bright cherries when I lick them. It does work, they shine so much.'

Ruth, as if to quickly clarify her companion's comment said, 'She has a habit now. She licks her lips all the time.' She mimicked the action of Mary licking her lips and making a cheeky pout.

She then threw her head back and laughed. It prompted the others to join in. Ruth, encouraged by the laughter and attention, added, 'The more she licks, the more the ceruse disappears, so her face is like snow and blood.' She giggled, but had gone too far.

Mary was glaring at her and Lady Charlotte was showing her disapproval of such a brazen outburst. Kathleen gave a little gasp of disbelief in her daughter's vulgarity. Jack and Oliver grinned as they stared at Ruth's face, red with embarrassment, but Henry was brazen. 'She didn't mean any harm.' The other two stopped grinning. Frances gave a momentary glare in Henry's direction and he briefly looked at the floor. He should not have spoken out to give his opinion. Ruth hung her head in shame, remembering her status, that of a low birth. Mary raised her eyebrows, then her chin in an expression of arrogance. There was an awkward silence before Frances faced Mary.

'When did Master Griffin say such a thing to you?'

'He frequently says it. I didn't like him at first but he's very kind to me now. He knows of secret hideaways in houses and told me of some very clever ones…and…he likes unusual things.'

Ruth, daring to speak again, recalled the event. 'That was the day he was discussing hidden treasures, not just hiding places. I thought you told him too much about how precious and valuable my mother's herb box was, adorned with jewels.'

'Ruth!' warned Kathleen, shocked at this second discourteous outburst from her daughter.

Mary retaliated. 'Nonsense. Ruth, you should never speak against me, especially in the company of others. You must say you are sorry.'

Ruth, her face a brighter red, looked in the direction of Lady Charlotte, then back at Mary. 'I am sorry I was ungracious, Mary. I am sorry, your ladyship.'

Stone-like, Lady Charlotte was in no mood to continue this distasteful conversation.

'We have lost the spirit in which we were in a short time ago but before we leave the matter I am curious, Mary, and must ask you, did you discuss hiding places at any length with Master Griffin?'

'Indeed, madam. He was so interested, but there was no detail. What ails you so?'

'Hither Mary, let's go nearer to the fire.' Lady Charlotte took hold of her daughter's arm and, as they strolled, she whispered, 'I trust that you did not reveal our chapel?'

'Of course not, madam.'

Her mother did not want to hear any more, in case of a sudden attack of her melancholy on this, a happy occasion. But she was uneasy regarding the attention that Edward Griffin bestowed upon her daughter.

''Tis wearying me, daughter. Thou should'st continue to decorate the house. Look there is more holly. Perhaps you can both find other places?

'Yes, madam.' It was a polite dismissal. As the girls approached the large fireplace where a pile of holly lay, they soon started to argue again in low voices about the jewelled box.

Lady Charlotte sighed and took hold of Frances's arm to lead her to the great hall.

'Ignore the girls, Frances. I have said to myself this morning that no incident today will serve to anger me. I do need to speak with you. The earl and I are leaving for London the day after tomorrow. I want you to keep an eye out for Master Griffin and his conversations with Mary.'

'Of course, my Lady. Will you be going for long?'

'Just a few weeks. I want to see my sister and her family.'

Frances noted the look of concern on Lady Charlotte's face.

They both held suspicions that the new tutor was scheming. He had expressed his concern over the use of the ceruse, saying it could carry poisons and yet he encouraged Mary to lick the skin around her lips, knowing that the white lead mixture on her skin could easily be ingested. Had her mistress also detected Griffin's dislike of Mary? So why was he now being charming? What was he up to?

*

Hearty, herby, sweet and spicy smells emanated from the scullery, wafting all over the house, intoxicating to the merrymakers who were now sitting either side of the long table in the dining room, busy making decorations for the table later and for the next day, Christmas Day. The earlier incident was forgotten and Ruth and Mary had settled down, to the relief of Kathleen.

Frances and the Lady Charlotte were returning from the garden when Margaret came bustling in with a tray of mead and freshly baked quince pies.

'Join us for one of your pies, Margaret.' Lady Charlotte smiled. 'It is Christmas and you should sample what you give us anyway.'

The boys had become giddy and raucous, sticking bits of holly into one another. Oliver, feeling very mischievous, risked his mother's wrath.

'Madam, do you think Margaret may want to poison us? Are you going to watch her digest her pie before we partake?'

Although he laughed he was keen to see that his comment did not upset his mother. Lady Charlotte merely scowled at him, remembering the promise to maintain an air of calmness if she could not muster frivolity.

Margaret thanked her mistress and sat down at the end of the table nervously. She could not recall being asked to eat a pie with them on previous celebrations and this invitation triggered an odd sense of embarrassment. She spotted Henry and, as he was close by, she nodded and smiled at him. 'You look like a proper gentleman, lad.' He smiled back at her approval. She ate self-consciously but soon jumped up excitedly.

'Oh the goose, I must go and baste him, before he gets too tough and chewy!' Everyone chuckled and showed pleasure in the mead and pies. There was also a large jug of wine for anyone to help themselves.

Lady Charlotte rose after eating and excused herself to go and check that the goose was not spoilt.

Now that the mistress had left the table, Anne felt the urge to express her protest at what she saw as the snubbing of Edward Griffin. Bending her head towards Frances who sat next to her, she whispered, 'Why has Kathleen been invited and not Master Griffin?'

Frances whispered to Anne while directing her gaze to her lap. She was conscious of the fact that Ruth and Jack may hear the conversation. 'I don't think Lady Charlotte thinks it is the proper thing to do, with all the trouble about the thrashings and all. In any case, Master Griffin does not live here.'

'And neither does Kathleen.'

Frances glared at her and snapped in a low voice instead of a whisper. 'Would you want to create a rumpus today of all days and in front of all the children?' She rose from the table before Kathleen and her children looked over. 'More wine, Anne?'

Anne was forced into silence. Arguing with proud Frances over the festive period was unlikely to be successful; she was even more arrogant today.

The woman disliked Master Griffin so much, Anne thought. She was simply jealous that she was unable to attract a man herself. Perhaps, deep down, she even liked Griffin and had hoped he would court her.

*

Griffin had secured lodgings in a three-storey house in the village, but he wanted to escape his interrogating landlady. She wanted to know too much about him and that could be dangerous. He would make merry in the inn, drinking ale, mead and spiced wine. He would celebrate his future.

The wool industry was beginning to take hold in the area. He had sought to buy sheep and sell wool, and had made a good start drawing up larger enclosures for the sheep. The earl was too busy to check his accounts. Griffin was gratified that his plan meant that he would one day prosper. The land enclosures for the sheep and the resulting disappearance of the villagers' livelihood had upset the yeomen however, who had been paid a paltry sum for their land. They now faced hardship, especially during the winter.

The new tutor had said nothing about the disgruntled men to the earl. He felt the amount the earl was paying him was insufficient for his efforts. He would make sure the accounts balanced, but he would have his fair share. In his sights was land of his own: that which was denied to him by his father, then his mother. He was becoming an adept merchant, but a greedy one.

Now as he entered the inn and looked around him, he was reminded of the differences in people's statuses. The inn was a dark, unruly place, with a few candles set in metal wall sconces of little use in illuminating the room, which was heavy with smog and rank air; no fresh straw laid for weeks.

There was a smell of sweet sickly ales, old cheeses, sweaty bodies, drunken men's vomit, even dogs' urination and excrement. A few unkempt dogs were scrapping for leftover food, before flopping to scratch vigorously at their fleas.

The inn vibrated with a cacophony of raucous and high-pitched laughter, some obscene and lecherous, some vociferous and vile. Buxom women, some sitting on the laps of sweaty men with their legs akimbo, bared their bountiful breasts and dipped their nipples into the ale jugs before offering them for tantalising arousal. The inn was vibrant but vulgar. Griffin despised their conduct, but today they were all free to do as they pleased. There was no law or order. The harassed landlord had given up on restraint and, apart from throwing bones at the snarling dogs while swearing and cursing, he had enough to do keeping his customers happy by attending to drinks, pies and great platters of cheese.

Griffin abandoned his feelings of distaste. He drank heavily, caught up in the atmosphere of merriment and Christmas. The feeling of disgust for these people dissipated as he joined them, singing carefree and bawdy. He started to swagger as he joked with other men and flirted with passing women.

He came to a halt as he saw two well-dressed men at a corner table. They were playing hazard for money and drinking quietly. The landlord glanced over but he obviously turned a blind eye to the illegal gambling, Griffin thought as he watched their game. When one of the men in the corner looked up, Griffin recognised the face.

'I know you, sir.' He strode nearer and bent over the table to face the two men, but overbalanced. The drink was blurring his vision and weakening his legs.

The second man answered. 'Thou art disturbing our game, methinks sir.'

Griffin glared at him before he leaned closer to the man he recognised. 'Thou art known to me, sir. I never forget a face...ah, the name doth come to me...thou art the heretic.'

The men looked at one another, aware of the dangers if some people had overheard this comment. Father Peters stayed calm and stood up to face Griffin squarely. He took a cursory glance to check if anyone was watching or listening to them.

'If you wish to seek counsel, good fellow, why don't you join us in our game? That is of course if you have the means?' Father Peters knew that, if Griffin refused, he would lose face.

'Of course I have the means,' he slurred. Father Peters and his compatriot, Father Morley, watched as he seated himself unsteadily on a stool and grappled with the coins in his purse.

Father Morley—who, like Father Peters, had learned to be discreet about his religious beliefs—was dressed as a wealthy yeoman or a merchant might. Like Father Peters he was involved with other Catholic conspirators, including those who arranged the construction of priest holes.

They were both only too aware of the dangers. Discreet Catholics knew of the tales: many priests suffering from gaol fever, imprisoned in cells, sharing their space with rats, caked in grime and virulent fleas, suffocating by heat and stench or by bitterly cold winters. Others tied to leg or arm irons were subjected to stretching on the rack. Death was a welcome relief.

The game commenced. Griffin was excited by the prospect of winning money.

He shouted for more ale, his exhaled breath already overpowering. He squinted as he tried to get the landlord's attention. Father Peters won another round of the game and took the winnings from the table. He looked at Griffin, perspiring and fidgeting nervously.

'Another game?' Father Peters said. 'You are the caster this time.' Griffin's means had come to an end but he still ordered more ale. Father Peters and Father Morley thought they had better call an end to the gambling.

As they tried to close the game, Griffin abruptly stood up and banged the table in fury. He swung his body round to face the rest of the inn and shouted.

'This man has cheated me and stolen my money. Hark! Thou should'st be aware that he is a Papist and a man of deceit. Such men should be imprisoned for treason. Who is going to help me to banish him from our midst?'

As he finished shouting, he tipped the table furiously towards the lap of Father Peters, his eyes narrowed with hate. Father Peters swiftly got out of the way.

His frenzied accusation was only heard by a few of the revellers, however, and a toppled table was nothing to be surprised at in this inn. Father Morley signalled to Father Peters by a quick nod of his head, to leave swiftly but quietly by the back door.

Father Peters straightened the table and poured ale for Griffin, coaxing him to sit back down. He spoke with deliberation.

'Thou art a man of high reputation, sir, being Lord Oliver's tutor. Thou would'st benefit by keeping your demeanour calm.

People and walls have ears. Tidings of a drunken schoolmaster for the Earl of Becton's son will not bade well.'

Griffin looked at Father Peters through eyes that he knew were deceiving him. His vision was blurred, his hearing was marred and the room was swaying. He was aware of the priest leaving but he suddenly felt faint and nauseous.

'He has poisoned me,' he mumbled into the table, before falling off the stool completely, his ale soaking into the straw.

Father Peters asked the landlord to let him sleep it off in the corner. 'It is, after all, Christmas.'

The landlord was unperturbed. 'He will have to stay there. I am heavy with this lot to attend to.'

'Aye,' nodded Father Peters. 'Should he seek counsel, refrain from speaking of his actions. He is not privy to my good companion or myself. Do you understand?'

The landlord agreed. He just desired an easy Christmas.

Chapter Eleven

September 1957

The sensation of suddenly losing your footing under water which is actually pulling you so you become completely submerged is probably the most terrifying thing ever; coupled with the fact that the water is filthy, rat infested, dark, utterly cold, and putrid.

Our arms thrashing and grabbing the other made it harder as we struggled for air, trying to catch our breath. The very act of trying to open your eyes to make sense of surroundings while you are believe you are drowning is nothing short of horrific. What was worse was that, one minute we were paddling and noticing the rat, then we were suddenly pulled into this very deep water.

I swallowed, hoping it was merely saliva. 'Can you swim, George? We have to swim!' I glanced round quickly to gauge the space. The tunnel had widened a bit, say about six feet or so across and was oddly circular. It remained very low, almost claustrophobic. The roof here was made of brick and was arched. George was panicking. His clenched fists were fighting the space in front of him as if he was being attacked.

'I can't see, Tom. Everything's blurred—my glasses have gone... and my torch! I've dropped it somewhere. I can't feel the bottom!'

His neck was arched and extended above the water level. Just for a couple of seconds, his eyes protruded like those belonging to a demented frog, before he sank again. I grabbed him. He popped up again and he spat out something green and stringy from his mouth.

'God, this water…'

I thought he was going to drown as he became submerged a second, then a third time. I needed a better grip of him.

'Tread water George. Tread water, for God's sake!' I yelled; it was bloody hard pulling him to the side, but then I discovered a brick ledge. At some time this must have been a constructed wall. Thrashing people, even little people, can suddenly become very heavy. Thank God it wasn't the width of a swimming pool. 'Hold onto this ledge, George.'

He was hyperventilating.

'Take slow deep breaths, George.' At least I could remember something from the first aid course I did when I was a boy scout. My torch was still working even after the dunking it had received. While his breathing recovered, I looked around. It appeared as if this particular bit may have been constructed as a standing space. It was perfectly circular and there were signs of the wall being chipped away.

Assessing the way ahead however, boulders popped up above the water level, making me think it was shallow.

'Get your breath back. I'm just going to that bit there; it looks far less deep.'

After a few more yards I felt my feet dragging on rubble, possibly once steps that had collapsed over the years. Once again being hunched was the only way to negotiate the tunnel, which now seemed to bend to the left, perhaps around the back of the house.

I stopped and watched George take a deep breath, let go of the side and doggy paddle the few yards until he reached me. Because he was tiny, the crouching along the low tunnel was easier. When we were side by side I noticed him panting again.

'You're okay, George. You're okay.'

'Yeah. C'mon, we'll carry on. I'm just breathless. I'm not a very good swimmer.'

'Hmm…you don't say,' I kind of muttered. 'Hopefully, mate, there won't be any more surprises. Crikey, the stench is worse down this end. What do you reckon, we're near the cess pit?'

For once George didn't answer and I realised he was shivering and looking like death. I didn't want him fainting on me, so I thought we'd better turn back. I told him to take deep breaths and, while he concentrated on his breathing, I looked ahead, wondering how long the tunnel was and where it went to. It was at that moment I detected movement, but resisted focusing my torch upon what appeared to be a hooded figure. I was about to alert George when I thought better of it, except I couldn't go back without shining the torch. This time I saw only a thick pillar, probably supporting the roof, and I dismissed the movement as shadowy light on that construction.

George shivered more.

'C'mon, let's get out of here.'

We turned back, panting, paddling, swimming, wading and then climbing up the iron struts, this time crawling to the left on the horizontal passage, until finally falling into the cupboard of the front bedroom. Rolling out onto the bedroom floor, we didn't know whether to laugh or cry; there was definitely immense relief, as well as foul water everywhere flowing and seeping into every crevice. It was then that George threw up.

I slammed the cupboard door shut. The sound of Mickey's claws clattered into the room and, when he saw us, his tail wagged vigorously until the constant swaying from side to side caused him to slip on the water now mixed with vomit. Mickey started to sniff the floor.

'Hey, he's after your leftover apple pie, George.' I wanted to humour him to check he was still alert. He'd gone pretty quiet, but managed a grin.

We couldn't steady Mickey—he was too excited—but it seemed a relief to be finally laughing.

'Hey, I've no idea of the time. Your dad might be here soon and you're bloody soaking.'

There was the sound of footsteps.

We listened. Someone was coming closer. Shit, we hadn't got into dry clothes and the room was a nightmare.

'God, I stink!' I whispered.

George responded, 'We both do. Are you going to tell your parents about all this?'

'You what?'

The door opened. I was well and truly snookered. Small fingers curled around the door…Annabel.

'Jesus Christ! What have you two been up to? I can't believe this mess… All through slug hunting?'

Whenever George got nervous, excited or embarrassed, he babbled…a lot. This incident evoked all three emotions and off he went into a tirade of reasons for the floor, the smell, the state of us. Some were nonsensical but others true as he gave an account of the secret underground cave and the effects of erosion, for God's sake!

I interrupted the onslaught of babbled words, 'Actually George, I also saw what looked like a priest, well a hooded figure, but I didn't want to scare you anymore.'

'A ghost? Even more exciting, but I could have taken it Tom, really, you don't need to nursemaid me.'

I shook my head. He wanted to be the big hero in front of my sister.

Annabel was squinting with her hands on her hips.

'If you don't believe us,' he said, 'come down with us next time.'

My mouth shot open: not a chance.

'Okay then,' she announced, 'I will do, 'cos I don't believe a word.'

Shaking my head, I left the room to get clean clothes and towels. I threw George a dry shirt and some trousers. I couldn't hear Mum and Dad so assumed they were still on their walk. God was on our side.

'Annabel, you won't like where we've been and you're not

coming with us; we might never go again anyway, so you'll never find out the truth.'

'Oh yes I will. I'll tell Mum and Dad.'

I chucked the towel with mopped up vomit against her, 'Get out and take Mickey with you.'

'Ugh…what's on that towel?'

I slammed the door shut, to hear her yell, 'I'll snitch.'

Chapter Twelve

Winter 1598

Since the New Year, Edward Griffin had barely used the birch on Jack, or at least that's what Kathleen had been led to believe. Jack might have lied to her; she remained suspicious of Edward Griffin and suspected that nothing about the man would ever make her think any differently.

Jack had admitted to her once that he watched Griffin's twitching fingers lots of times but Kathleen knew that the tutor had been warned against resorting to harsh actions and her son was missing out on an education, knowledge that she desperately wanted her children to receive. The man had a good position at the house and would not want to risk it.

*

Shortly after Anne became the governess for the Lady Mary and Ruth, she began to suffer with pains in her head and limbs. Kathleen treated her with a specially formulated aromatic balm and it seemed to soothe her. She used it frequently and Kathleen often checked on her welfare as well as the progress of young Ruth. The pair could be seen frequently in conversation and a trusting relationship grew.

Anne's developing friendship with Griffin however was looked upon with increasing ill repute. One day, Anne commented on Griffin's higher status, the nature of which she wasn't allowed to disclose, but nevertheless he was performing a duty for the earl and excelling.

Kathleen pondered this 'secret job'. If his wealth was increasing, this had to somehow be at the expense of the earl, a kind man but perhaps too easily duped.

She also suspected Anne hoped to marry Griffin. There was no doubting her excitement when she spoke of him and her desire to be rich.

Her passion used to be solely for high standards of education, but now it was driven by a desire for material wealth. Influenced by Edward Griffin.

As Kathleen prepared her herbs, she reflected on the waning friendship between her and Anne. Kathleen could never like or trust Griffin and that was one reason why she was unable to tell Anne about Father Peters staying at the cottage with her. Most people did not know, and Kathleen didn't want to invite gossip. She already had to deal with suspicions about her medicines. If her cures did not work, some people were resentful and bore a grudge. These were the very beings who might consider her a witch. Lately there had been talk of people receiving cruel penalties. She recalled Griffin's verbal abuse in the kitchen that day with Margaret, the accusation of being a witch.

She lived with the constant fear of the possibility of being shorn or pressed as other women labelled as practising witchcraft. Some had drowned in the river on the ducking stool, others were hanged.

It was rumoured that those in Scotland were often burnt. She had to be careful.

Sighing, she assessed the quantities of saffron, ginger, cloves, cinnamon, lily root, arsenic, rose water, rosemary, lavender, feverfew and mint sprigs. She had lots of vinegar, aniseed, honey and clary sage. Over the fireplace coarse cloth bags holding the ground plants mixed with honey and spices slowly filtered into pots below. Sweet, sour and bitter intoxicating aromas filtered through the tiny cottage.

Kathleen listened whenever a physician visited anyone in the village, hoping to learn from them. They respected her interest and help when they were busy. A few years previously, one of these physicians had taught her to read English as well as Latin. She was a good student and had been very sad when, a year later, he had died.

With Father Peters' help, she kept notes about her successes and failures of her treatments inscribed in Latin on vellum. She kept these at the bottom of the jewelled herb box Father Peters had crafted for her. The jewels were obtained from the dissolution of the monasteries, left to him by Father Murphy. Father Peters had taken a long time in setting the jewels into the Elizabethan cross.

Some, she discovered, were obtained from underhand dealings on ships, just docked when returning from the New World. Father Peters had disclosed this in trust, having admired her hard work and ambition, especially for the children. Kathleen suspected he was concerned regarding her income, but he assured her that, should anything happen to him in these dangerous times, she would be his beneficiary. At least of the jewelled medicine box.

She admired her herb box, often polishing the stones until they dazzled when sunlight struck them. Emeralds, opals, rubies and diamonds, were all set into the elongated cross of Queen Elizabeth and welded into the silver box.

Only she and Father Peters could open the box. Although it had a keyhole, it was opened by a tiny hidden lever at the back. Some of the herbs and mixtures were potent and only Kathleen and the priest knew of the effects and the dangers of the contents.

In certain cases, negative effects might well be required. Kathleen always placed the toxic ones at the bottom of a two-tier arrangement and under that her notes. She intuitively felt that, one day, the poisonous mixtures would be needed.

She peered through the window at softly falling snow. Her thoughts were jolted by a sudden and loud knock on the door.

She was not expecting anyone and was glad Father Peters was elsewhere. Who might this be?

Before opening the door, she asked who was there.

'Oh, for the sake of Jesus Christ, let me in here, Kathleen, it's so cold.' Kathleen opened the door to see Anne shivering on the threshold.

'Thou art disturbed, Anne. Wherefore has't thy come to my house?'

Without answering, Anne took off her cloak to warm by the embers, too cold to speak.

She vigorously rubbed her hands together then faced her palms to the glow in the fireplace and tutted. 'Oh, Kathleen, has't thou only got these embers?' Kathleen did not answer but poured her some warm mead from a jug resting on the hearth.

Anne reached for the welcome drink.

'Ah…that will indeed help.' As she sipped the mead, she slowly lifted her face towards Kathleen and began to whisper as if saying something slanderous. 'The Earl and Lady Charlotte are staying awhile longer in London. There are tidings that say the Queen is ill. She has been behaving strangely from the beginning of this year and some fear her death will soon be upon us.'

'What do you mean, behaving strangely?'

'She is heavy with melancholy. Some say from woe, others say different. She has ceased to eat or drink and takes herself to her chamber, wishing to see no-one. She won't lie down lest the demons take her, but she is weak, Kathleen, weak with apathy.'

'Her death won't affect us, Anne. We will carry on even when Elizabeth has gone. Thou should'st worry less.'

'Aye, but you may be wrong about her death not affecting us.' She moved closer to Kathleen and looked around as if suspecting eavesdroppers.

'Some educated men say it is the mercury and lead in her face powders and lip colour. They say she has been using more of late, layer upon layer to disguise her ageing years.'

Kathleen looked perturbed. 'Nay, the queen has used the face mixture for years.'

'Aye, but there is a physician who is saying the poison in the powders dulls the wits. If this be true, we must not allow Lady Mary to use it anymore. If she became ill, Kathleen, thy would be to blame.'

Kathleen looked concerned, until footsteps startled both women. A tall shape appeared in the room.

'Forgive me...the door was ajar, hast thou not felt a draft here?' Edward Griffin's sardonic grin was foreboding, Kathleen thought, as she watched him glance from her to Anne.

Anne became flustered. 'How long hast thou been here, sir?'

There was a hint of a smile on his face. Kathleen thought Anne was afraid of him. She suddenly stood stiff and fiddled with her hands as if she shouldn't be there with her friend. Kathleen was angered by Griffin's delight that, should Lady Mary become ill, her own livelihood would be threatened.

Neither dared ask what he might have overheard. Kathleen was sure he had heard them discussing the concern of the lead face powders. The man would have most likely heard every word, he was that kind of man. She watched him walk over to her box, cursing that it had been left in a prominent place.

'What a beautiful specimen! Where did you get this from, Mistress Kathleen?' He came close and examined the precious stones.

'I have had it a long time.' Kathleen broke his concentration, stepping to face him with a steely glare. 'Why are you here, sir?'

'Why do most people visit a herb wife? I have constant headaches and have been told you are good at what you do.'

Kathleen felt her stomach churn in this man's company. She thought perhaps Anne was right: there should be no more ceruse. She didn't want to cure him of anything, only to harm him before he harmed her. She knew he would slander her in no time if she gave him nothing, so she gave some opium juice and some feverfew.

'Go back to your house, sir. You can sleep early this evening. Keep your windows open.'

Griffin half smiled again as he thanked her.

He turned to offer Anne his arm in readiness to leave. He looked at Kathleen as she was about to close the door behind them, narrowing his eyes.

'I am to return if I feel no better?'

Kathleen tried hard not to say 'never' but calmly replied, 'If you feel better, sir in the morning, you need not visit me again. This one treatment can be free, sir.'

He nodded before adding, 'The boys' old tutor…Father Peters, isn't it? You remember him I'm sure. I have unfinished business with him. Do you know where he resides?'

Kathleen tried again to keep calm. 'No, sir, I have not seen him since you replaced him.'

Griffin did not seem convinced. 'Hmm… Well I am sorry, madam, to have disturbed you. Forgive me but you look in need of medicine yourself, so heavy with woe. No doubt you have much on your mind. I will find the priest, don't worry about that. One further thing. Methinks, madam, you should hide that beautiful box of yours lest it be stolen. So many jewels…'tis a mystery how you have come to own such a fine specimen. Adieu madam.'

At that, he patted Anne's arm and escorted her from the cottage. Anne frowned as she quickly glanced over her shoulder at Kathleen. Griffin's demeanour was so dominant over Anne. He was the one using witchery. She was totally controlled. Kathleen took a deep breath. She did not welcome his interest in the box or his meddling in her affairs. She closed the door and realised she was close to tears. There were many questions in her head. Could it be true? If the powders were dangerous, she was in trouble, but that devious, malevolent man was up to something.

Chapter Thirteen

October 1957

The incident in the tunnel had been alarming for George but at least he didn't vomit any more, thank God. Of course, he had to go home in my clothes. How we managed to evade my mum's beady eyes on us when his dad turned up, I'll never know. I had nicked her perfume bottle to spray a bit in the front bedroom and swung the window wide open. Towels and my clothes went into a garden sack. I would have to wash them when she was out again.

After George had left, Annabel asked when he was coming again.

'Maybe next Saturday.'

She looked thoughtful. 'It will be difficult. Gran's coming to stay and she'll be in that room.'

I groaned.

On the Sunday afternoon, I told my parents about the detention the following Friday evening. This, as I should have expected, required a whole explanation with bells and whistles.

'I told you, for the umpteenth time, there are boys who pick on George for being small. We just had a fight, that's all.'

I had stormed outside, frustrated, and picked up Dad's spade. I had dug like mad near the summer house, chucking dirt everywhere; it was a good way of banishing anxiety.

I dug deep until I saw something shiny. The tin cup; the very same goblet with a worn away inscription that the raven grabbed from my hand. I'd forgotten all about it. I gave a cursory glance in the air before stuffing it into my trouser pocket. No sooner had I done so, when that bloody bird launched himself at me, screeching. I covered my face with one arm while trying to strike it with the other and run back to the house at the same time. He continually heckled me but my fear was turning into rage and, just before I reached the door, my elbow connected with his body so he screeched even louder but flew higher, allowing my swift escape. Once inside, the door firmly shut, it was me who was hyperventilating like George did. I hated that bloody raven.

*

By the Friday afternoon, in detention, I noticed that George put on new spectacles to replace the ones he'd lost in the tunnel. I commented that they looked fine.

'I still had to have thick lens and frames, NHS rules or something.'

'If you can see okay, George, don't worry.'

'Yeah. Mum wasn't pleased when I told her I dropped the old ones in a field, right into some cow dung, then trod on them.'

'Cow dung? Ha! What an excuse. I've still got to wash your clothes when Mum can't see me. What did she say about wearing my clothes, by the way?'

'She didn't see. I've got them for you at home. I'll bring them to your house.'

'Hmm. My gran is coming to stay apparently and she'll be sleeping in the front bedroom. Don't know when she's coming though.'

George smiled, 'It doesn't matter. We found the passageway but we don't have to come back that way, into her room. How long is she staying?'

'Dunno. But hey, I've got something to show you. It's that cup I told you about.' I pulled the cup, still crusted with dry earth, from my bag. I began to rub at it with my thumb.

'What, the one the bird stole from you? Let's look at the words. Ooh, hardly clear but we could read the Latin and translate it.'

'Quiet!' yelled Mr Stephens as he entered the room to supervise the detention. 'Two hundred lines this evening.' There was a collective groan before we put our heads down to write two hundred boring lines:

I must not fight on school grounds but think of other means to solve problems.

What a load of tosh.

'What did you have in your hand, Tom Winchett?' Mr Stephens was striding towards us.

'Nothing sir.'

'Yes you did.' He kept coming. 'It's there sticking out of your satchel.' He tutted. 'Let me see it.'

I handed it to him.

'Where did you get this?' He was bent over me, waiting for my answer when George leapt into babble mode.

'Tom's house is haunted, sir, and there's whisperings in Latin, well I think it may be Latin. There's a tall dark ghost, who Tom thinks is a priest from Tudor times. That goblet is just part of hidden treasure, buried since the Elizabethan period—his house has a priest hole…and…there's a secret tunnel, right under the house…and….'

I turned around to see Mike Thompson and his two cronies watching us from the back of the classroom. *Damn.* I started coughing uncontrollably and nudged George, accidentally on purpose. He saw my annoyed nod towards Thompson, big ears straining to know more.

Knowing what George could be like, Mr Stephens ignored him, but not before he examined the goblet.

'Hmm…quite a specimen.'

'Yes, sir.'

'Not that I believe a word of your adventure story. Nevertheless, it sounds like a very good plot…this secret tunnel…but another time.' He seemed to be embarrassed as he awkwardly dismissed us 'Now, carry on with your work or there'll be another detention next week.'

Thompson would be sniffing around for details.

At the end of detention, he blocked my exit from the room. 'Where's this tunnel then, and all that treasure, eh?'

'Ha, you know George. You mean you actually believed him? You clot. Go and read *Alice in Wonderland* if you want to know about life under the ground. Now get out of the way.' I heaved into his shoulder so he lost his balance, falling into the door.

George quickly scurried past him, but Mike grabbed hold of his blazer. 'Was all that fibs, you little squirt?'

'Yes, idiot.' He tutted. 'Some people are so gullible, it's pathetic.' George shook him off and caught me up.

'That was close,' I said. 'You really are going to have to learn to keep your gob shut.'

*

The next day, George was dropped off at my house and we waited impatiently for Mum and Dad to go shopping in Chesterfield.

As the old car drove away, we shouted for Annabel. She had persisted about snitching if we didn't let her go with us, so I had changed my mind. This could be fun.

'Yes, I'm ready for your silly game.' She was confident and happy to go second, between us.

I turned to George, 'Take off your trousers, George; better if we don't wear any this time. When he looked embarrassed and glanced in Annabel's direction I added, 'She won't look at anything.'

I turned to her, 'Look the other way!' She did as she was told. Then it was her turn to be embarrassed as I demanded that she take off her skirt.

'What? Just be in my blouse and knickers?'

This time George spluttered.

'I told you… There's water down there, drying a pair of knickers is easier than trousers or skirts. Take it off and we'll put them all under the bed, just in case Mum comes in. This is no time to get all girlie!'

I gave them each a long scarf. 'Tie this around your waists. We need to tuck the torches into something when we climb down. It will make it easier, especially for you, Annabel. And no shoes.'

'Huh!'

George decided to leave his new spectacles behind, 'It'll all be blurred so you two will have to guide me.'

Annabel still sounded confident. 'Don't worry, George. I'll keep my eye on you.'

I just knew her confidence wouldn't last. For a start, I could tell all this preparation was making her nervous. She giggled incessantly and fidgeted. She was afraid, all right.

She gaped at the chasm, then hesitated before turning round so that she could make the slow descent. 'Where are the struts? You said there were little stumps or struts or something, a kind of ladder?'

I'd just gone down ahead of her but now I was aware of the panic in her voice just above me.

'You have to feel for them. There's one just to your left…that's it, now use your hand to hold on to the one on the right and lower your right leg.'

She was so hesitant. If she fell, we'd be in big trouble. Her heavy panting showed how nervous she was. I tutted as she almost completely lost her footing half way down.

At that precise moment, I regretted bringing her.

'That's not the worst one. Get a good hold, the last stump is broken so take more care.'

Any calmness she had started with had gone. 'What?' she yelled, almost in tears. 'I can't hear you properly and I think I've cut my toe.'

I watched her without repeating my warning. She was so jittery; any more instructions would completely break her nerve. I really didn't think she was listening.

I felt such relief when she landed at the bottom, giddy with nervous energy.

'See, I did it. A piece of cake…just one small cut on my little toe, that's all.'

George, as ever, was polite. 'Yeah, you did really well.'

I bit my tongue.

She surveyed the water. 'Oh, this isn't that bad. I could have kept my skirt on. it stinks though.'

George and I grinned at one another, our faces strangely shadowy in the torchlight.

'C'mon, then.' I said.

'Oh God, it smells foul and it's cold. '

'Annabel, stop moaning. We told you it stinks.' *What does she expect an underground tunnel to be? A fairy grotto?*

It wasn't long before we reached what I thought was an old chamber, the deep part. By this time, Annabel had re-gained some confidence and waded past us. I was about to warn her about the much deeper bit when she disappeared under the surface, just like George had last time.

'No!' we yelled simultaneously.

Too late. In a panic, she surfaced, gulping for air.

'Can't…' she gulped again, extending her neck.

Her hair plastered to her face, she resembled a deep sea monster, mouth pursed tightly and cheeks bulging to keep out the foul water. Then she spat out, 'Can't… swim!' before she went under again.

'What? You had swimming lessons!' I yelled.

'She can't hear you. We'll have to grab her and pull her to the side.'

It was easier with two of us pulling her. She panicked as she saw something dangling from her sodden hair. 'Urrgh, what's that? There's a rat on my head!'

'Just a weed, silly.' I picked it off. 'You stay here and hold on to this ledge.'

'You can't leave me here!' Annabel pleaded, gasping for air and shaking frantically.

'You can't swim, so what else are you going to do?'

George was more sympathetic. 'It's only a few yards before it gets shallow. We can pull her through it.'

'I might drown, I might drown, no!'

'Shut up!' I was furious. 'Okay. Grab one arm and I'll take the other.' I snapped at George, and then shouted at her, 'Keep your head high above the water and try kicking out your legs behind you. Didn't you listen when you had lessons in the swimming baths?'

She had no choice but to do as I said as we dragged her forward through the water, until she yelled, 'Ouch, my legs. I've hit some hard rocks, oh no.'

'At least you can't drown now. Shut up!'

It was the bit where we had to crawl like crabs and she bubbled again, her snotty nose disgusting. 'Oh, what do I have to do now?'

As we breathed again, I had another 'go' at her. 'Just crawl. Why didn't you swim back there? You had swimming lessons, didn't you?'

She was still gasping for breath and looked hurt. 'I didn't finish them. I was ill, remember, and never got the certificate.'

'Why didn't you say?'

'I didn't believe all this!'

George interrupted, 'Leave it now, the pair of you. We've got to move on.' We were so busy arguing; we hardly noticed how dark it had become.

George's head was a mere outline as he said, quizzically, 'I don't remember it being this dark, Tom.'

Of course, that spooked Annabel.

'Oh I'm frightened. I want to go back.' She was about to burst into tears. I had to be harsh.

'Shut up,' I yelled. 'You wanted to do this, remember.'

She stifled her sobs, while George reassured her. 'It doesn't last.'

Annabel yelled again, 'I want to go back... Now!'

'Get hold of her waist, George and help her. I'm going on a bit further.' Annabel was getting on my nerves.

'Oh, God, what is that? I can't stand it, something is tickling my leg, argh!' Annabel shrieked.

'Just keep going!'

'It must be a rat. They carry disease. Oh my God, hurry.'

'Or it might be an adder.' I couldn't resist one last jibe. 'I'll catch you up; just want to go a bit further.'

'Argh…quick, quick.' Annabel was causing frantic echoes; '*quick…quick…quick…*'

George wanted to wait for me, 'Hurry up Tom. We'll wait at the foot of the ladder.'

Feeling a bit under pressure, I crawled along the stones and lapping water until I spotted three stone steps on the right hand side of a wide vault. The steps were obviously once a way out into the garden. It was hard to judge the distance but I had a wild guess it would open out near the old shed.

The water became a bit deeper nearer the steps and it was then that I stubbed my toe on something really hard. Shining my torchlight downwards and putting my hand in the water, I pulled up a metal box with a decorated top, an elongated cross of what appeared to be gemstones. As I examined it, someone tall bent closely right over me, blocking my torchlight.

Chapter Fourteen

February 1598

The Earl of Becton and Lady Charlotte finally returned from London at the end of January. Queen Elizabeth had welcomed them at Court for festivities up until the twelfth night, but many had noticed her weariness and melancholy. Some courtiers wondered if her condition had anything to do with the lead-based make-up: rumours of the physician's theories were spreading fast.

After the earl and his wife had returned to Charlotte's sister's house, however, they were notified by a messenger that Queen Elizabeth had made a good recovery from whatever had ailed her. The physician's claims had been ignored and his beliefs about ceruse being poisonous were deemed to be plain nonsense. Her illness was nothing to do with the painting of her face.

That afternoon, in the girl's schoolroom, Anne found herself unusually challenged. Mary could not concentrate, was fractious, and at times drowsy. She noticed that Ruth had been pestering her to help find some hidden treasures, but Mary was so irritable that she snapped at her alarmingly. 'Find them yourself. You just want to be rich from what belongs to me.'

'Mary… that is enough. What has become of you? You never used to speak this way,' Anne said.

The following morning, when Anne saw Lady Charlotte in

the garden, she approached her and asked to speak with her. She thought her ladyship looked very tired and didn't want bothering. Perhaps she was expecting to hear more complaints about Edward Griffin. Lady Charlotte's response showed her irritation.

'Oh Anne, I hope this does not regard Master Griffin? I am weary of hearing about how strict a master he is. The man has had his warnings now and I find gossip tiresome.'

'Oh no ma'am, it's not about Master Griffin. I wish to speak with you about Mary.'

'Should I be concerned about my daughter's progress?'

'No, ma'am, she is doing well, although more tired of late.'

'Then what seems so urgent, as I read in your face?'

'The white face mixture and cinnabar on her lips. Some are saying that this is dangerous.'

Lady Charlotte smiled and shook her head. 'As I have said before, Anne, these worries are unfounded. The Queen recovered well: there was no substance to the rumour that the lead powders can do any harm.'

'Her lips are very sore, ma'am, and I think it is better if she at least stops colouring her lips.'

Lady Charlotte sighed deeply and shook her head.

'Very well, I agree. No more lip colour and we will see if her lips heal. Now go along with you.'

Anne briefly curtseyed and returned to the house, where she planned the afternoon's lessons for the girls.

It was her intention for them to translate some Latin phrases into English. She welcomed these opportunities to improve her own knowledge, being aware that her status was not as high as that of Master Griffin. However, she tried very hard to keep one step ahead of her charges.

*

She decided it was best to dismiss the girls early and, seeing Master Griffin in the hall, could not resist confiding in him, including details of the girls' conversation. He reassured her that she had done the right thing, to tell Lady Charlotte of her concerns.

Smiling, he said, 'You look quite beautiful, my dear, when you are deep in thought. Won't you walk with me later when I have finished with the boys? We can talk some more.'

She nodded and returned his smile.

*

Later, Anne wrapped a woollen shawl tightly around her shoulders before walking out to meet with Griffin. He stood calmly waiting for her near the stables. They walked along the hedgerows in the cold dusky air.

'Tell me my dear. Do you enjoy working at the manor?' he asked.

'Of course. Why do you ask?'

'No particular reason, my dear. Of late, it has come to my attention that secrets lay hidden in the house. Ruth said something to Mary and, when they saw me, Mary hushed her.' It has just made me think, my dear that's all. Are you of the opinion the house has secrets?'

Anne laughed. 'No.'

Griffin smiled and they walked in silence for a few minutes

'I cannot deny, Anne, that Mary licking all that lead ceruse is of concern to me as well as you. Howbeit that the herb woman would not know the actual harm this substance may cause? Lead can poison the system and play tricks on the mind. You have noticed strange behaviour. I have noticed strange talk.'

Anne stopped walking and looked at him.

'She tells me of lots of treasures from the old priest, but surely not. The priest does not strike me as a wealthy man, So you see, I suspect Mary's mind is muddled, perhaps even verging on lunacy.'

'I don't know why she should mention treasures, except for the spoils of the monasteries from the old king's ruination of them all, but I wouldn't know if the earl has any. Father Peters was a shrewd man and knew many of the Abbots who maintained the chapels. He would be the one most likely to have treasures, I would well think.'

Griffin nodded.

The path grew dark ahead of them as dusk fell. Griffin sensed a slight nervousness in his companion.

'Are you afraid of the dark?'

'No,' she hesitantly replied, laughing nervously.

'You are with me; you have no need to fear the dark.'

He stepped closer to her, holding her hand. With a sudden gesture that startled her, he drew her near to him, pushing her back against a tree. She gasped and felt his warm breath on her cheeks as he gently pinned her against the bark. He lifted her chin so her gaze could not escape his.

'Dear Anne,' he whispered, bending lower to kiss her lips, softly at first, then with increasing passion. His breathing was heavier, his warm body was pressing even more closely to hers and his hand gently caressed her left breast.

'What are you doing?' It was a young voice in the near vicinity.

They broke apart hastily, embarrassed to see Mary staring at them.

'You should not be here, Anne. I have been looking for you, everywhere.' Mary's gaze swiftly focused on Griffin. 'Master Griffin, I will need to speak with my father about this.'

Anne stepped forward to protest, 'No, Mary, there is no need to speak to…'

Suddenly, Mary's knees buckled and she slumped to the ground.

Anne rushed to her 'We have to take her back, Edward, quickly. She is ill.'

Griffin swept Mary up into his arms, hoping that Anne did not detect his annoyance at this intrusion.

As he lowered the girl onto her bed, Anne went to fetch Frances. Mary's eyes opened and she glared at Edward Griffin.

'You will not keep your post, sir. You are deceitful. I heard what lies you said to Anne. will see to it that you leave in haste.' The voice was just a croak, but the look was one belonging to a demon, Griffin thought. What was she really thinking? He had been trying to gain her trust to find hidden treasures but now he wondered how long she had been following them. What exactly had she heard? Was it the reference to her weak mind or the hidden jewels? He now recalled her saying that they were a matter of upmost secrecy.. He had no time to seek his answers.

Footsteps were returning to the room. Griffin feigned concern.

'Mary, you must rest my dear, just rest.' He glared back at her, his smile demonic.

Anne and Frances ran to the bedside.

'This is not like Mary. She is very sick.' Frances dithered, straightening bedclothes while she pondered what to do. She noticed how sunken Mary's eyes had become, her eyelids red and heavy, the girl fighting to keep them open.

After a short while she began to utter words in a weak and stunted manner.

'I feel…very tired, so…I think…I must…sleep. Could you… help me? I feel weak…' She drew in a sharp breath in order to speak again, adding '…no strength…'

Anne brought a bowl of cool water to bathe her, noticing that her skin was clammy and cold but her head was hot. She shivered violently then she cried out, her limbs becoming rigid.

Oh, Mary…Mary, oh Jesus Christ!' Anne tried to get a response as she held her, but the rigid body forbade it. The girl's limbs, now shaking, rejected any interference and her back began to arch disturbingly. Her head rocked, teeth chattering as blood and saliva oozed from her lips, her face turning purple.

'Get the mistress, quickly!' Frances cried.

Anne ran out onto the landing. From the top of the stairs, she spotted Henry below, carrying bread. 'Henry, Henry, fetch the mistress quickly, Lady Mary is ill. Quickly I said!' Henry gawped up at her, before running at speed, some of the bread rolling across the hall.

Edward Griffin had slipped into the corner of the room,

transfixed by the sudden seizure but showing no emotion. Then it stopped and Mary lay limp and exhausted.

Frances mopped her brow, trying to rouse her. She was feeling so helpless when at last Lady Charlotte, the earl and Oliver entered the room.

'Oh, what has happened, what has happened?' Charlotte and the earl hurried to their daughter's bedside but then became almost motionless in shock at the sight of her.

Lady Charlotte told Anne to fetch Kathleen. 'Send Henry. Tell him to ride Sabre, as quick as he can.'

With everyone's attention on Lady Mary, Griffin took the opportunity to edge out of the room; however, Lord Becton caught sight of him.

'Why are you here, Griffin?'

Anne was entering Mary's chamber.

'He helped me, my lord. He carried the Lady Mary when she became sick and watched over her, while I went to fetch Frances and then the Lady Charlotte.'

The earl looked at Griffin pensively but said nothing. Griffin responded, 'It is true. Anne could not carry her, my lord. The Lady Mary has been lethargic of late, her studies affected by lack of concentration. The white powders are of some consequence, my lord, I am sure. Lady Mary applies it thickly and it easily becomes ingested. In my opinion…'

'I am not interested in your opinion, sir,' snapped the earl.

Oliver jumped up from a chair to address Griffin. 'My sister said you encouraged her to lick her lips.' He turned to his father. 'She licked them so much father, that she must have licked the white powders each time.'

But Lady Charlotte walked forward to face Griffin. 'If you really believe that they make you ill, why did you encourage this?'

There was a soft moan from her daughter and Charlotte, turning towards her, no longer seemed interested in Griffin's reply. As attention was again focused on Mary, Griffin left the room without answering, quickly glancing at Anne, who followed him.

Oliver saw them depart. 'Why are you taking your leave, Master Griffin?'

The earl was losing patience. 'Let him leave, Oliver. I will deal with him later. Mary, I am sure, has falling sickness. She can be cured of this.'

Frances watched from the doorway. Anne was spending too much time with Griffin. He would lure her into his web of deceit to get what he wanted from this life. Anything the man did was of noxious intent. Her thoughts were quickly banished by repeated anxious cries from Mary.

'Some water, William. She feels hot. Fetch some water, she must drink.'

The earl did as his wife commanded and fetched the pitcher of water from the table by the window. But Mary was too unresponsive to drink.

'Mary, you must drink. Try to take some water.'

She hardly stirred, her body hot, but she muttered something about her head.

Charlotte turned to her husband. 'She has a bad headache, and she is not breathing well. We must get some lavender to spread on her pillow, quickly. Oh where are the servants when you need them immediately?' She was almost crying with frustration. 'Frances, where are you?' Frances was looking out of the window, distracted again by the departure of Edward Griffin and Anne.

'I am sorry, my lady,' she dithered, before quickly composing herself.

'Don't just dally, girl. Help us, for the love of God.' Lady Charlotte remained irritated. 'I need lavender, lots of lavender water. Where is Kathleen? It's been ages since Henry left.'

'He has taken Sabre, the quickest horse, Charlotte. Try to calm yourself,' the earl said as he strode across the room to look out of the window. As yet, there was no sign of Kathleen.

Frances brought the lavender and stood close to Mary's hot body. As she watched her, Mary began once again to arch her spine, her neck extending further backwards and towards the bed so her body was stretching out as the blade of a scythe. A few wet strands of hair stuck to the waxy hollows of her face.

She was sweating profusely, her skin marbled red and purple, her thin gown pasted to her like another layer of skin. Her spasmodic shrieks shook the walls of the house, alarming all who were in it. Her eyes occasionally opened wide but then sunk into deep red sockets. There was only inescapable torment, each piercing scream releasing bloodied saliva down her chin and neck, all the while her stiff limbs jerked wildly and uncontrollably. Frances gasped, thinking, *This is not Mary but a stranger, a wraith, a demon, perhaps bewitched.*

Oliver touched his mother's arm. 'Is she going to die, mother?'

'No, Oliver, she will survive. She has always been a fighter. People recover from the falling sickness.'

She turned towards Frances to vent her anger. 'Don't just stand there, you fool. Fetch more lavender and some cloths. Cool her.' Frances was startled by her lady's commands. She had never seen her so frantic, but then this situation was indeed dire and Lady Charlotte knew every second counted if her daughter was to recover.

They took turns to bathe the now blotchy skin, their urgency causing the water to splash haphazardly on the wooden floor. At last the sound of galloping hooves could be heard, increasing to a clatter on the flagstones in the yard below. Then footsteps, the noise of crunching gravel and lastly the sound of heavy boots on the stairs.

Kathleen rushed in with her jewelled herb box, followed by Henry carrying further bags of medicines. She studied Mary with wide fearful eyes. She could see there was no time to lose. She felt her brow, looked at her pale fingers and frowned.

She sent Frances to get feverfew and rose water from her box, also some of the green jade precious stones within a cloth bag under the vials and little herb bags.

Although her instructions were responded to promptly, Kathleen knew it was probably too late. The girl's damp skin was a mix of blue and red, with increasing threads of torn blood vessels. Her powers were not sufficient to cure this. She had never performed cupping, which would release some of the blood. She placed the stones around Mary's neck and in a line down the centre of her body, then dabbed the skin around the stones with rosewater.

She placed crushed feverfew around the girl's nostrils and across her forehead. Mary was unable to swallow but Kathleen still applied the feverfew to the insides of her mouth, trying to encourage swallowing by massaging the cheeks and the throat. The child did not protest, breathing was still present but now spasmodic, the spittle gurgling in her throat, until another desperate scream alarmed them all, cutting the air and resonating throughout the entire house and beyond. Charlotte and the earl held each other, fear etched onto weary faces.

Kathleen turned to them. 'She has passed the stage where I might have healed her. You must call the physician without delay. She may need to be bled. This is beyond my capability, I am sorry to say this to you.'

At first they both stared at her with disbelief. They had put their faith in her. The earl came to his senses.

'Where is Henry? He must ride to the physician's house.'

Frances shook her head and tried to steady herself.

'I will send him, my lord.'

All they could do while they waited was to carry on bathing Mary's skin using fresh, cool water. Margaret had brought fresh water from the kitchen but she was uncomfortable around such profound sickness. She had lost a friend to the dreaded pestilence, remembering only too easily the raw horror when the matrons in their vinegar-soaked garments entered the homes of the sick to check for buboes.

Anne returned, receiving a stern look from Frances. 'Where have you been?' she hissed. Anne glared at her and then introduced the physician who was close on her heels.

'I was helping Henry to fetch him.' She smiled at Frances.

Mary's condition had worsened and her body lay limp and

lifeless. The physician didn't believe that cupping, purging or bloodletting to release the hot blood would help. This, he thought, was the falling sickness: he had seen it before. He said he thought it may be due to poisonous vapours of some sort. He asked Lady Charlotte whether there wasanything different that Mary may have eaten, drank, touched, or perhaps smelled.

Lady Charlotte, very quiet and thoughtful, stood staring at the floor when suddenly she needed to sit as she felt quite faint. She looked up at Anne, who immediately knew what she was thinking. It was only a few hours since their conversation in the garden that morning and even less since Oliver's accusation towards Griffin of the dangers of licking the white powders.

'Could it possibly be true?'

'My lady?' Anne was buying time to think of her response.

Lady Charlotte rose from the stool. Slow, shaky.

'You remember…this morning, what you had heard about the ceruse?' It was a cold, accusing stare.

Anne swallowed hard. 'Yes, my lady, I remember, but…'

She was interrupted by the earl 'My dear Charlotte, this is all mere gossip, we understood from the Queen's recovery that this powder is not poisonous.'

The physician listened intently to the conversation, adding further distress to the group when he said that he too was becoming wary of these powders and that, in the last few days, reports had come to his attention that the Queen was once again ill with severe melancholy.

The earl questioned him further. 'Why do you heed this talk of poisonous powders? Many women at court thus adorn themselves to no ill doings. They have remained robust. There's something else wrong with Mary and it is your job, sir, to know what that is and treat her so she becomes well again.'

The physician shook his head. It might be just hearsay but he believed that over time there was something in the face powder that affected the balance of the four humours: yellow bile, black bile, phlegm and blood. His medical training had taught him that all four should work in balance within the body. He suspected the blood was somehow affected, but knew not how. He chose his words carefully.

'There is a belief, my lord, that these powders block the vapours and the body's energy is thus sapped. We do not know for certain and usually it is because the powders have been ingested, my lord.' He fidgeted, uncomfortable at this admission of uncertainty.

The earl hung his head low, but Lady Charlotte now released some pent-up emotions and sobbed, putting her head in her hands as she sat down again. Her words were fearsome for Kathleen.

'This is your doing, Kathleen, giving my daughter this poison!' Lady Charlotte's hands slapped her sides as she viciously turned on the herb wife. 'If my daughter dies, you will pay for this, do you understand? You will pay! You will be pressed or burnt to death, I will not care!'

She turned to leave the room, her cries now the hysterical shrieks that the family were used to. Anne and Kathleen were stunned into a speechless shock. Frances knew Edward Griffin had encouraged Mary to lick her lips so that they stayed a brilliant shiny red. Could this action have caused the ingesting of the lead? Why would he wish her to be ill?

The earl instructed them to continue bathing Mary before hurrying after his wife. He suddenly remembered the physician and turned back towards the room to speak with him.

'Please stay. Mary must live; do whatever you feel may save her life.'

The physician was at a loss. There was no known cure for ingestion of the white powders, if indeed it were true that they cause such a profound illness.

He looked at his curette, the instrument he would need to cut the skin to bleed her. He stayed, studied her body, monitored her condition and pondered. An hour had passed when he noticed a change. There was a stirring. Mary's back arched upwards again but then was suddenly thrust forward as she retched severely, before projectile vomiting.

The physician asked Anne and Kathleen to help him turn Mary onto her side, so the foul liquid drained.

Mary cried out in pain. The physician interpreted this new incident as a disorder of the digestion or flux. So, in order to show that he was at least attempting to cure Mary, he rubbed the inside of her mouth with ginger, the new hot spice known to be an anti-emetic.

'Now she has been purged we will see an improvement, I'm sure,' he said.

Anne and Kathleen remained speechless and horrified. Kathleen cleared up the vomit and wiped little Mary's mouth clean.

The physician went downstairs to report to Lord and Lady Becton that all would be well as the body had purged itself, then he hastily announced that he must now leave.

Lady Charlotte felt relief and wanted to sleep. The whole event had exhausted her and she retired to her chamber, requesting that Frances and Anne share the duty of sitting through the night to watch over Mary. Oliver remained by his sister's bedside, dumbfounded.

'Oliver, return to your room now. Mary is in good hands with us. We will care for her over the night.' Frances said.

Oliver kissed his sister. 'She will die, won't she?' he asked Frances.

'We are doing all we can, Oliver. You need to rest.' She watched him walk away, his head low. She felt a strong urge to cradle him as she had done when he was a baby. She hated to see him so sad.

Frances and Anne decided to stay awake together, neither sure of what to do should Mary weaken again; but now she appeared to be sleeping comfortably. Would this anguish ever end?

Kathleen gathered her medicines, fighting back tears of dismay, unable to treat Mary.

She gathered her medicines, dismayed that she had not been able to treat Mary; but then neither had the physician. It was the body's own mechanism to purge itself from this scourge, whatever it had been or, indeed, whatever it still was.

*

It was almost midnight. Kathleen hated to walk in the dark. She borrowed a lantern so that she could see her way home.

The light swung from side to side as she walked briskly along the path through the woods. The sound of cracking twigs and undergrowth startled her from time to time and she increased her pace, looking behind her every few seconds. *It's just animals looking for food*, she reassured herself. She hoped that Father Peters was at the cottage with Jack and Ruth, and prayed that candlelight from the cottage would soon be in view.

She was starting to feel more positive when a sudden movement startled her. A tall figure appeared from behind some trees and faced her abruptly.

She gasped, stopping dead in her tracks, unable to move.

'You seem in a hurry, madam.' It was Master Griffin. Her heart sank.

'I must make haste to get home, sir.' She recovered and walked on, stepping around him.

Master Griffin was persistent.

'Allow me to help you. Let carry your precious box. You would not want to drop that, would you? It is of great value.' Kathleen stopped and faced him.

'Master Griffin, I do not require your assistance, thank you. Leave me be, to make haste.'

But Griffin continued to harass her. 'I know, madam, what has upset you. I know of Mary's illness and that if she dies, you will be blamed.'

Kathleen was irritated by this reminder and that he seemed so knowledgeable regarding the incidents of that evening. She sighed but repeated, 'Please Master Griffin, just take your leave.'

'If she dies, madam, you are answerable, but I can help you. I will testify that the substances are indeed harmless and you are in no way to blame for what has happened to Mary.'

Kathleen threw back her head. 'And what will you be asking for in return, sir?'

'Ha, you are a clever merchant after my own heart. You will give me the jewels from this box. I think that is fair. You can keep the futile stones you use and your silly herb bags, but the jewels will be mine...for my silence and co-operation. Think of it, madam: being scrutinised by another cunning man, one who could order your drowning in a sack, your hands and feet tied together or... even...committing your sweet little body to the stake, to burn as a stuffed pig, your skin blistering, your screams piercing and your lovely hair brilliant red with the flames of the devil, until just your bony skull remains.'

He grinned at her, adding, 'Your lovely daughter may also join you, as she is your accomplice, is she not? Furthermore, you enlist the help of a thief: a Catholic priest who resides with you. People will not respect that, will they, witch!'

Kathleen was now upset, frightened and very anxious. 'Go away, Griffin. Get away from me.'

He held her arms tightly. 'Listen to reason, witch: you are doomed. The cook will testify that you cursed me. Do you recall that, madam...? Well?' His breath upon her cheeks was foul as he drew closer to her. 'I can forget that ever happened, but you must agree to my conditions. Do you want your daughter to die?'

Remembering the scene in the kitchen, whereby she did curse Griffin, made her feel sick. She was desperate to get home and speak with Father Peters. She was deeply afraid.

He pressed his fingers harder into the flesh of her upper arms and stared coldly into her terrified eyes. She had to get away. Her fingers felt in her deep kirtle pocket for the smooth cloth bag, loosely tied. She forced the tie apart with her index finger plunging it into the small bag, then swiftly pulled out the grinded poisonous herbs. Freeing herself from Griffin's hold with a swift rising of her right arm, she furiously flung the mixture into his face.

'Aargh!' The powders entered his eyes and nostrils and he started to cough. He released Kathleen and she gathered her pace. A villager had come out of his cottage when he heard the commotion just in time to see Kathleen scurrying along the path. He turned his attention to Griffin, his lantern held high to illuminate the scene, and shouted angrily.

'What's going on here? Take your leave!'

Griffin now started to vomit, steadying himself against a tree. He gasped but found his breath and straightened his body.

'Your neighbour is a witch. She has cursed me and has evil medicine at her disposal.' His words then became louder. 'You have to beware of this woman, a servant of the devil!'

The man watched Kathleen hurry out of sight and then looked at Griffin again, unsure of what to do. He decided on nothing, as Griffin began to stagger back towards the centre of the village.

Kathleen rushed into the cottage. She poured out everything to Father Peters, glad the children were asleep. The old priest sat down and rubbed his chin thoughtfully.

'He will not do anything, Kathleen: it would risk his position. You are highly regarded. You said yourself the physician could not cure her.'

'But the ceruse, Father, and the cinnabar. Anne warned me of tales from London, that the Queen had become ill because of poisons in the powders. Lady Charlotte blames me!' She sobbed into her cupped hands. 'I wish I had never made it and given it to her, Father. What am I to do?'

Father Peters stood up and placed his arm around her shoulders.

'We will overcome this evil man who has been touched by the devil. You will see.'

Chapter Fifteen

1957

Ithink the scariest bit in the tunnel was when I found the silver box. Crouching on those wet rocks, with drips of water catching my hair, the dark presence standing over me was grisly. I glanced at it swiftly, my eyes looking up as far as I dared before looking down again. It was someone tall, but shadows can be tall. Maybe that's all it was and I simply imagined a hooded figure. It neither spoke nor touched me.

I crawled back towards the shaft without looking back and swam across the deeper part, the, box tightly gripped against my chest.

'What is it Tom? You look kind of spooked. What's that under your arm?' George was too inquisitive.

'I'll show you when we get back.'

Annabel couldn't wait to get out of the tunnel. George climbed the struts after her but, in her haste, she trod on his fingers and then she dropped her torch. I was less irritated. I couldn't get the dark shape out of my mind. Nothing, or no-one had touched me; but I had felt a powerful presence in that vault. Recalling what Mr. Haslam had said about the raven and a priest hating one another, I could well imagine how horrific their squabbles may have been. When the raven tried to attack me, he could have pecked my eyes out.

Annabel rapidly escaped to her room but, although George admired the box, he announced that he was starving and I asked him to go downstairs and bring up some drinks and biscuits as he knew where they were kept.

I sat on the bed and polished the box to reveal colourful and precious gemstones outlining an elongated cross. Originally it must've been very ornate and beautiful and it had something to do with the history of this house. Textbooks can tell you about historical facts, but this fascinating object made me aware of the power of the privileged, the quest for extreme wealth, the obsessions and mystical beliefs of the time and then…those who were oppressed and persecuted. Teachers had told us of prisoners being hanged, drawn and quartered, but now, with this box in my hands, I saw them, I heard their cries and saw their guts dispelled.

Silence. There was an odd feeling of people watching me, there in my own room. Voices were faint but it was as if they were trying desperately to communicate with me. Gingerly, I got a pen from my bedside table and wrote what I heard as best as I could:

'Sancta Pater, Sancta Pater, audi nos, libera nos, et nos cum mater nostra.'

George came in shortly after, with the tea and biscuits, shattering the aura. I couldn't hold back the incident with the dark presence looming over me, so I told him. I wasn't sure I was ready for his babble. 'You say nothing was said and nothing happened. Maybe you were lucky it was a ghost and not a poltergeist, Tom. A supernatural being supposedly responsible for physical disturbances such as loud noises and objects being moved around, even levitation. They can punch and kick and really hurt someone, if they want to. I've read it somewhere…'

*

For Bonfire Night, Dad had saved lots of old stuff for us to burn, including a mattress.

Mum didn't want to upset the garden. She had planted some bulbs and said she couldn't remember where, so we would have to go to the field at the other side of the track. There was a small gate and she had seen some boys already stacking wood for a bonfire.

'There's plenty of room for another bonfire so take your wood and rubbish over there.'

Mum made toffee apples and parkin as well as baking large potatoes. Dad had reluctantly bought some fireworks including rockets.

When it got dark we all trudged over, each one of us carrying something, whether it was food or a stool

The fire soon became a tall bright blaze, wood cracking and spitting, chestnuts roasting around the sides, our faces burning.

Annabel was whirling a sparkler in the air when, through the star-like twinkling, I saw the silvery shape of a woman with long flowing hair, sort of suspended in the distance.

'Look!' I shouted to Annabel as I pointed to the woman. Her head followed my gaze but she had gone.

'What's wrong with you?' asked Annabel.

'There was a woman… '

'Not again, Tom. It's a trick of the flames; a bit like when you see dogs and lions in the clouds…stupid!'

'Ha, made you look though.' I felt like I did when I had discovered the secret panel. No-one would believe me then. I did not pursue it.

The woman, the dark shape, the box, the voices and the bloody bird, were all running through my head that night.

*

The following Saturday, George was coming again. Annabel and my parents had taken a great liking to him, so he was almost like another member of the family and his weekend visits were regular. I was starting to realise he wasn't very happy at home.

We waited until my parents left to go shopping in Chesterfield and then the three of us investigated the ground behind the summer house. There had to be another way to access the tunnel. I was becoming obsessed with finding it.

'This is where I found that cup—well, goblet—and I just have a hunch that the tunnel is under here somewhere,' I told the others. The bending to the left of the tunnel and the estimated length of it indicated that perhaps there was some evidence of it below the ground.

George did his calculations. He walked from the tall outer chimney over a mound-like stretch of garden and, analysing the hump, decided that was the top of the tunnel. He announced that I was probably correct in my assumptions because the mound ended just feet away from the shed, a short distance from the outside lavatory.

We dug and dug for hours, but all we found of interest was old fragments of horseshoes, just like Dad had. Daylight was fading fast and the air became chilly, a winter breeze starting to bite.

'I hate early winter evenings. It gets dark too soon,' George groaned.

'Well, we'll carry on just a bit longer.'

Then I saw a light in the house.

'They're back.'

It was at that point that Annabel's spade struck something hard.

'God, what's that?' she asked.

George and I ran over to her. I took the spade and struck the ground again. There was a loud grating sound.

'We have to move all this soil...wait a minute.' I heard a noise, a loud and constant knocking in the garden. At the same time, an anxious but muffled yelling. Then it stopped.

'Is it the voices?' Annabel asked.

I was too interested in discovering what was so hard under the ground that I carried on digging.

It started again. 'Listen...stop digging, Tom,' demanded George.

But the wind, now whipping around the shed, made it difficult to hear.

'Please help, help!'

'Well, it's not in Latin this time and it's hardly whispering.' said George.

We crept out from behind the shed. The voice was coming from the outside lavatory and there was a glimmer of light seeping under the door.

'Oh, don't tell me, there's a ghost in your lavatory, Tom,' said George. 'That's a woman's voice. Might be the woman you told me you saw on Bonfire Night.'

We crept closer.

'Maybe the end of the tunnel is under the lavatory and the woman has just come up to have a wee.' laughed Annabel.

George laughed but I just muttered, 'Very funny.'

We got nearer and listened.

'Who's there?' I demanded.

'Who do you think it bloody well is, Robin Hood?'

'Gran!' We didn't know she was coming today.

'I can't get off this seat, Tom. It's far too low and I've dropped me stick.'

'Hold on, we'll push the door. Heave!' It gave way and George fell straight into Gran's lap, having tripped over a torch, its beam directed outwards and then her stick.

'Oh my God.... Never mind... Thank goodness I've not done anything smelly and I've pulled me knickers up.'

George, going bright red, looked horrified, but then he saw the funny side and laughed.

'Are you all right, Gran? I'll get your stick and pick up the torch.' Annabel was now fussing over her.

'I'll be fine, I just need a wee drop of something in my next cuppa, that'll do it!'

*

Gran's my mum's mum. Her name is Dorothy but she is sometimes referred to as Dot. She's seventy-five and, since grandad died five years ago, she's lived on her own. She's got a council house in Sheffield and she manages all right now, but it took

her a long time to get used to living on her own with no one to say good morning or goodnight to, share the crosswords, argue about politics and share all the chores.

Her only ailments were arthritis of the knees that stopped her from getting down too low and getting back up again. She also liked a nap in the afternoons and a tipple of brandy or whisky now and then, which she told people was merely medicinal for her arthritis and circulation.

The invitation to stay with us was well received and she had only visited Becton Manor briefly, before the electricity was installed and the roof was repaired.

She was looking forward to a family Christmas and possibly staying longer. If my dad lost his job, she told him she would help out with the bills. Dad was quite impressed with that.

Hobbling into the kitchen, flanked by George and Annabel, Gran smiled at my mum's quizzical gaze.

'What happened?' My surprised mum placed the drained potatoes on the table before she dropped them.

'I was rescued from solitary confinement in a small place. I dropped my stick on the floor. That loo of yours is so low, I couldn't stand up. These three helped me out, thank goodness, but the lock will need fixing, I'm afraid. I was rattling it so much that it fell off.'

My dad groaned. 'Another bloody job…and I suppose you'd like a new raised toilet seat, Dorothy?'

'Oh well, yes, thank you Albert.'

My mum distracted her from Dad's annoyance. 'I'll get you a mince pie with your tea eh? Thought I'd bake an early batch so I could perfect them by Christmas.'

'Don't forget a drop of brandy, eh? I'm really shook up, love. You have got brandy haven't you, or whisky?'

'Well, actually not yet, we'll get some later.' She glanced back at Dad. 'Won't we, dear?'

'I expect so, if the snow doesn't come; the forecast is for overnight, another problem with this isolated spot and a rough track outside.' Poor Dad sounded tired.

Mum sighed and watched him go into the kitchen.

'He gets a bit on edge, Mum, with everything we have to do and fear of losing his job an all, but at least he's not limping.'

Dad shouted back: 'There's some whisky.'

There was no hesitation from Gran. 'Oh that'll do fine, but if it's a single malt, I'll have it separately, dear.'

Mum and Dad exchanged amused looks, but Mum then looked concerned. I heard her whisper to Dad, 'Hope she hasn't become a serious drinker.' She giggled. 'Oh well, it is Christmas.'

Mickey was excitedly wagging his tail, circling Gran and looking into her face, all doe-eyed.

'Hello, Mickey, it's so lovely to see you. Do you like this house, then?' She always spoke to animals as if they'd answer her back.

Mickey cocked his head on one side then the other and gave the hint of a whimper as she gently massaged his ears then, noticing him watching her eat and salivating profusely, she sneaked him a bit of her pastry.

She was smiling at George while she dropped a few more crumbs for Mickey.

'I've not seen you before, young man.'

'I'm George.'

'Hello, George, I'm very pleased to meet you but so sorry that you had to meet me in a lavatory.' George smiled as she went on. 'Do you live nearby?'

'Well, not really. I live about three miles away. My mother brought me today.'

'Oh, you've got a car? You are very lucky, not many of us can afford a car. Albert's car is very old and not too reliable. He should be looking for another one.'

'Not something else, dear mother-in law,' Dad groaned.

'Hardly anyone had a car when I was a young girl and now quite a lot of people are buying these televisions. A lot of money, they are.'

'Don't ask me to buy one of them!' Dad snorted.

'Times change so quickly. I bet everyone will have a television and a car in the future, you'll see.' She swallowed her whisky in one gulp. 'Any more whisky, Albert?'

Dad's face was a picture. He muttered something under his breath as he went back into the kitchen with her empty glass, but luckily Gran and Mum were too busy talking to hear him.

I looked out of the window. It was too dark now to do any more digging and soon George's dad, Arthur, would come to pick him up. In fact, there he was. You knew it was Arthur because he knocked in a rhythmic style, the same five beats every time, followed by a miserable expression on his face.

Gran opened the front door and introduced herself.

'Err, it's Arthur, missus,' he introduced himself. 'George's dad.'

'Yes, hello, come in, Arthur.'

George went ahead of me as we both heard his dad arrive.

'Found any more treasure, have you?' he asked his son.

'What treasure?' asked Gran. I got the impression from her raised chin and scrutinising expression that she didn't quite like him.

'Oh, haven't you heard, love? They found a goblet, I reckon it's a goblet anyway. Lots more where that came from, I wouldn't wonder, in a house like this.' His head did a sort of half circle as he looked all around the hall and up towards the galleried landing.

My gran's head cocked to one side. 'Really?'

Arthur looked a bit embarrassed and hurriedly said good night, ushering George into the car.

Later that evening, Gran stopped me at the bottom of the stairs just before I was about to go up.

'Is that true, Tom, about a goblet?'

'Err…Gran, are you going to your room? I'll show it to you but it's all a secret.' Once in the front bedroom, I brought the goblet to show her. She looked amazed.

'Tom…this is worth something, I'm sure. I'll buff it and make it shine. This needs to be valued.'

'You will keep it secret, won't you, Gran?'

'If it's a secret, how come Arthur knows about it and not your dad?'

'George obviously told him. Mum and Dad…don't believe any of what I say. There are ghosts here, Gran, I'm sure. I haven't seen him properly but I know he's a hooded figure; might once have been a priest. Then there's voices, low voices, more like whisperings and last week, I found a box in the tunnel…'

'Ghosts? A priest? A tunnel?'

Had I said too much? Would it scare her?

'There's a long shaft, right next to the chimney which goes into a tunnel under the house. So technically the ghost isn't in the house, but somewhere under it.'

'Wait…how do you know this? How did you get into a tunnel? Tom, you had better not be playing games with me.'

I hesitated. 'I'm not playing games, Gran. I climbed into a passage that runs behind that cupboard.' I pointed to the cupboard in her room. 'It seems there a lot of passages, secret ones: priest holes. That particular one goes to the back of my room.'

Her eyes rested on the cupboard. 'That cupboard? In this room? My room? I've got to sleep in here, where a man might come through that cupboard: a hooded man? Have you lost your mind, Tom?'

I couldn't help but chuckle. Typical Gran reaction.

As I stared at her, she fished inside her bag and swigged a large gulp of whisky from a hip flask. I was at a loss for what to say next but just managed some reassurance.

'We're on to it, Gran. George and I think it's a sad spirit and so does the man in the newsagents in the village.'

'He knows about a ghost in this house?'

'Yes, his friend used to live here when they were kids and some eerie things happened. Not only that, Gran. There's a weird big bird here, a raven and sometimes he swoops really low and tries to peck you; like he doesn't want you here. The man in the newsagent said the bird was some sort of curse. The boy was starting to find out what happened when his family had had enough and they moved away.'

'Hmm. I'm not surprised. Come to think of it, your Uncle Charles said strange things happened on a particular night— Midsummer's Eve, I think it was—but, ah, Charles was always on the rum!'

'Gran…that's also what the man said: "*It all happened on Midsummer's Eve.*"'

Gran now looked very worried. '*What* all happened? What did he mean? Didn't you ask him?'

'Don't think he knew properly. We don't know, but George and I—and maybe Annabel at times—want to find out. The other thing is, there may be another way to get into the tunnel. When we got you out of the lavatory, we were digging and Annabel struck something hard. I think we may be on to something, but we need to keep digging.'

'Don't dig deep holes, Tom. It could be dangerous.'

'Don't worry, Gran.'

*

Over dinner, Gran had hardly been able to contain herself. I knew she wanted to spill the beans. Mum had commented on how quiet she was and Gran had looked at me as if wanting permission to disclose everything I had told her. I subtly shook my head.

When the table was being cleared, she came close to me. 'I can't take my eyes from the cupboard Tom. My whisky flask needs replenishing, 'cos of what you have told me; it helps me sleep. It's difficult to keep all this secret, not to be telling your mum and dad. You must.'

'Not yet, Gran.'

A stick had been placed where we last started to dig, in case there was more snowfall.

I thought that this must be a trapdoor of some sort. At one end it appeared to be lower, as if it had started to sink at some point. Whenever Gran saw me, she quizzed me on our progress. But one day, Mum heard her whispering.

'What are you whispering about, Mum?'

'Oh…Alice…just asking Tom if he's got a girlfriend. He's that age now, he could have a secret lady.'

That was a good one for Gran; I was impressed. 'I told her I have several, Mum.'

'Oh that's nice,' Mum said, disbelieving of course, and went back to the kitchen.

Then, later that same evening, there was an early snowfall. It was only mid-November but it had been unusually bitterly cold. I was on my way to my room, when I spotted Gran napping in the hall chair.

We were both startled by the front door being flung open. Dad appeared, in a very bad mood.

'That's it! All finished! The mine is closing for good. Not making any money so we all have to be on the bloody scrap heap.' He stormed upstairs, straight past me without acknowledging me, but yelled down to Mum. 'Now your mother will have to help pay these bills or we move house again, something bloody smaller.' He slammed the bedroom door behind him.

By this time, I was at the top of the stairs. I looked down. Gran was standing at the foot of the stairs, having been joined by a worried-looking Mum.

I will never forget their faces as they stood and stared at me. We had been learning about the Second World War at school and their expressions reminded me of a passage that Mr Wilson had read out, reciting the words of Neville Chamberlain announcing that Britain was at war and showing us pictures of stunned people as they listened to the radio.

'It's going to be all right, you know.' Gran said to her daughter, before giving her a big hug.

'But you knew it might happen, Mum.' I said.

It didn't seem to help. 'Yes, I suppose so. I'll put the kettle on.'

That's it, I thought. *Put the kettle on, it solves all sorts. Tea and whisky.*

That night as I lay in bed, I realised I wasn't as much concerned about Dad losing his job, but at not yet finding the other tunnel entrance. I suppose, at sixteen, the implications of being broke with a large house to maintain just didn't register.

My dad walked around as if he were wading in treacle, his head low and his face set in a glum expression. He stopped joking or even talking very much but did get irritable and started to grow a beard.

Everything was an effort; the puffing and sighing became tedious. He didn't have the heart to get interested in Christmas preparations and was miserable to be around.

One morning at breakfast, Gran offered to give him money for petrol to take her into Chesterfield.

'Why don't you call on Alice in the library and pick yourself a book, eh?' said a cheery Gran.

Dad shot her an indignant look. 'Why do I want to read a book?'

'You've never given yourself the chance to read properly, have you? Your generation left school early and started work, then there was the war of course, but now you have the time. I know you're looking for work but just go in and have a browse. You might find something of interest. Tom can go with you. It's half term after all.'

*

While Gran ambled around the shops, I accompanied my dad to the library. Mum saw him, 'Oh, Albert, glad you've come in. I'll make us a cup of tea. It's nearly my break. Why don't you go over there in the quiet part and I'll be over in a jiffy.'

Dad moseyed around, glancing at the books on the shelves. I stayed with him, wanting to know what he was interested in.

'What am I doing in a library, Tom, for God's sake?"

'Books can be really interesting, Dad. Keep looking.'

Then something grabbed his attention: the word Becton, on the narrow spine of an old book.

All the books in this section were old and now he read a sign above the shelves: *Local History and Folklore.*

He picked it from the shelf and flicked through the pictures, stopping as he noticed a very old, yellowed photograph of our house. He sat down and noticed the words: *Thought to be haunted.*

He slowly mouthed the words again out loud. 'Haunted.' Then it became a question: 'Haunted?'

'Albert!'

Dad almost jumped out of his skin. Mum came to join us with a tray of tea.

'The boss said she didn't mind if we didn't linger too long. We're not busy but I will have to get up and see to people if there are any queries,' warned mum. 'Found yourself a good book?'

'Actually I have, yes. There's a picture of our house. Look. It says it's haunted.'

They looked at the picture with interest. 'Oh, what a shame.' Mum announced. 'You can't borrow this one, dear, it's for reference purposes only. Complete rubbish about the hauntings, anyway. We haven't seen a thing. It's probably accurate to say that the house was much larger in its original state but the ghost thing is laughable.'

At least Dad still looked interested. 'What are these priest holes dating back to the late sixteenth century?'

Gran walked in and looked over dad's shoulder. 'Can't find much in the shops. Oh…you've got a book about Becton Manor, your very own house, how about that?'

Dad nodded then, breaking his words into manageable syllables, he slowly read out: 'And mani-fest-ations on Midsummer Night's Eve?'

Gran looked at me quizzically. Now we might have to tell the tale.

'Oh dear Albert…that's what Uncle Charles said, but I thought he was simply on the rum. Don't worry, there are things they can do – there are exercises to get rid of spirits.'

'Exorcisms, Gran.'

'What?' Dad sighed. He'd had enough of ghost talk. 'I'm off, hearing all this about where I put my head at night is just making me feel worse.'

Mum was irritated. 'Albert, it's high time, you drove Mum and Tom back before the traffic builds. Enough of this fantasy nonsense.'

But Gran had another browse on the way out and noticed books on antiques. She chose one which had pictures of Tudor goblets, except the word used in the book was *'chalice'*.

She remembered the markings from when she'd polished the goblet I had found, the stem featuring a barley-twist design, and looked for a similar picture. After a couple of books, she found one giving approximate values at auction and then her eyes widened. She beckoned me over to read it:

The majority of chalices from the Tudor period, as this one is, were destroyed following the Dissolution of the Monasteries in 1530. The chalice is silver but the Latin inscription has been worn down so is illegible. The base has a tongue and dart decoration around the rim of the foot. The stem is of a barley twist design. There is a band of arabesque engraving around the rim. Various inscriptions refer to the 'blood of Jesus Christ'.

Approximate value: £1,500.

'Oh my God,' she whispered.

'Are you two coming?' asked Dad impatiently. She nodded and then turned to me. 'Tom, if that story about Midsummer Night's Eve is true, we have about six good months. Because, by the sound of it, when that time comes, Becton Manor may not be a nice place to be in.'

Chapter Sixteen

Spring 1598

Mary remained unconscious, prayers held every morning and evening to beg for her to recover. The earl sat one side of her bedside and his son on the other.

'Will she ever greet me again, Oliver, in her beautiful red dress? She is desperate to get to court, you know. I don't know why. She prefers to run wild and free, like Sabre. She watched you all the time as you were growing up. She so wanted to join in your games, to be strong, climb trees and catch butterflies and moths.'

A tear escaped from Oliver's pooling eyes.

'Yes, father. She was better than me at catching insects. So quick.' They managed a weak smile but neither could sustain it.

Lady Charlotte did not stay long away from her bedside. She now joined them, occasionally giving way to loud wails. 'I cannot bear this, William. I cannot bear it.'

Oliver sobbed. His mother hugged him close, before he suddenly broke from her clutches and ran from the room.

Frances stood at the back of the room in attendance. She wanted to run after Oliver but knew she must stay where she was in case her mistress needed her. Lady Charlotte sat opposite her husband.

She and the earl each held a delicate white hand in theirs. Then Mary suddenly called out in a piercing shriek: a banshee from another world.

Her body writhed and struggled with God-only-knew-what. Blood, mixed with spittle, oozed from her tightly clenched teeth. Urine dripped onto the floor after the sheet could no longer absorb it, and the bedhead rhythmically creaked at the strain of her tormented frame.

'Tell Henry to fetch the physician, now… Now, I said!' Charlotte screamed at Frances. The horrified housekeeper was jolted into action.

'Yes, my lady.' She turned and ran down the stairs. The earl was helpless. He knew the physician could not help her.

As suddenly as it had started, it stopped. She was lifeless: her lips blue, her body mottled.

For a moment, Lady Charlotte's astonishment froze her to the spot, staring with anguish at her beautiful daughter. Mary's chest no longer rose and fell. She slowly stood and shook her daughter's shoulders, protesting vehemently at this sudden end.

'The demons cannot have her, they cannot take her! No…no!' She put the palms of her hands together and looked up to the heavens. 'Mercy, oh mercy!'

The earl walked around the bed and placed his arm around his wife.

'Charlotte…it is not to be.'

Charlotte swung her body round to reject his supportive arm. She raised her voice. 'Don't you see…? This is divine retribution, William! Punishment for letting Father Peters go and for renouncing our faith. Don't you understand? What have we done?'

No one answered her questions. She hung her head low…until she rose and announced: 'It was her, wasn't it? Kathleen and her poisons?'

There was a demonic look in her eyes.

'She has to suffer, the way I am suffering now. She will never come here again and people must know that she is not to be trusted.'

Her words resonated. Oliver ran across the landing towards the bedroom.

'No, no, it can't be, it can't be. My sister can't be dead, she can't be!' He went close to Mary's face and clutched her hands. 'Mary, Mary, wake up. Mary, you must hear me. Wake up, I said!'

At the foot of the stairs the servants heard every word. Anne feared for Kathleen. Frances had just told Henry to ride Sabre to get the physician as fast as possible... It no longer mattered.

*

The days that followed were solemn and grim. Margaret's infectious laughter ceased; Frances was even more austere. There was only the sound of the servants' footsteps, going about their business.

Anne asked for permission to begin some further tuition for Ruth, at least for a short time but, as soon as she asked, she quickly gauged her mistress's angry response.

'How dare you even ask that of me? The daughter of that murderer will never come to my house again! You will help Margaret and Frances until I discuss with the earl what duties you shall have.'

'Yes, my lady,' said Anne humbly and walked away. *So I may be dismissed.*

*

The earl had received condolences and a pardon from his duties from the Queen, but he felt that he would rather be at Court, busying himself, than in this house of sadness and death.

Nothing would ever bring Mary back to him. Her brightness and energy would meet him no more as he returned from court. She would no longer dance and giggle, play the flute or dress up and play imaginative games of growing up into a beautiful lady. A beautiful lady she would have been, too.

He recalled the endless nights of her restlessness as a small infant. She had cried every night and her appetite had been so poor that they had gone to many lengths to fatten her with bread soaked in eggs and milk, and even warm ox blood and honey. She had eventually surprised them by growing stronger and wilful. How can that time now be wasted? Tears fell without effort or control from red eyes set in a grief-stricken face.

The earl's reminiscing ceased as sobs from above travelled through the house. Charlotte was groaning, 'You must come home to me, Mary, you must come back home, come home my sweet child, come home. I cannot bear this.'

The sound broke his resolve and he gulped painfully. He bent his head low into his cupped hands and sobbed. He could stand no more. Tears now burst from his eyes in abundance. His face contorted, his chest began to heave and his body shook with uncontrollable sorrow.

The howling was heard in every room. In the scullery the servants stopped what they were doing and solemnly looked at one another as they listened.

Margaret's lips trembled as teardrops ran down her cheek. She had held back too long and now needed to release her pent-up misery.

Her emotions were infectious. Frances and Anne wept. Ged and Henry stood watching but they also needed comfort and release. They hugged one another. They all hugged one another. There was nothing else they could do. Lady Mary had gone; gone forever.

'Come on,' said Frances, sniffling then wiping her nose, before restoring her familiar decorum. 'This won't do. We cannot help, by crying like babies. We have duties to perform. None of us can bring Mary back. She has returned to her maker. God rest her soul.' They made the sign of the cross.

Chapter Seventeen

Christmas 1957

I frequently saw Gran studying the chalice. She often handled it and now voiced her thoughts, 'Wonder who has held this, Tom? How often do you think it was used?' She was fascinated.

We talked about keeping secrets and now she wanted to share her new knowledge and prompt her daughter and son-in law to become involved with my mission of discovering what happened in our manor house. I had looked concerned, until she promised me she wouldn't mention the tunnel.

'Wait and see,' she said.

I nodded, 'Okay, just the goblet—chalice, rather.'

That evening over dinner, she sat down excitedly.

'I have something in my apron pocket I haven't told any of you yet, but what I found out at the library is intriguing and I can't wait to share it with you. Tom of course, is well aware.'

Silence. Gran fiddled in her pocket.

'Hurry up then, mother, the potatoes will go cold.' Mum was irritated, as if anticipating another tale of ghosts in her house.

'Well, here in my hand is a beautiful piece of history…and it belongs to you.' Her eyes scanned us all. 'An actual Tudor chalice. Of course, what I read in the library was a mere estimate of its value; the picture was surprisingly similar though.' She paused.

'And…?' My mum was becoming anxious. I wasn't sure if she was eager to know the value or worried about her cold potatoes.

'Well, it's definitely of Tudor origin.'

'How do you know it's Tudor?' asked my mum, lifting the lid from the tureen of potatoes to check their temperature.

'The markings: there's a Latin inscription. I'll get it properly valued, but I've done a good job of cleaning it and I'm pretty certain it is indeed valuable. The one very similar in the antiques book was valued at £1,500.'

She turned to Dad.

'Albert, this could be your salvation. The children say there's more treasure. We should be helping them. It's not just imagination. Something happened in this house centuries ago and you should keep digging, love.'

'Huh!' Dad started to eat his braised beef and potatoes, seemingly uninterested.

Then, with a mouthful of food, he looked up. He ate while he looked at the chalice. After he swallowed his food, he showed some interest.

'Let me see that, Dorothy.' He held it and for the first time in ages, he looked inspired. 'Hmm. I'll think about it.'

Mum wanted to hold it as well. 'It does look like a fine specimen. You really have cleaned it well, Mum. I hope it's worth something. We need the money.'

Annabel and I grinned.

Mum, now that everybody was eating her food, seemed relaxed and excited. 'Think about it, Albert. £1,500, eh?'

An animated Annabel squealed, 'I can have a new Raleigh bike.'

Dad shook his head.

I, too, started to think of what I would like but, strangely enough, nothing of any material worth came to mind.

*

George was invited to Christmas Eve dinner. In the previous weeks,

Annabel and I hadn't made much progress with the digging. She got too cold and fed up and Dad had been against it, but I wanted to resume it and knew George would be enthusiastic.

The tall Christmas tree, adorned with sweets and fancy baubles, glowed from candlelight that flickered from tiny candles held in holders at the end of the highest branches in the soft evening light. Mum didn't want them too low in case someone knocked them.

Masses of brightly coloured paper trimmings hung low from each corner of the dining room, meeting in the centre of the ceiling and swaying gently in the warm air.

The fireplace looked spectacular as it sparkled with red and orange flames. The mantelpiece brimmed with holly and bits of conifer decorated with baubles and bells.

The cracking of wood reminded me of Bonfire Night: not the fireworks or the spuds, but the ethereal image of the woman with flowing hair. Just like the face at the window, it lasted a mere couple of seconds, leaving you with the impression that you have an overactive imagination.

I recalled the familiar sight of the candles on the first evening in the old house but now it was much cosier, the damp fustiness had disappeared. The smell of freshly baked pies and cakes wafted from the kitchen. George was smiling broadly.

'This is great, Tom. My Mum and Dad never make a fuss. Say it's too damned expensive. This feels like a proper Christmas.'

Mum had arranged a few early presents under the tree, and George was given his. He opened it eagerly to discover a new torch with differently coloured beams but, in his delight, he forgot himself.

'Oh, Mrs Winchett, this is great: far better than the one I dropped in the tunnel, eh Tom?'

There was a silence.

'Oops…' George muttered.

Mum stared at him.

'Ah, was it a blue torch by any chance George?' She held his horrified gaze. 'Only I was searching for my blue torch the other day and couldn't find it anywhere' Group silence... then mum asked, and what tunnel might that be?'

George had turned bright red. Dad, sensing an awkward moment, quickly ushered us to the table.

'George, you can sit here across from Annabel and next to Tom, eh? We can all carry on opening presents after we've eaten eh? Dinner is ready, isn't it Alice? Do you want any help dishing up dear?'

My momentarily dumbfounded Mum took the hint and went to fetch the food: a large ham, potatoes, carrots and peas. Gran helped her and, as they were returning to the room, I heard her mutter, 'Don't get agitated Alice. George is having a really nice time. Don't spoil it for your guest.'

Mum dished out the meat.

'Help yourself to the vegetables, George.' But she still wanted answers and couldn't resist. 'I didn't quite catch your answer to my question, George. Did you lose my blue torch in a tunnel?'

Dad chipped in but it made no difference, 'Alice, leave the lad alone to eat his dinner, eh?'

George, surprisingly, was ready with a response.

'I took the torch home Mrs. Winchett and by accident I dropped it into a pond in an underpass. Sorry, but you can keep the one you bought me to replace it. I won't mind.'

Gran kept opening her mouth like a bloated fish: wanting, I assumed, to spill the beans. I glared at her.

Dad now wanted answers. 'And why do you kids look so guilty?'

'Okay,' I said, taking a deep breath. 'I know it's not fair to keep you in the dark, but you have to believe what we have to say for a change.'

Gran nodded with approval.

'I have a feeling you know something I don't,' Mum questioned Gran.

She shook her head and shrugged her shoulders.

'Oh go on, Gran, say what you have to say, you've wanted to for ages.'

'Well…are you sure, Tom?' I nodded and she seemed relieved as well as excited to be able to give her account. 'It was quite by accident. You see, it was Arthur, really. George's father. He mentioned a little cup that Tom had found in the garden. I quizzed Tom. George must've told Arthur about it, but never mind.' George looked guilty. Gran hesitated. 'Actually, I think it's better coming from the children.'

'Tell them, Tom,' Annabel said to me, and a sheepish George nodded in agreement.

They sat listening hard to the account of the tunnel. Once or twice Dad or Mum laughed with utter disbelief. Dad asked if all this had to do with the hauntings but, like Mum, he was in denial. 'Ah, it's a new Christmas story. Another Charles Dickens.'

Mum sighed. 'I get sick and tired of all this stupid chatter about spirits. They simply do not exist. How do you expect me to accept that living creatures from the past are messing about in a tunnel under my house? This game is ridiculous, Tom.'

Gran reassured her. 'I don't think it is a game, Alice, but it's not as bad as you think. It may not be a creature at all. Tom thought he saw a dark shadow, that's all and probably imagined a hooded figure. You know what kids are like. At first when Tom told me of secret passages, I was afraid that something would enter my bedroom through the cupboard, but nothing has ever happened. Silly, isn't it?'

Dad laughed out loud. 'This sounds like you all belong to a secret fantastical organisation that's duped you into believing this stuff is real. Ha! I can't believe what I'm hearing. Monsters in cupboards, I ask you! For God's sake.'

Gran was unperturbed as she confronted my dad.

'There has been some good come out of the digging, Albert. Look at the chalice…and you have to agree, you live in a very old house with a rich history. Isn't that what you're proud of, Alice?'

'Of course, mother. But that doesn't mean dark shadows and voices all around us, for God's sake.'

Then we all starting talking at once, trying to get across our own analysis of events which we experienced, about how people became bewitched, but then Mum's voice raised above everyone else's.

'Some people have vivid imaginations and see things that don't exist and actually believe that humans die but come back as somebody else, or even a creature. It's plain madness, people either read too many Dennis Wheatley type books or they have little excitement in their real lives. Anyway, that's my opinion!'

George, thoroughly encouraged by Mum's prattle, could not resist a debate and shot into 'babble mode', giving his reasons for ghosts, the difference between a ghost and a poltergeist, and the history of priest holes. He hardly drew breath, but all around him the family were all ears.

You could do nothing else once he started, because he rabbited on to match the speed of light. He was so animated that his eyebrows remained arched and almost reaching his hairline throughout the entire speech. He was loving it.

When he finally stopped before he expired, Gran clapped and we followed suit; even mum was grinning. Gran rose from the table deciding we all needed a drink.

'There's a large bottle of Tizer for the children, some beer for Albert and some whisky for me. I will have lemonade in it, dear, don't worry.' She winked at her daughter. 'And for you, Alice, I have bought some pink champagne.'

Dad rose from the table. 'Dorothy, I'll get the drinks. And thank you. Tom and Annabel, you put some mince pies on the table, please.'

There was a hive of activity. I had to admit a great sense of relief in getting all that eerie stuff out in the open. Most of all though, it was just great to see George so ecstatically happy.

The drinks started to flow. We were still sitting around the table but the transformation in everybody was amusing. Dad had forgotten that he didn't have a job.

After a couple of glasses of pink champagne, Mum wasn't too upset about a possible resident spirit under the house and Gran was visibly relieved not to be keeping secrets any more.

We raised our glasses many times to drink to Becton Manor and its treasures. This house was my home. This was now a quest, a joint quest, with everyone on my side. There was more to come, of that I was certain.

After dinner we played Charades and Monopoly. Gran's vision after too many whiskies was playing tricks, and she believed Annabel when she agreed to buy all her houses on Park Lane and Mayfair from her, which were in fact hotels. We ate lots of chocolate and giggled at the slightest thing.

The doorbell went. It was George's dad. Annabel let him in. He kind of whooped into the dining room, emitting a strong smell of whisky.

'Merry Christmas all.'

'Merry Christmas, Arthur.'

George looked disappointed at having to leave us, but he remembered his manners.

'Thank you, Mr and Mrs Winchett for a really lovely Christmas Eve dinner.'

It had been a very memorable evening. That night though, I still polished my box and became acquainted with the momentary soft voices within the walls. Something happened in this house, many hundreds of years ago, and someone wanted me to find out.

*

Compared to Christmas Eve dinner, Christmas Day lunch was just too peaceful. Perhaps we needed George's presence. For some reason we didn't discuss the treasures further, or the ghosts of the house. Maybe Mum and Dad needed time to digest it all.

A couple of days after Christmas the sun broke through and the ground was not so frozen.

Dad kept his promise to dig deeper behind the summer house and gave new spades to Annabel and me. With all the striking she had done at the stone object below, Annabel had broken one of the spades. Dad's fury, though, had now subsided. We dug vigorously with intent and purpose, shifting heaps of wet, muddy, heavy soil tinged with grey sodden snow, but the ground remained hard and the stone object larger and more sunken than we thought.

Dad at least showed some interest.

'You're right, Tom. Seems like there's a flagstone here all right.'

He walked to the shed and came back with his large pick.

We hurriedly cleared away more soil until it was exposed; about three feet by four feet long. Dad hooked the pick on the edge of the flagstone. It came loose and lifted; revealing the sound of water trickling below, like a cave. As we all peered into the hole, the damn raven swooped, in an apparent rage, brushing the top of our heads.

'Make it stop! Make it stop!' yelled Annabel.

'Cover your eyes, the pair of you!' Dad shooed it away. The bird squawked loudly and flapped its huge wings, inches over Dad's scalp. 'Oh, God, what have we started, here?'

I couldn't resist a quick look into the hole, now filling with spilled soil. Below the ground were the steps I had discovered, but also something new: I glimpsed another tunnel off to the right of the vault.

Chapter Eighteen

Spring 1598

The return to normality at Becton Manor, following the death of Mary, was indeed difficult for all who lived under its roof. The earl and Lady Charlotte hardly spoke to one another or the servants. Lady Charlotte failed to comment on the new growth on her shrubs, the signs of spring and new life in her garden, something she usually delighted in.

Kathleen was full of remorse and Father Peters spent hours trying to reassure her that her medicine and the methods she used worked, but that the Lady Mary had simply gone too far. The physician could not cure her either, he needed to keep repeating to Kathleen in her depths of woe. Lady Mary would not have survived from any of the known treatments.

Jack and Ruth felt a sense of loss as they stayed in the cottage, not knowing what to do with themselves. Jack would soon resume his studies but Ruth would no longer enjoy the privilege of being educated.

In addition, Ruth felt guilty as she felt a wave of resentment that Mary had died. Mary never did help her to find the hidden treasure of Becton Manor. She thought about asking Father Peters directly but doubted he'd tell her. Her dream of having something of value was lost.

*

Early one morning, as Henry was attending to the horses, he heard a commotion in the nearby field.

He ran along the track until he came to a small gate which enabled him to peer through.

Hundreds of men and boys were tearing down fencing, shouting with a frightening urgency. Further in the distance, some were setting fire to the fences. Henry could smell the burning and hear the wood crackle and spit.

He turned back to the house and almost flew through the door, panting furiously. Breathlessly he shouted to Margaret in the scullery.

'There's a mob on the field across the way. They're setting fire to the fences and tearing it all down. There's hundreds of 'em!'

He was speaking so fast, Margaret struggled to understand. 'Henry, calm down, for the love of God.'

As soon as he was able, he slowly repeated what he'd said. Margaret said he must tell the earl, and she went with him to knock on the study door. The earl always rose early and was now sitting at his desk. He looked up, surprised, as Margaret entered followed by Henry.

'I am so sorry to disturb you my lord, but Henry has something of importance to say.'

Henry looked nervous. It wasn't often that he had an audience with the earl.

'Well, speak up, lad, what tidings have ye?'

As soon as Henry had told him the barest of details, the earl turned his head to the window.

He opened the nearest one and listened to the commotion. Breathing deeply, he could smell burning wood. He grabbed his hat and, with Henry close behind, rushed to the field.

A man in the field shouted, 'There is the man who has ruined our livelihoods.'

Several men started to run towards the earl, who stood his ground. They were waving sticks and Henry was afraid for the earl's safety. He wondered why the earl just stood there; he had no hope of fighting all these men. Henry did not know what to do except keep shouting, 'No, no! The earl has done you no wrong.'

One man, disregarding status, pounced upon the earl and dragged him to the ground, holding him down with his left hand while wielding a stick in his right.

'You think you can destroy our lives, you greedy lot of high-borns?'

The stick waved menacingly in the air until Henry intervened, grabbing it away from the man and kicking his shin. The other men gathered to watch this encounter, some laughing at the boy's efforts but others egging the man on to 'finish him off,' ready with their sticks to continue attacking the earl. Henry jumped onto the man's back but the man, big and brawny, just threw Henry off, dumping him to the ground.

'Get yourself off, ye little scoundrel.'

Henry stumbled as he tried to get up.

Another man was running up from the rear, shouting loudly.

'Wait, wait, do you want to be in prison or hanged for murder? That won't help you or your families. Stop! He will listen to me.'

The earl, wiping mud from his face, looked up to see who was shouting. He knew this man as Yeoman Thomas of Barley, who was a hardworking, honest man. They had a good relationship and respected one another, or so the earl had thought. He slowly stood up, brushing mud from his breeches and doublet, and faced the big man who had attacked him.

'I could easily have you hanged, man. Name yourself!'

Thomas of Barley winced at the threat of death and quickly interrupted.

'We need to speak, my lord. These men have good reason for their intrusion.' The earl had spoken kindly to him and his family in the past. There had to be a better way.

Once he had caught his breath, the earl looked piercingly at

Thomas. Raising his voice, he stepped towards him. 'If there is strife, Thomas, why did you not seek my counsel?'

Thomas answered clearly. 'Perhaps I should have come sooner, my lord, but these men have had enough of high rents and seizure of their land for your sheep! Some are near starvation: no land, no crops, nothing to sustain us. You have your profits from your sheep, wool, milk and meat, while we starve. Do you know what our lives are like, without a crumb on the table, while you eat venison and drink French wines?' There was a pause. 'These men are very angry!'

The earl was dumbfounded but knew this had to have something to do with Griffin.

Thomas agreed to halt the mob until he had spoken in private with the earl and they marched back to the house.

The earl thanked Henry for what he had done. In truth, Henry had enjoyed the scrap. 'I'd do it again, sir.' The earl smiled at the animation on Henry's face.

In the parlour, Thomas explained.

'These men, my lord, are just a small number of those who are getting angrier by the day. Your rent increases and the land you enclosed for sheep robs us of our livelihoods. We are unable to sustain our living, my lord. The price of grain is rising but we have precious little land left to grow crops. We were told by a man who represents you that we would benefit in the profits from the sheep: there would be wool, milk and meat to trade and we would all have a share, including a supply of butter and cheese. Truth is, my lord, we cannot wait for that day.'

He nodded to the window.

'Some of the small farmers out there are beginning to starve. Young Harry Osborne has four children now and he cannot feed them properly. His wife trembles with fear of what tomorrow may bring. She frets so much that her milk to nurse the little one has dried up. They are unable to take anything to market or to buy from others. You must listen, my lord. I have told the men you would listen.'

The earl was indeed listening and very thoughtful; Griffin was on his mind. Had this man turned out to be a scoundrel? He hadn't mentioned raising the rents.

He recalled his wife coming to him with complaints of the man's demeanour with the boys. He recalled his daughter Mary wanting Griffin dismissed, for sheer arrogance. He recalled that Margaret and Frances disliked him intensely.

Had he been missing something? Or had he chosen to ignore what happened around him, as he ignored Charlotte's complaints about the children and the servants? Could it be there was torment enough for him, with troubles at court?

The fact remained that he had put his trust in someone he hardly knew and had not checked this man's actions. He gave his head a brief shake: he had made mistakes, mistakes that might be costly. He should take more note of what was said and done.

He said to Thomas, 'I will see to it that some of the fencing is taken down, so the villagers can take back land on which to grow crops. Before I do that, I will look for myself at the enclosures and speak with the villagers. But you must give me your word of no further attacks, either on my land or on my person. If there are any other disturbances, I assure you: there will be hangings and bodies will be gibbeted.'

Thomas of Barley shuddered.

The earl strode to the bottom of the stairs and called up, 'Master Griffin, would you come down here a moment?'

Griffin had watched the commotion from an upstairs window, forbidding the boys to leave their desks. He was nervous.

'Yes, my lord?' he asked as he entered the parlour.

'I understand you have met with the tenant of Barley Farm: Thomas?'

'Yes, my lord.' Griffin observed the dried mud on the earl's face.

'Pray, explain to me, Master Griffin, what dealings you have had with this man.'

Griffin looked uncomfortable. Thomas was saying nothing, but there was a look of discontent on the man's face that led Griffin to believe his explanation should be diplomatic and conciliatory.

He cleared his throat and offered his tale of the encounter with Thomas and the other villagers.

When he mentioned a venture that would benefit all the smallholders in exchange for most of their land, the earl interrupted.

'Oh, what benefits are those? When might they come into effect, I wonder? You see the mud on my face, Griffin? The attack that I have just been subject to should have been on you, sir! A pity you did not hear the commotion from your study and come and join in the scuffle, eh?'

The earl waited for his response but Griffin remained quiet.

'Well, Master Griffin, what are you going to do to make amends? Already, some of your fences have been destroyed this morning, some by fire. Worse than that, people are starving because you have not delivered your promise to the villagers. I am more angry, Griffin, that you did not report to me what you were up to!'

There was a long awkward silence before the earl shouted again. 'I will repeat myself, Griffin: what are you going to do?'

Griffin finally turned to Thomas. 'With respect, sir, you appeared not to have listened well to me. You are correct: when we met, I gave you my word that I would share the dividends of the sheep trade, but you must understand business. Lord Becton has not yet received payment for the wool I despatched to Nottingham and Lincoln. As soon as that is in Lord Becton's hands, you will benefit.'

Lord Becton stepped nearer to Griffin, his anger obvious.

'That does not solve the problem of the land being taken from the villagers and as a consequence they are losing their livelihoods, sir.'

He paused to check the tutor's reaction, then he continued with increased wrath.

'You have not discussed this with me, Master Griffin. You will give back the land to the people…that is what you will do. How dare you bring further grief to me so soon after the death of my daughter? Come and report to me your actions on Friday and bring the accounts. I will decide your future when we have discussed them. Now go back to the boys.'

The earl turned away from him and looked at the floor. How much of his money was taken up in these wool dealings?

At the end of the day's lessons, Anne walked with Griffin as he left the house.

'I will most likely be dismissed, Edward. I will have no work soon. With Mary gone and Lady Charlotte's refusal to have Ruth in the house, I am no longer needed as a governess. Lady Charlotte will shortly leave for her sister's house in London. I think she will take Oliver with her, which means that you will not be working for the earl either. We will both need to find employment.'

Griffin barely listened. He refused to accept that his scheme would fail. He had nowhere near the amount of money needed to set himself up in business. He had to think about this – he must have more money. He focused on the plants in the hedgerow, the belladonna leaves that lay in wait for their beautiful purple flowers to bloom. The baneful belladonna.

*

On the Friday evening, he strolled along the track at the back of the manor house, heading for his meeting with the earl. Resentment continued to burn within him. He would need to do something fast and pull himself up by his wits.

He was greeted at the house by an icy Frances. She announced his arrival to the earl, then came back to the hall to show him into the earl's parlour.

'Sit down,' the earl commanded, scrutinising him before seating himself opposite.

After an awkward pause, Griffin began to explain how he would compensate the families for loss of land with food provisions until profits started to come in, of which he was sure they would. He detected irritation in the earl and wasn't sure if he was fully listening.

'Do you have the accounts?' asked the earl.

Just then, Frances knocked and entered with the earl's evening brandy.

'Leave it on the table by the window, Frances.' said the earl with a dismissive wave of his hand.

As soon as Frances left the room, Griffin clumsily dropped all his papers. He gathered them up.

'I will sort these in no time, my lord.' He took them to the table by the window, leaving some on the floor by the earl's feet. The earl tutted but bent down to pick them up.

'It will not take me long to order them, my lord.'

'Oh for God's sake, man!' The exasperated earl impatiently picked up the rest of the papers. Griffin turned his back, tidied the papers, then passed the earl his brandy. The earl, still irritated, took one large swig from the goblet. Griffin's eyes widened, his grin slight but wicked.

The earl began to study the accounts, which were now haphazard. 'Go away, Griffin, and get these in order. I want proof that you are increasing my profits, sir!'

Griffin bowed his head as the earl continued.

'My daughter did not like you, sir, and that makes me wonder why. My instinct tells me to dismiss you now, but I am giving you one more chance to redeem yourself. My wife will be visiting her sister in London and taking Oliver with her, so you will be relieved of your tutoring for at least two weeks. That gives you time to concentrate on my accounts. You are working for me, Master Griffin, not yourself.'

Just before Griffin turned to leave, he watched the frustrated earl finish his brandy. He closed the door hesitantly. What was done was done.

Chapter Nineteen

Spring 1598

The next morning, Lady Charlotte and Lord Oliver left for London. Lord Becton bade them farewell, hiding the signs of acute nausea from which he was suffering.

Not long after they had gone, he was heard violently vomiting. Frances was reluctant to send for Kathleen, knowing that Lady Charlotte would not want her in the house. But she felt that something needed to be done quickly for the earl and knew of no one else other than the physician, who was hard to get hold of. She sent Henry to fetch her.

Kathleen rushed in to the earl's bedroom and set down her jewelled herb box. She felt his forehead. He was indeed sweating and irritable with fever. She tried to calm him and instructed Margaret to boil some leaves and the root of marshmallow together with fennel.

She added some barley flour to the mixture, slathered this onto a muslin cloth and applied it gently to the belly, covering it over with a warm blanket. Margaret was asked to prepare some sour apple juice. When she returned from the kitchen, Kathleen poured some into a goblet.

The earl gripped it with trembling hands and sipped it with quivering lips.

Margaret's words were a warning.

'Whatever you choose to do, Kathleen, I hope it is effective. After the death of Mary, I fear you will suffer tragic consequences if the earl does not recover. Not only that, but I will be dismissed as well as Frances for allowing you into this house.'

Kathleen glanced upwards, fear on her face. She must use the correct mixtures. She could do no more; she knew the sweating meant that the body needed more fluids in order to balance the humours.

'Lots of the apple juice, Margaret. I will return tomorrow.'

On Sunday, the illness was contained, but on Monday the earl deteriorated. The vomiting and now bloody diarrhoea persisted. The retching could be heard in the kitchen. Then he called out and Frances rushed up the stairs.

Edward Griffin had also arrived early on the pretext of leaving some accounts at the house. Frances, having been told that his presence was not required for a few weeks, was disappointed with this intrusion and reluctant to let him enter.

'The Lady Charlotte informed me you were not required for tutoring in the next few weeks, sir. What brings you here?'

'I have notes to prepare, madam. The earl is aware of this. Now allow me to enter.' He stepped over the threshold, not waiting for her reply. On his way to the schoolroom, he heard a soft mumbling from the earl's bedchamber. Frances hurried to the room. Griffin left the schoolroom door ajar, to listen.

'Frances…fetch…Father…Peters…do…you…hear?' the earl feebly uttered, barely audible.

'My lord, I do not know where he is to be found.'

Griffin crept nearer to the edge of the door and strained his ears to catch the words being spoken.

The earl spoke softly again. 'He resides with Kathleen.' Then it sounded like a gasp for air. 'Send Henry… I believe it is time… To meet with my maker.'

'Don't speak like that, my lord. This will pass.'

Edward Griffin loitered in the schoolroom. He grinned maliciously, nodding to himself. Here was proof the priest resided with Kathleen. A most unholy union: a priest and a witch, both hiding treasures. People would want to know of this.

Griffin kept his head down, pretending to scrutinise the accounts until he heard the sound of horses' hooves along the track, a short distance away. Soon, there was a loud clatter on the gravel just outside the house as the horses came to a halt.

Henry rushed in, followed by Father Peters. Griffin squinted as he watched from the slim crack of the slightly opened schoolroom door. Footsteps hurriedly mounted the stairs and Griffin caught sight of Henry carrying the priest's bag.

*

The upstairs was not usually part of Henry's domain and, as he entered the earl's chamber, he was shocked by the sight of Lord

Becton lying motionless in his bed. As he slowly stepped nearer, he was struck by his master's bony cheeks, the white skin stretched taut and his chin prominent and pointed. What had happened to the strong and jovial earl?

He recalled his own uncle looking almost the same before the end. *Lord Becton is going to die.*

He stepped closer still to examine the earl's face and check if he was breathing. His lips were gently quivering and then he suddenly opened his eyes, stretching out his dithering angular fingers towards Henry, until they managed to cling onto his arm. The presence of Father Peters reassured Henry, who felt suddenly afraid of this unknown figure on the bed: a once strong man, now a frail enigma.

'Come here, lad...' the earl pulled him closer.

Henry glanced at Father Peters, who nodded. The earl continued. 'You've been good to me.' The voice was raspy and the words stunted. 'You should be proud of yourself. You are a brave young man. Stay brave, Henry, and you will do well. I wish I knew what had befallen me. I don't get sick.' He gave a short laugh before drawing in air, his chest only able to rise with a great effort.

Henry smiled at him apprehensively but remained speechless.

The earl turned his attention to Father Peters, who now bent to embrace him.

'My dear lord, we are as brothers in the same family. Do not fear, William. Our faith is strong. We will pray and drive out these demons.'

'The demons are too strong this time, my good friend. Please forgive me, Robert. That man is a scoundrel. I should never have let you go. Can the good Lord ever forgive me? I have sinned, Robert, against you and against the faith. Charlotte was right: this is divine retribution.'

'Nay, William. The good Lord is not punishing you; you have kept your faith, your commitments to your family and lived according to God's will. Our Holy Mary smiles upon you. The devil we will beat. We must fight this.' Father Peters looked up for an instant and slowly closed his eyes as if averting tears.

He suspected the devil was amongst them, and he knew who that devil was.

'My Lord, I must ask you. Did you partake of any food that was different for you or drink anything unusual?'

'No…no, nothing different…except…there were some odd dregs at the bottom of my glass of brandy.'

'When did you drink this?'

'The night Master Griffin came to discuss the accounts with me.'

'Master Griffin…'

Henry crept silently out of the room, so the earl did not hear him.

The schoolroom door was still ajar, but Henry detected a slight movement. He furtively crept towards the schoolroom door and peered through a small hole in the middle of a crack in the wood. His eyes widened as he watched Griffin removing a large loose stone from the wall, before placing it on the table. He then turned again towards the secret cavity and lifted out a small black chest. It was then that Frances shouted him from the bottom of the stairs.

'What are you doing, Henry?'

Henry saw Griffin hesitate as he heard Frances shouting, so he quickly jumped back from the door, feeling panicked. He recalled the words of the earl: *'Stay brave'.*

As the schoolroom door opened a little wider, Henry angrily pushed it hard against Griffin.

'Thy poisoned the earl!' He shouted at the schoolmaster. 'Thou art an evil murderer.'

Margaret and Frances stood at the bottom of the stairs.

'Oh, Good Lord. What is happening?' Margaret bellowed, astonished at Henry's outburst.

'He poisoned the earl,' Henry yelled back. 'I saw him pick poisonous plants from the hedgerow. I saw him from the stables… the night he was coming to meet with the earl. He put it in his brandy. The earl knows of this, he saw the dregs of the plant. I heard him say. He should be hanged…hanged for this!'

Edwin Griffin laughed. 'The boy is deluded and the earl is so sick he doth not know of what he sees or speaks.'

Was it possible that Griffin might have put something in the earl's brandy? Frances thought. She tried to recall the eve that Griffin had visited and, where the brandy was. Surely the schoolmaster would have been noticed placing poison in the brandy, right in front of the earl?

Father Peters, also disturbed by the commotion, came out of the earl's chamber, closed the door behind him and stood listening on the galleried landing.

He and Griffin narrowed their eyes as they came face-to-face. In a low voice, Father Peters asked him to leave.

'You cannot command me, sir. You, a Papist, a thief and a witch protector.'

Margaret gasped.

Frances, fearful of a confrontation, came slowly up the stairs. She spoke to Griffin.

'We are an honest household Master Griffin. Did you at least pick the plants to which Henry refers?'

Griffin gave a sardonic laugh.

'How dare you ask me such a foolish question, madam?'

'I ask you again to leave.' Father Peters stepped towards him.

'You owe me money…papist,' Griffin growled. 'Money which you and your papist associate stole from me.'

'I owe you nothing. Leave this house!' His tone was robust and powerful.

Griffin was undeterred. 'I know you reside with the witch. You have no evidence against me, but I have ample against you, sir: you and your witch harlot. I will see you both hanged. It is she who has bewitched the earl with her medicine. She who killed Mary with the white powders. She will be tried and so will you, not only for unlawful union but stealing from the Crown and failing to swear the Oath of Supremacy.'

Empowered, he strode nearer to the priest. Frances wrung her hands together. She was afraid that Griffin may strike.

Father Peters' eyes narrowed. Griffin's fingers twitched as he matched the priest's cold penetrating stare. The onlookers were tense, but Griffin resisted the urge to hit the priest. His words had given him the upper hand and would continue to do so.

'The earl is dying. Your witch will have killed him with the same tainted medicine as she surely used on his young daughter. You both shall suffer! If not at my command, the Lady Charlotte will see to it.'

The pair stood facing each other like hostile bears until the earl's door swung open and both were distracted by the gaunt figure peering across the landing. With enormous effort, Lord Becton took a few strides towards the angry men and pointed his finger to the schoolmaster.

'You are my murderer!' he cried hoarsely. 'You heard Father Peters, get out now! Your body will hang on the gibbet.' He coughed.

Henry felt a strong urge to protect the earl, as he recalled his words: *'Stay brave, Henry'*. They gave Henry the impetus to lunge at Griffin.

He heaved against him, pushing him to the stairs. Griffin lost his footing. Frances who was still standing a few steps down, quickly got out of his way. The man fell down half the stairs before scrambling to his feet by grabbing the banister, but by then Margaret had released the dogs and rushed to hand Frances a stick. Frances beat Griffin down the remainder of the stairs.

Griffin punched the barking dogs in an effort to defend himself, but was overwhelmed when his coat sleeve was ripped by the most vicious of the snarling dogs. He cried out in pain, taking another swing at the animals, but this action triggered more aggression. He was forced to run from the house, snarling dogs in pursuit.

Frances followed into the courtyard, where Ged was calling back the dogs.

'They will rip him to shreds, Mistress Frances. 'Tis your good self who will suffer.'

Frances was angry.

'Be on your way,' she yelled at the schoolmaster. ''Tis thee who will suffer: the good Lord will see to it that justice shall indeed prevail.'

She slammed the front door and slumped onto the settle in the hall, whereby she fought the urge to cry.

The earl had fallen against the door frame, exhausted, and now lay propped up against the wall. He turned to Henry.

'Again…you helped me, lad. You will not be forgotten.'

Father Peters and Henry gently lifted him to his feet and gently ushered him back to his bed.

'You must rest,' Father Peters urged the earl. 'The man will not return.'

He did rest. He slept and slept until his breathing became weak and spasmodic. He asked for his wife and son. Frances had sent word to London. It would still be another two days before they arrived home.

Lord Becton could not hold on. The day before Lady Charlotte and Oliver were expected to return, in the early morning, William breathed his last.

The servants came solemnly to stand by the bedside. Henry fingered the silk shroud, recalling his own deceased uncle, wrapped only in coarse cloth. He recalled Christmas, when he was allowed to attend the family dinner, so proud in that white linen shirt, smart doublet and breeches. It felt so different. It made him feel proud and important. Although death smelled the same, some people were born to privileges, while others would never have anything, all their hard working lives; but all lives seemed futile in death. We all must die, he thought, but first we must live, and he was determined in that moment to achieve something in life. He desired wealth and power.

The others quietly left the room. When Henry reached the schoolroom, he opened the door and looked inside. He saw Griffin's box still on the desk. Everyone had been too distracted to notice it. He stared at it for a while, before looking round to make sure no one saw him. He tucked it under his arm before tiptoeing down the stairs and back to the stables.

The house was once again solemn and silent, as it had been following the death of Mary. The dogs sensed their master's passing and pined. Margaret felt sorry for them; they had enjoyed many walks with the earl. She allowed them into the kitchen but, when she threw scraps, they didn't eat.

*

On the Friday morning, the sound of horses' hooves on the gravel broke the eerie silence. Lady Charlotte and Oliver climbed out of the coach, weary from their journey. Once their feet reached the ground, they hurried inside.

Father Peters met Lady Charlotte in the hall.

'I'm sorry, my lady. It was yesterday. He wanted to wait for you both, but he was too weak.'

The priest saw her face crumple and her legs buckle. He steadied her and she took his arm, before they slowly climbed the stairs, heads bent. Oliver walked behind them, fear etched on his face. He was fighting back his pooling tears of emotion.

Father Peters knew he was trying to be brave. It had been ingrained in him that noble men do not cry or show emotions as women do. Poor boy, it was only a short time ago that his sister died. Now he would need to take care of his mother alone.

Father Peters allowed them time at William's bedside. As Lady Charlotte sobbed, Oliver asked him, 'When do the spirits take father away?'

Charlotte heard the question, swallowed a lump in her throat, and took her son's hand in hers. She began to answer and Father Peters smiled as he listened to her, speaking gently but with deliberation.

'They have gone already, with his soul. You see his body, but he is not there anymore. He has gone to Jesus now. He was a good man, generous and kind, so good that the demons could not pull him away. I know he has left with the angels. Sometimes there is a struggle between the evilness of demons and the angels, but if sins are confessed, you are free from eternal damnation.'

She looked at her son, suddenly fearing for his future, then whispered, 'Your father has gone to Heaven with the angels.'

'Will we see Father again as a Holy Ghost?'

'Perhaps. He will always be close by, watching over you, even though you perhaps won't see him. Mary is with us at times. I can smell her, Oliver. I search for her. I don't see her, yet she is here. We must all pass to God's secure haven, a place that will be our eternal sanctuary...but I miss her so much...and now your father has left me...'

She stopped abruptly, her speaking stifled with extreme emotion. She dropped her son's hand, took a deep breath as she threw her head backwards and then brought it forward again to rest in her cupped hands and began to sob.

Father Peters laid a hand on her shoulder.

'The Lord God have mercy.' He then walked to Oliver to embrace him, but Oliver was infuriated.

'Forgive my blasphemy Father, but I find it hard to believe in the holiness of Him. He has torn my family apart.'

'You must be strong, my boy. You are the man of the house now. You have much to learn about the ways of the Lord.'

*

All the servants except Anne solemnly entered the room for prayers.

Anne could not be found. Frances was not surprised. Griffin had tried every day since the earl's death to get back into the house. He'd said he needed to take away some accounts. She had threatened him with the dogs.

Anne had been acting strangely. She had been seen snooping in the schoolroom. Frances wondered what it was she was looking for, but whatever it was, she didn't appear to have found it.

Father Peters sprinkled the room with holy water and used his sacred oils to anoint the body of the earl. The intense silence was broken by his words, softly spoken:

'Pax huic domui: et omnium habitantium.'

'Peace to this house and all who dwell therein.'

'Glora Patri, et Filii, et Spiritui Sancti.'

'Glory be to the Father and to the Son and to the Holy Ghost.'

After the last blessing, the gathering chanted The Lord's Prayer before Father Peters said, 'May the Lord Jesus Christ protect you and lead you to eternal life.' Then he made the sign of the cross, followed by the others.

As they all quietly left the room, Henry tugged at Father Peter's vestments, then quickly looked around to ensure no one was listening.

'I wish to confess something, Father,' he whispered.

'Now? What troubles you, Henry?'

'I stole the money chest, Father, belonging to Master Griffin.'

'Did you count the money?'

'Aye, there are fifteen gold shillings and some silver ones. I am sorry. I'll bring it to you.'

Henry turned to go downstairs but Father Peters rested a firm hand on his shoulder, giving a cursory glance towards the door to ensure no listening ears.

'That money was no doubt stolen in the first place. Master Griffin was fraudulent, my son. It will largely belong to the earl. He thanked you many times for coming to his aid… Keep it, my boy. Keep it for your future and say nothing. Had the earl lived longer, I know he would have said the same. In this world, you will one day need it. Keep it safe and when the time comes to invest, seek my counsel.'

Father Peters grinned, before adding, in a serious tone, 'Go without guilt, my son.' They both crossed themselves.

'Thank you, Father. You have my word.'

Henry's wish of a better life was coming true. *Go without guilt.*

As he descended the stairs, he was surprised to hear Lady Charlotte's raised voice from the hall below. She was facing Frances with a thunderous tone and a harsh face.

'Tell me the truth. Was my husband treated by Kathleen? Tell me now: how did my husband become sick?'

Frances hesitated. She knew that Kathleen had not been allowed in the house since Mary died.

'I…I…' she stammered.

'She was here, wasn't she? You allowed her to treat my husband. How could you?'

The venom of blame was directed at Kathleen. An angry Lady Charlotte walked away from Frances but then she swiftly turned back. 'That woman will suffer. She is a witch; I have no doubt of it.'

Frances watched Lady Charlotte walk briskly towards the parlour. Troubles came one after another, she reflected. Times were bad. She worried for Kathleen, and for all of them.

As Henry hurried down the stairs, she called him over and sent him off to the village. It was market day; they still needed to eat, whatever happened. She saw Father Peters emerging from the earl's bedchamber. Had he heard the wrath of the mistress?

*

Henry welcomed the opportunity to leave the house. He didn't run, he dawdled, daydreaming of what he should do with all his money. *It's mine and I'm not to feel guilty.*

As he approached the market, he heard a rumpus from the inn. Men were shouting. He climbed up onto a step to look through a window at the side of the building.

He gasped. There was Griffin, sitting with Anne.

So that's why she hadn't been with them all for prayers. It was disrespectful, he thought, for her to be here, in an ale house of all places.

Wide-eyed, he watched Edward Griffin stand and address the crowd.

'I urge you all, if you truly care for your children, to heed my words. We have no time to waste. That witch has killed Lord Becton with her hocus pocus medicine, just as she bewitched and murdered his young daughter, the Lady Mary. How can we tolerate a witch and a Catholic priest in league with the devil? Co-habiting as joint sorcerers against the religion of our sovereign? Their medicine, it has been proved, is black and evil. They not only abuse our sovereign's law, they abuse the law of the Holy Father Himself. I say we cannot wait for the Assizes. We have a duty to our loved ones, to our children, to hang them now, without further ado.'

Henry watched people nodding and shouting in drunken agreement. There were calls of 'Aye' from bawdy men and one shouted for the witch to be pressed. He suddenly slipped on the stone on which he was standing and crept round the front of the inn. As a few men left, he slunk just inside to listen.

The landlord spotted him.

''Ere, young lad…what are you up to? Stealing your game, eh?'

Edward Griffin looked in the direction of Henry and lunged at him. Henry ran as fast as he could through the streets, dodging the crowd. Then he dashed down an alleyway and hid behind a stack of barrels to get his breath. He peeped out and Griffin was immediately upon him, hands wrapping around his throat. Henry could not speak for the strangling hold and felt his legs buckling beneath him.

'Let go of that lad. Let him go!'

Two huge women wearing grubby aprons waddled towards Griffin, the smell of grease and sweat on their bodies putrid as they got nearer. One struck him with a stick and the other wielded a heavy pan.

Griffin let go of Henry and struck one of the women with the back of his hand. As he did so, the other one spotted a dead rat by the side of a barrel and, picking it up by its tail, flung it wide to slap directly across Griffin's face. Then she rushed forward and brought up her knee harshly to his groin. The first woman was back on her feet and now she punched him in the chest, while the other picked up a stone and struck the back of his neck.

Although still struggling to breathe, Henry wasted no time running back to the Hall, glancing back from time to time, imagining Griffin close on his heels.

Anne disliked sitting alone among roaring men, and ran out to find Griffin. She shouted at the enraged women.

'Stop! What are you doing? This is a respectable schoolmaster!'

'This "respectable schoolmaster" was strangling a young boy, for your information, Miss High and Mighty!'

'Let go of him. I will see to him now.'

The second woman waddled up to Anne.

'Aren't you the governess at the big house? Surprised you keep the company of the likes of him.' She gestured to Griffin, straightening his body and shaking off dirt. 'Wouldn't be surprised if it's your own pretty neck he's squeezing, one day.'

The two women glared back at Griffin as they began to walk off, muttering to one another.

Then one picked the rat up again and threw it at him. It landed right in the middle of his back. They giggled as they went off, arm in arm.

Edward Griffin noted the look of horror and disgust on Anne's face.

'That boy accused me of poisoning the earl. He is dangerous… to us, Anne. Listen to me. I want us to be wed, but first I must make myself a worthy man, as is only proper, to give you everything I should.'

There was a pause as he held her arms tightly by her sides and studied her response.

'Our future together is at risk unless we prove that witch is to blame. I need her wretched box of medicines, to prove my innocence, and I need that papist to return my money to me. They should both meet their end: for our sakes, for our future. I cannot wed you, only to look forward to a wretched and poor existence. We are worthy of more.'

Anne looked at the pathetic pleading figure before her,

dishevelled and filthy. She didn't really want him to touch her. He had been furious when she told him she couldn't find his money chest, so much so that she thought he was going to strike her, and now the comments from that washer woman served to deepen her mistrust.

For the first time, she felt afraid of the darkness in his face, the coldness in his eyes.

She must banish thoughts of his greed and evilness. She must believe that he was a man of honour: ruthless, yes, but men with ambition always are.

'I will help you, Edward. We will get your money back, one way or another. We will not be defeated.'

She would help. He was right. She wanted the security of marriage to a wealthy man and he knew it. He wanted the box he'd carelessly left in the schoolroom; he wanted the jewelled chest and he wanted the money that was stolen from him at the inn.

He was obsessed with the desire to see the witch and the priest hang. Perhaps after that, he would show his desire for her. It had to be done. Then they could escape to start a new life.

Chapter Twenty

March 1958

Lifting the stone slab with the shrieking flapping raven disturbed my dad for the next few days. He didn't say much, but I had a hunch that these were the kind of incidents he didn't want to meddle with.

I heard him talking to my mum one evening after dinner.

'To hell with discovering the secrets of this damned house. It might be wiser to leave well alone, cover the hole and seal that bloody panel once and for all. What happened then, all that bloody time ago, has nothing to do with us...and furthermore, that bloody bird is insane, I'm telling you: insane!'

He'd been excited when he saw the chalice on Christmas Eve, and he'd agreed that we would all work together to investigate the strange incidents. Now, he forbade any further digging or going into tunnels and would seal all 'holes' as soon as the warm weather came. I felt tethered as if bound by rope. Dad being out of work meant that he would keep a close eye on me.

Over the next few weeks, although George came to the house, we just played board games or cards or went for walks. Some of our friends had the new television sets, but Dad had said no to us: 'No job, no television.' He just got tetchier and watched us closely to stop any exploring.

One weekend in early March, Arthur brought George. Gran opened the door.

Arthur asked to speak to Dad.

'Good news, mate. There's a job for you if you want it, working with me and Harry, who did your electrics. The company want some old mills clearing for renovation. I reckon it's about £560 a year, but better than nothing. There might be overtime…that's if you don't dig up any more buried treasure in the meantime!'

He threw his head back laughing, before adding, 'Why don't you come to the Old Gatehouse tonight for a few pints? Celebrate, like.'

I saw Gran scowling and then Mum hurrying into the hall, wiping her hands on her apron.

'Oh Albert, I don't think you should go, dear. You haven't been out drinking in ages.'

'No, I haven't, have I? In fact, not since coming to live here. All the more reason to go, Alice.'

I don't think Dad wanted Arthur to think he had to do what Mum told him to do. Which was actually what did happen most of the time.

'Right then,' said Arthur. 'See you there about seven?'

'Aye, I'll have the car. I'm just about keeping it on the road. Bread and jam on the table though.' He gave a little excited laugh. 'I'll see you both there.'

As he went upstairs, Mum said in a low voice to Gran, 'Oh, we can run to a few drinks in a pub, especially with the find of the chalice. If what you say is right, Mum, we'll manage all right. Not that I really want to sell it, mind.'

*

Dad was only a few hundred yards from home when the accident happened. We all heard the collision and ran from the house. The mangled wreck was smoking, the bonnet pointing skywards, and the side of the car had a half moon dent where it had been rammed against the tree.

There was broken glass everywhere and Dad was slumped over the wheel, the horn loud and continual.

'Oh my God!' exclaimed Mum. 'Run down to the telephone box, Annabel, and call 999. Tom, you help me try and lift him out.'

'No!' shouted Gran. 'He mustn't be moved, Alice. He's breathing but we don't know the extent of the damage. It's important to keep talking: he might be able to hear. He is breathing, though. Shallow, but he is breathing.' She tried humour, 'Just like my son-in-law to worry us! No more going to the pub for you on a Friday night!'

Mum anxiously repeated, 'Oh my God, Oh my God.' Her hands cupping her cheeks.

It wasn't easy for the ambulance to get up the dirt track; Mum was hoping it wouldn't get stuck in mud as it was still pouring down. She heard the siren coming closer and then saw the blue flashing light through the trees. The ambulance men worked quickly and efficiently while cursing the foul weather.

They were able to force off the driver's door and then, protecting his head, neck and spine carefully, lifted him out of the car and onto a stretcher. They talked to him, but again no response.

One shone a torch into his eyes, while at the same time shouting his name. The other warned about the use of oxygen as he could smell burning.

'We have to hurry, mate,' he warned his associate. 'We'll give him oxygen in the ambulance.' He turned to Mum. 'Are you his wife?'

She swallowed hard. 'Yes.'

'He's in good hands now, love. Come in the ambulance and sit down a bit before you collapse. We'll need some details.'

Mum climbed into the ambulance but looked back at her mother. 'Look after the kids,' was all she could say.

'Don't you worry,' a dripping Dorothy reassured her. 'They'll be fine and so will Albert; you'll see.'

Chapter Twenty-One

June 1598

After the earl was buried, Gilbert was keen to scrutinise his brother's accounts. He felt disturbed by what had been going on. His sister-in-law defended the schoolmaster against accusations of poisoning, and blamed the deaths of her husband and daughter on Kathleen Melton. But he listened to others, who were convinced Edward Griffin was guilty. He would need to go through the ledgers in detail; something was seriously amiss.

He recalled how Griffin had been eavesdropping the day he'd discussed the accounts with his brother. He was now deeply suspicious of the arrogant young man and, being aware of Charlotte's dark moods and desire to get her own way, he worried about the fate of the herb wife. He'd listened while she vehemently denounced Kathleen as a witch and stated her intent to alert the magistrates.

There was relief when she went back to her sister in London, taking not only Oliver but Henry with her as his companion. She had given orders that Frances was in charge of the house. Margaret and Anne were to leave with an allowance and Ged was to look after the garden, the horses and the dogs.

She did not know when she would return.

Gilbert was impressed with her clarity of thought after so many years in the past, when she'd often pleaded with her husband that she was unable to cope with household affairs. Now, her absence would give him essential time to examine the situation at the manor.

Gilbert settled down in the peace of the evening to study the accounts. He strode to the cabinet to pour himself a brandy, then hesitated, remembering the accusations of poisoning. He sniffed the top of the pitcher and shook his head. He called Frances to wash the pitcher, just in case something still lingered. This Edward Griffin had caused such grief.

*

On Sunday morning, the villagers were gathering outside the church in Becton's neighbouring village. Services there, as in many others of the parish, were always well attended, especially those days, when failure to do so resulted in a shilling fine.

As the last couple entered, the vicar saw a stranger approach. A tall, shabbily dressed, hooded man staggered to the door.

'I have not seen you before, good fellow. Are you a newcomer to this village?'

'Yes, vicar. I hope I am welcome?'

'Of course you are welcome. You look forlorn, sir. Do you need help?'

'I have lost my job and my coin. I am near to starving.'

'We may be able to help you, come in. Our parish overseers will decide who will benefit, but we have little funds, you must understand. Many farmers now suffer, deprived of land now used for sheep.' He waited while the stranger nodded before adding, 'The Earl of Becton took on a new representative who drives a hard line. A reedy man by all accounts.'

'Yes, I have heard of this atrocity.' The man shook his head as he entered the church and sat quietly at the back of the congregation. A few heads turned to look at him.

He listened to the sermon and, when it was over, the vicar

asked those who wanted to claim from the parish poor rate to come forward. He asked the newcomer to stand. He reminded the congregation of the need to be humanitarian towards others, those new to the parish who had fallen on hard times.

People turned again but were suspicious. No one welcomed vagrants in the village and many suffered the stocks. The vicar looked around the congregation. He did not want trouble.

Kathleen Melton watched as the man standing at the back lowered his hood. She gasped with horror: Edward Griffin.

He saw her and, focusing on the vicar, quickly spoke.

'I thank you for your kindness. Your sermon spoke of judging and ridding the village of evil. I feel it is my duty to bring something to mind, in this holy house.' He then paused to ensure he had everyone's attention. 'The Lord God does not suffer witches...in the book of Exodus. Am I right, good vicar?'

The vicar nodded but looked worried. Griffin continued. 'Well, good people, we have one in our midst.' There was a gasp of horror from some in the congregation as Griffin pointed to Kathleen. 'There she is: the herb woman. She cursed me and made me ill by the side of the road. I warn this congregation; she is a deceitful sorceress.'

The church echoed with the murmur of shock, but what was worse for Kathleen was the sea of accusing eyes around her.

Griffin continued: 'It is her medicine that has caused the deaths of the Earl of Becton and his daughter Mary. Can we feel safe while this woman, who is actually a demon, is free to kill our children?' He looked back to the vicar.

He spotted the man who had seen him vomiting after his confrontation with Kathleen.

'Ask the people, Father, for confirmation of this. What about you, man?' He pointed to the man he had seen. 'You came out of your house and saw that I was sick. You heard her curse me; you were there!'

The vicar turned to the man in question. 'You are in the house of God, my good man. You must be honest. Is this true? Did you see this man get sick after being cursed by Mistress Melton?'

The man was very quiet but, prompted by the words of the vicar, he stood and faced the congregation. He was an honest, God-fearing man, and he looked over to Kathleen, not wanting to do her any harm. Eventually he spoke.

'This woman has done me no harm, but I have to say that yes, one evening I did hear a commotion outside my house.' He paused.

'Go on, my good man,' encouraged the vicar. 'Did Mistress Melton curse this man?'

The little man paused, then stuttered, 'She did curse him, Father'. There was another pause while the congregation gasped again.

He continued, pointing towards Griffin, 'And this man was violently sick. She threw some seeds or something at him.' He did not relish accusing Kathleen, a neighbour, and hung his head low rather than look in her direction.

Kathleen looked down and felt her stomach sink. The shrewd Griffin did not let the congregation see his brief grin as he bowed his head. He lifted it quickly, looking forlorn and needy.

All heads now turned towards Kathleen. A second man stood up and admitted that his daughter Jennet had died after she had visited the house of the herb wife.

Kathleen shot up to her feet. 'Jennet had been a good friend of my daughter for years and had visited Ruth often. She was already very ill on the day she came to my cottage. I did not use medicine.'

The man angrily pointed his finger at her.

'Jennet got worse and died the same night that she had been with you.'

Kathleen, still standing but feeling unsteady on her feet, badly wanted someone to speak in her favour.

'Who can speak for me? I am not a witch. I seek counsel from many physicians. I have cured many of you of sickness. What say you?'

One woman stood.

'Kathleen Melton is a good woman. She has helped me many

times when I was with child. My children are all fit and well. I say she is no witch.'

A few more women agreed but there remained tension and a sense of fear on the faces of the congregation.

The humming sound of low whisperings sounded like a swarm of bees trapped inside the church. There were mutterings mentioning the Earl of Becton and Lady Mary. People were looking at her accusingly.

Sitting beside Kathleen, Jack held her hand to steady her nerves.

'Don't listen to it, mother.' Ruth was close to tears.

Kathleen felt on trial so, as silence now descended in the church, she spoke again. 'I am not guilty of these things. I work as a healer.' She paused. 'The earl's death is not my doing, but his.' She shot out her arm to point at Edward Griffin. Anger now drove her. She was shouting. 'This man poisoned the earl with belladonna. Let him be on trial.'

There was another loud gasp. The vicar looked perplexed but quickly recovered his composure. He felt that it was his duty to calm the congregation. Looking at Edward Griffin, he began slowly to question him.

'What motive would Mistress Melton have had, to interfere between you and the earl, sir?'

Edward Griffin scowled. It did not take him long to shock the people again, 'I took my position from a recusant priest. The very same with whom this sorceress unlawfully resides.'

There was yet another collective gasp, with all eyes turning towards Kathleen.

The vicar gulped. This was indeed exceptional.

'I believe this is a matter for governance outside these walls. These accusations are of a serious nature and must be reported to the magistrate. The parish cannot judge a man or woman guilty in this, the Lord's house.' He turned to Griffin. 'Witchcraft, sir, is a pagan belief. One to which I do not subscribe. Of course witches of a true nature would not be welcome in this House, but Mistress Melton has done a lot of good here.'

There was a further general low humming inside the church, such that the walls seemed to gently vibrate.

'We will all now leave peacefully. You must understand…' He now paused to look at Kathleen, then Griffin. 'What you have both revealed has to be reported to those of a higher position than myself.'

The congregation departed in a babble of gossip, all turning to stare at Kathleen as they went. Kathleen fought back tears.

These accusations had indeed aroused a public detestation. She needed desperately to speak with Father Peters.

Edward Griffin was seen patting the shoulders of Jennet's father, who was nodding. This had been a conspiracy. She was furious.

Griffin was now pursuing them, shouting loudly before the congregation dispersed.

'You are racing home to your indecent bond with your Catholic recusant, witch! You will hang or burn if justice is done. The Lady Charlotte is consumed with hatred for you, madam.'

Kathleen hurried on. Once at the cottage she grabbed her jewelled herb box and wrapped it tightly in coarse cloth. Her body shaking uncontrollably, she checked the windows to see that Griffin was not there, then tied it to Jack's back.

She then wrapped him in an old cloak so he looked like a pedlar with a hump back. She also dressed Ruth in a similar cloak so they both looked like beggars. Father Peters was staying at the cottage of Father Morley for a short time. She wasn't sure how long for, but she hoped that he would still be there. They had all been there on several occasions, so Jack and Ruth knew where it was and it wouldn't take longer than two or three hours if they hurried. They could be there before dark.

'You must be safe. Now quickly go and make sure that you are not followed.' As an afterthought she thrust a small sharp dagger into Jack's belt. 'Only use it if you have to.'

As they left from the rear gate, she rushed to bolt the front door. She was afraid. Griffin had incited hatred both at the inn and the church. He would see the death of her and seize the jewelled box.

How had this cunning fox managed to destroy her life? Her deep revulsion triggered a constant nausea.

Chapter Twenty-Two

Easter 1958

My dad was in an iron lung: an artificial breathing machine to rest his brain. He had sustained a nasty head injury and had to have immediate surgery to remove a clot that was causing pressure in his skull. We were warned that he may be in hospital for several weeks if not months.

You could tell Mum was beside herself with worry. She had mentioned to Gran how sitting by his bedside listening to the whirring and puffing of the breathing machine just made her jittery. Once back at home, her head was full of anxiety. Gran cooked meals for us but Mum hardly ate a thing:

'Strange,' she said one evening. 'Who would have thought that a machine could keep breathing for you? Will he ever be able to breathe without it, I wonder?'

Gran reassured her. 'This sort of injury, to the brain, I mean, takes ages, dear, to heal, but I'm sure he'll come round and breathe without a machine and be all right in the end.'

Mum gave a smile of appreciation and patted Gran's hand. 'I'm sorry, Mum. You're keeping the ship afloat here and I'm just being miserable and all wrapped up in myself. I am grateful, y'know. When we took on this big project, I didn't consider anything like this might get in the way. Oh…he never really wanted to live here,

Mum.' She started to cry. 'It would never have happened had we stayed where we were.'

'Now, now, that's not going to help. Don't worry yourself. I'm enjoying keeping things running smoothly. I haven't felt this needed in a long time and I feel so alive. There's something magical about this place: the kids keep me young. You just concentrate on getting to the hospital and staying with Albert and…stop feeling guilty because it's not your fault.'

*

George's dad and Harry the electrician called round with a 'Get Well' card. They felt guilty for letting my dad drink so much when he wasn't used to it. I was always suspicious of Harry. I thought he was a prying creep. In fact I did wonder whether him getting Dad drunk was intentional; whenever he went over the limit, he got pretty damn verbal. An ideal situation for revealing any 'secrets'. Harry, I am certain, thought the manor was a hidden goldmine of Tudor treasure.

George was embarrassed, and stayed away from us. At school he was so subdued that I was surprised to find myself wishing for the normally irritating 'babble' mode to start again.

'Look, George, it's not your fault that Dad's in hospital. He could've said no to all those beers and whiskies, y' know. Why don't you come again next weekend? Weather's not bad now. Dad can't say anything about us going back into the tunnel or digging outside. We can do what we want. Mum and Gran will be easy to get round, but if I see that priest when I'm on my own and he kills me, think how sorry you'll feel then!'

That last statement got to him. His eyebrows shooting up to his hairline, he had to grin. I made a silly face, which made him laugh.

'I knew you wouldn't let me down.'

*

It was six weeks since the accident. Mum started back at the library; it was a much-needed diversion for her, but she was increasingly fractious with me and didn't want to hear anything about the mysteries of the house. She just wanted to know who would pay all the bills. Gran couldn't help on a pension.

So she eventually asked if I could leave school and get a job or just a paper round. My studies did not matter. What did matter, she emphasised, was a steady income. Mum was panicking, but some of that might have been worry that Dad would not recover.

Dad remained stable but that was all. How much longer would it take before he recovered? How long does it take the brain to get enough rest? They said some stimulation may help, but how on earth do you stimulate someone locked into a breathing machine?

Gran reassured Mum.

'He'll be okay, Alice. Look, I have a surprise. Look everybody.' Gran fetched a large brown package and put it on the table. 'Help yourselves.' Inside were five very large chocolate Easter eggs.

'I thought everyone needed a treat. I bought these earlier today.'

There was a circle of wide eyed smiles and a chorus of 'thanks, Gran'.

Then she added:

'There's something else. I called in the library and read that book Albert had picked up in the folklore section. It was all about Becton, but he didn't read it properly: only the bit that said this house was haunted. Anyway, I wrote down the words, the history.'

She took a large sheet of paper from her apron pocket.

'I'll read them to you.'

The oldest house in the village is the Tudor manor house, Becton Manor, which dates back to the late sixteenth century. The original owner was the Earl of Becton a courtier of Queen Elizabeth. The Queen had granted him the position of Earl of Becton in 1585. He married Charlotte Mary Porter of Staffordshire, lady in waiting to the Queen.

There were two children of the marriage, Oliver and Mary. Lady

Charlotte was still suffering from the death of her daughter Mary when her husband also died suddenly, after a suspected poisoning.

She laid the blame for both deaths on the medicine of a local herb wife, Kathleen Melton, who was subsequently accused of witchcraft and of living in an unholy union with a Catholic priest.

The name of the priest was Robert Peters.

Kathleen Melton was burnt at the stake close to the Hall, on Midsummer Night's Eve, 1598. It is assumed her children, Jack and Ruth Melton, perished in a fire at their cottage on the very night of their mother's death.

Soon afterwards, Becton Manor fell into disrepair.

For many years, subsequent owners have reported strange happenings at the house and no one appears to have lived there for very long. It is also said the house contains priest holes.

There are, however, reports of a feathered deterrent; sightings of a very large raven have been regularly documented by a number of the house's owners. The bird, legend has it, appears to protect the house and able to pluck the eyes of anyone loitering. Some reports say the bird is actually the Catholic priest who was associated with the herb wife accused of being a witch.'

'Wow! This really explains a lot,' said George.

We each read Gran's notes, digesting the information. I emphasised the relevant points which linked to our existing findings.

'It just could be that the dark shadow I saw—well, sensed—in the tunnel, was this priest, this Father Peters. So, according to folklore, he lives again as a raven, making sure no one steals the treasure. That would make sense, why the bird won't let us get near the tunnel.'

'Sounds too mythical, Tom,' said Gran. She left the room to put the kettle on. 'Tea, anyone, with your chocolate?'

We nodded. 'Hmmm.'

George was still analysing, 'So the whispering you hear, could this be Oliver and his sister Mary, who was poisoned by that convicted witch?'

Annabel speculated, 'The witch was burnt close to the hall, it reads. Could it be the field the other side of the track, where we had our bonfire?'

'Yeah… don't you remember? I thought I saw a woman with long hair sort of glide through the flames then. I did tell you but you didn't believe me. People were getting tired of my so-called wild imagination, so I didn't say anything. She was gone in a second anyway.'

George looked pensive. 'I didn't say that I didn't believe you when you told me at school. Wish I could have been there on Bonfire Night, to back it up; that was Mum not letting me come.'

'What difference would it have made? No one ever believed me then.'

Gran now tried to be conciliatory. 'Now, boys, that's enough, I didn't buy chocolate eggs to eat and then argue. We are making progress and you have to keep positive. Things like this don't get solved overnight, and finding that information in an old library book is a gift. Don't you think?'

My mum nodded. 'Gran's absolutely right, boys.'

George turned his attention to the chocolate egg.

'Go on,' Mum said, before laughing. 'Get tucked in. We're close, eh, to solving the mysterious events in this wonderful house! We have a silver Elizabethan chalice of great value. Now, we just need Dad to get better.'

It was a good time to reveal my other object of certain value, so I made an announcement, 'I found some more treasure: a box in the tunnel. A metal box with a cross on the lid and lots of jewels all around it.' I ran to fetch it.

Gran was smiling broadly as I left the room and I just noticed her squeezing my mum's hand. I was pleased to see my mum a bit more positive.

George's cheeks were soon bulging with too big a mouthful of chocolate, but it didn't stop him making a suggestion to Mum. 'You could take the chalice to the hospital and show it to Mr Winchett.'

'You could take this to the hospital as well, now.' I announced as I ran back into the room. I was very proud of the box even though the lid had jammed solid. It was very heavy, but was that the metal or what was inside it?

Everyone gathered round to touch it and admire it. Bit by bit I had polished it, over and over again, although the silver was still tarnished.

Gran took hold of it. 'My God, this is magnificent. Yes Tom, I can see what you mean. It is tarnished but after the good job I did on the chalice, I think I can bring it to life.'

Mum actually looked impressed, 'This must be worth a lot more than the chalice. It must have been beautiful. Where did you find this Tom?'

'Err... in the tunnel, Mum.'

'All right. I accept there is a tunnel and you are fascinated by it. What I do want to know, though: is this tunnel dangerous?' You were given instructions not to go down.'

'No, Mum, just smelly. Think the deposits from the cess pit gets into it and some rainfall...' I was sharply interrupted by George.

'Oh there's lots of parts that are badly eroded, but over hundreds of years, what would you expect? You know I read somewhere that the earth...'

It was my turn to interrupt, 'Not now George. Anyway Mum, yes, it's damp but definitely not dangerous.'

Annabel opened her mouth. Knowing the idiot might say otherwise, I gave her the most evil expression I could muster.

'Hmm. I don't like the sound of the contents of the cess pit getting into it. Tom, that's foul, don't go down again or you'll be ill with dysentery or something. Ugh.'

'I don't swallow it, Mum.'

'Wish we could have a bathroom put in.'

'You could, Alice, if you sold the chalice.' Gran beamed.

For some reason, I didn't like the sound of the objects being sold.

Annabel, after glaring back at me, was excited about the box.

She and George were discussing how it opened, in between eating chocolate. We had no key and I heard Annabel say it shouldn't get damaged.

'Or covered in chocolate!' I had to say, realising I was quite possessive about my find.

Gran's thoughts were on its usefulness for dad. 'The doctor wants all the senses to be used, to encourage Albert to wake up, so that means hearing, touching, smelling and sight. We have touch and hopefully sight here at least.'

'There is another sense, I've read it...' George beginning to enter babble mode.

'We know, you read it somewhere.'

'I was just thinking of the sense of 'taste', Tom, that's all, but of course it's not relevant here, unless you put some wine in the chalice. Ha! That'll wake him up.'

'Oh, George...'

Mum gave a polite chuckle, 'Don't argue, boys. I'll take it and we'll see. Anything is worth a try. He just has to wake up.'

Chapter Twenty-Three

June 1598

Jack and Ruth kept looking behind them on their way to Father Morley's cottage. Jack fingered the sharpness of the knife in his belt. He imagined plunging it into the belly or even the heart of Edward Griffin. Yes: it would need to be the heart.

The memory of his mother's expression in church angered him beyond measure. He almost wanted Griffin to jump out in front of him again so he could rush at him with the knife, angled to puncture straight through his heart. He would not be merciful.

They arrived at Father Morley's cottage as dusk was falling. They were in good time. Father Peters was just about to leave, when Father Morley saw the children approach.

'Were you expecting Kathleen's children?'

'No,' said Father Peters simply. 'There must be some trouble.'

Father Morley welcomed Jack and Ruth, but Father Peters was deeply concerned.

'What is it? Where is your mother?'

Jack explained all that happened in the church and Griffin's accusations. The priests looked at one another. Griffin would not waste time scheming.

He had truly incited enough fury for the vigilantes to come after poor Kathleen. Tonight was Midsummer's Eve: the time for bonfires and the burning of witches. He had to hurry. He must turn the tide of hatred towards this man, who should be tried for murder, justifiably found guilty, and hanged, drawn and quartered.

As if reading his thoughts, Father Morley offered to look after the children while his friend made haste. Father Peters thanked him and mounted his horse to ride back to the cottage.

As he neared the summit of the hill near the cottage, he could see a golden glow enveloped by a sinister darkness on the horizon. The smell of burning grew stronger and he soon heard the crackle of timbers and saw sparks rising. He steadied his horse to survey the valley below. The scene below shocked and sickened him.

Kathleen's home was fully ablaze. He rode quickly on, but the closer he got the more intense the heat, the angry dancing flames reaching for the evening sky. His horse neighed as they came too near to the cottage on fire.

A small crowd of people were trying to put out the blaze, using simple pails of water. There was panic and yelling. Where was Kathleen? He tied his agitated horse to a tree and strode briskly up to them.

'Where is Kathleen? Where is she?' he shouted, as the building started to collapse.

One of the men threw his pail of water towards the flames but it was clearly futile. He faced the priest.

'They took her. I don't know where. They looked for the children, but they must have perished in the flames. You are the priest they are looking for, aren't you? You look like a man of the cloth. They're hunting for you too, I warn you. A tall man came here with an angry mob; the same man who had accused Mistress Melton of witchery in the church. She didn't have a chance, poor woman. I don't think she's guilty, she treated my family all right.'

There was a pause before the man asked, 'Were you in an unlawful union?'

'No, never. I helped her with her work. The man you speak of is the evil one,' said Father Peters.

'Aye, I believe you Father, but I don't know what you can do.'

Two old ladies ran towards the man, carrying small pails of water. He nodded to them and took them, and they rushed back to the well to collect more. Father Peters watched him throw them onto the flames. They were useless against such an inferno.

The man shouted, to be heard against the roar of the fire. 'There were too many of them. They said she'd be tried in the morning for witchcraft, probably in the village rooms. You could go there, but they want your blood as well.'

Father Peters nodded and spurred his horse forward to the village rooms. He must stop this, no matter that his own life was in danger.

The small Assizes building was dark and quiet. He dismounted to investigate. Maybe she was inside, in a cell. The gloomy place was locked and no one was about, until a man's voice shouted from across the street.

'That's him! The priest who lives with the witch!'

Father Peters mounted his horse as fast as he could muster, cursing his ageing years. He galloped as soon as the road was clear and headed back to Father Morley's cottage, using the track through the woods which he knew so well. It was only when he came to a small clearing that he looked back.

A group of horsemen were lower down the hill, partly hidden by the woods. He needed to hurry back to the children.

A curse on Griffin. He would pay for this travesty.

At the cottage, he hurriedly dismounted, taking his horse into the stable. Puffing and panting, sweat running down his ruddy cheeks, he quickly entered the cottage, relieved to see his friend and the children.

'We have no time to waste, there are horsemen near.'

'We've already been visited, my friend. They are looking for you and the children. I had to hide them quickly. I don't know if we can hold out. It will only take one to barge in here and search every inch of the place.'

'Aye. I have to get them to the manor.'

Father Morley simply nodded. 'You need to be in disguise.

You must have a good story if you are stopped. Tomorrow is Midsummer's Day and there will be feasting. You are going to sell your vegetables in the market, but you want to be early so you are stopping with a friend for some ale. Here are some pedlar's rags... Been a while since you've worn anything like this, eh?'

Father Peters chuckled. 'Ha! You have always had a trick up your sleeve, Francis, as long as I have known you.'

Francis Morley's smile flickered for just a moment. He was too worried to laugh.

'You are not far behind me, Robert, with your schemes, devising all those holes at the Hall. I swear you are as much a genius as Father Owen. Now you must use that art to hide the children. Cover them well with sacking and straw and then some of my vegetables and fruit.' He was busy assembling the load. 'If Griffin has alerted the mob and that man is right, they'll be looking for Ruth, at least, as Kathleen's apprentice. Go the back way to the house. It will be rough in places for the wagon but this horse will manage it. The moon is strong but then it could also give you away. You must take care.'

'Is my mother safe?' Jack asked Father Peters.

Father Peters hesitated. He'd have to tell them what happened, but now was not the time. God forgive him, he'd have to keep their mother's fate from them for a while longer.

'We face dangers Jack; we must do as Father Morley suggests. I will explain later. Quick, both of you into the wagon.'

He ushered them in, looking all around and listening with intent for the horsemen. 'Stay still, both of you, as if every breath has left your body. You must not be revealed. Do you understand?'

'Yes, Father.'

They climbed into the cart and Father Peters covered them with sacking then lots of straw, vegetables and fruit. He gave them Kathleen's herb box to hold tightly and keep hidden.

'Do you really want us to stop breathing, Father? Jack asked. Although he chuckled, Father Peters couldn't stop the sadness welling within him.

'No, my son, but you must be well hidden.' He felt a strong sense of urgency, to get them to the Manor house and then on to the court to avert this dreadful persecution.

Jack was worried about his mother. There was something badly amiss. He had not been reassured that she was well.

Father Peters covered them again, ready to set off on his way.

'Thank you, brother.' He leaned forward towards Father Morley and the two friends embraced. 'Fare thee well, God save thee. I shall see thee anon.'

Father Morley gave a sad nod. 'Farewell, my good friend. May God be with you.'

Daylight was rapidly fading. Father Morley watched them leave with a heaviness in his heart. The sound of the wagon's wheels clattering on the stones soon ceased as it disappeared into the trees. It was not long gone when Father Morley saw horses approaching from the opposite direction.

Chapter Twenty-Four

May 1958

Dad's recovery was slow. I went with her one day, but found it a bit emotional to be honest. Seems sort of abnormal watching a parent in a hospital bed; especially when the weeks go on and on. I also found myself hating Harry and Arthur too, for buying him all that booze. I let Mum sit near him while I stood up, occasionally looking out of the window. Sounds bad, but I didn't really want to be there, listening to the hissing and puffing of the iron lung, even though I knew it was his lifeline.

Mum sat by his bedside counting the drops of saline that dripped into the chamber of the intravenous tube, keeping him hydrated. Encouraged by the nurses to talk to him, she placed the chalice and the box on his bed. Gran had done a superb job of buffing the silver and the stones, which now appeared as sapphires, pearls and rubies, set with perhaps diamonds. It must have taken a lot of time and patience.

'Hello, Albert. Isn't it time you were coming home?' No response. 'Tom found these treasures in our house. Well, in the garden and that tunnel. I know you didn't like it but…' She chuckled, 'Tom says the tunnel stinks of the cess pit. I've told him, though, he's not to go in it again… But you know Tom, he'll do it anyway.' She studied him. No response. 'We need you to come home, Albert.'

She held his hand and turned to me. 'He's quite cold, Tom. Perhaps I ought to say something.'

'He looks okay Mum.' I wasn't sure what to say to reassure her to be honest, but I did think he looked thin.

Mum shook her head, her voice suddenly unsteady,

'How life can give you a sudden kicking, when you are plodding along nicely.' She sighed. 'I miss you Albert, so much.' A couple of tears drew a thin line down her foundation cream as they spilled from her pooling eyes.

A nurse came in and comforted her. 'Go and get some rest, Mrs Winchett, you look worn out.'

'Aye, my mother is doing a lot of the cooking. We'll leave earlier today and give her a break. I'll leave this chalice and box with him, if that's all right. Err...they're very valuable. Can you make sure they stay in here?'

'Of course, Mrs Winchett.' The nurse's eyes and mouth opened wide as she looked at them.

I was a bit worried about them staying at the hospital, so I asked, 'Can they be locked away securely until my Mum comes again, do you think?'

'Of course. Can I ask you? Where did these come from?'

'We live in a Tudor mansion house. They were discovered... er...underground. Dad might be interested.'

'Wow! You look after your Mum, eh? I promise these will be kept safe.'

*

Back in school, I entered another restless phase. I was becoming frustrated at the lack of time or opportunities to solve what was going on in my own house and bored with lessons.

Mr Stephens accused me of being sullen, intolerant and downright cheeky. 'If it wasn't for your poor mother and what she was going through at the moment I would have you in detention again. You need to pull your socks up, for her sake, lad.'

Deep down, I knew he was right, but I didn't want to give him the satisfaction of saying it.

One afternoon, Mr Stephens left the classroom as the whole class were working on science projects. Bored with experiments with dry ice, George and I speculated on the information in the notes from Gran…but eager ears were close by.

'That tunnel again?'

Mike Thompson.

'Go and find your own amusement, Thompson. Nosy bastard,' I growled.

'Are you calling me a bastard?'

'I just did! You deaf or something?'

Mike made a fist, lunged over to me and swung his hand forward to hit me square on the face, but I ducked.

He stumbled forward and George put out his foot so that Mike fell over it and onto the desks.

Other boys joined in. The sound of furniture scraping the floor was deafening. The girl who was always smiling at me, Sally, caught the fish bowl just before it crashed to the floor, but she tipped the water and the goldfish deliberately over Mike Thompson's face. The fish slipped down his blazer just as the door was flung open and there stood Mr Stephens.

His mouth looked like that of the fish. He stood astounded until the class noticed his presence and quietened. The little fish fell to the floor from under Mike Thompson's blazer but was still flapping. Recovering his voice, Mr Stephens demanded the fish was rescued immediately and put back into some water. Sally made several attempts to grasp it, but it kept jumping and slipping from her fingers.

The others giggled, making Mr Stephens angry.

This time, we were suspended.

*

My mum went barmy. 'How could you do this? Don't you think I've got enough to worry about? Have you no thought at all? Well?'

'I'm sorry, Mum. Mike Thompson and his mates are bullies. It's so bloody irritating that we get punished and it's all their fault.'

'Don't swear, Tom.'

'Oh, you don't understand.'

Her eyebrows shot up as her wild eyes fixed on me. There was more yelling to come.

'I do understand!' she snapped. 'I understand that you're incapable of thinking about anyone else. That's what I understand! Go to bed! And another thing… I don't want to hear about that damn tunnel, 'cos you're never going down it again!'

She stormed off into the kitchen. Gran placed an arm around me.

'You know how to pick your times, don't you?' she said. I just shrugged and went slowly up the stairs.

The suspension was for three days. Mum went off to work, then she was going to the hospital.

Gran was going into Chesterfield. I gave her the piece of paper on which I had wrote the words, *'Sancta Pater, Sancta Pater, audi nos, libera nos et nos cum mater nostra.'* I just caught her in the hallway, putting on her coat, 'Are you going to the library Gran? Please cold you find a Latin translation book and tell me what these words mean?' She frowned and shook her head, the look was enough to convey that she thought I should give up.

The house was empty. I stared out of the window. I'd read Gran's notes over and over again and now an image of the priest walking on the garden was before me: the Tudor children were playing and the woman I saw in the bonfire was stood in the corner by a tree. The images sailed in and out of my brain all day.

Could any of it be true? Was the dark shape I saw the ghost of a priest and the whisperings those of the children who originally lived here? The Earl of Becton's daughter died, so maybe it was her spirit here, whispering to me, but there were two voices, I'm sure.

The library book never mentioned what had become of Oliver

or his mother, that Lady Charlotte. Then there were the so-called witch's children who were assumed to have died in a fire and that bloody raven. Where did he fit?

Just to complicate matters, the whisperings may even be children who had died in this house since the Tudor period, in the Victorian era, for example. My thoughts were circling and getting nowhere.

*

During the suspension from school, Gran had mentioned that I should learn to cook. I had helped to cut chips once, so I found potatoes and started to peel them and did what Gran did: left them in cold water. I then made a salad with lettuce, tomatoes and cucumber and placed it in a bowl. I looked in the fridge, not knowing what Gran had planned for tea, but, as soon as she came home, I would cook whatever it was. I suppose I partly wanted to get back into their good books.

Annabel was first in from school. 'Hey, lucky you. I wish I could have three days suspension. I'd stop in bed all day. What you been up to? Not gone anywhere near that tunnel I hope?'

'Nope.'

'Huh. Find that hard to believe. So you haven't discovered that the slab we dug up has been firmly put down again and sealed? That electrician, Harry, came here on your last day at school and said he'd put down a heavy iron sheeting. Gran said it took him ages and he was having a good snoop around. Dad had apparently asked him to come and do it before he had his accident.'

I was flabbergasted. Nobody had told me until now. I rushed out. There, over the hole with the steps to the vault under the ground, was a large sheet of corrugated iron set firmly with several bricks. Huh. George and I would quickly shift that, but why did Gran seem to think Harry was snooping?

I set the table when Annabel had gone upstairs.

Shortly after, Gran arrived. She had books in her bag and

came up to me, rather furtively, 'The words you wanted Tom.' She handed me the paper I had given her. I could see her own handwriting under my Latin words:

'*Sancta Pater, Sancta Pater, audi nos, libera nos, et nos cum mater nostra.*'

'Holy father, Holy Father, hear us, free us and unite us with our mother.'

'Quite powerful words, Tom, full of emotion,' she said. 'Where did you get these words?'

'They are the whispered words, Gran, uttered by children, in this house.'

She glanced around the hall. 'Seems really odd to think we're being watched, but why use the words *"Free us"*? It's certainly eerie. They want to be reunited with their mother...so is that the Lady Charlotte? Glad I don't hear them, hope it's not often, Tom?'

'No Gran, not often. I'm sure they are the children of Lady Charlotte Her daughter Mary died in this house after all. But I have a question for you Gran.' 'Why didn't you tell me Harry was coming to seal the tunnel entrance?'

'Ah... Tom, your mum asked me not to. She thought you would protest too much and she couldn't face it, quite honestly. She has a lot of stress on her plate, Tom, right now. Did Annabel tell you? I thought she overheard.'

'Annabel said he took a long time and you thought he was snooping?'

'Well, yes, I did actually. He disappeared from the hole and I saw him walking up and down the garden.'

'Hmm. Too inquisitive. What was he up to?'

Mum came home from the hospital. At last there had been some progress with Dad's condition. They had tried weaning him off the iron lung for longer and longer periods and now he was breathing spontaneously. Only the previous evening when Mum visited, he had begun to respond to simple commands such as being asked to squeeze someone's hand or open his eyes. The nurses were checking these responses frequently and shining a torch into his eyes to check that his pupils were reacting well to light. All in all they were very pleased. The nurse who was present when I went with Mum to the hospital had sat with him, encouraging him to touch the chalice and the box.

Mum said his speech was a bit slurred, but what concerned her was when she gave him a 'Get Well' card from Harry and George, he had frowned and painstakingly uttered, 'Don't trust them.'

Mum and Gran discussed his suspicions, Gran now telling mum how she didn't like the way Harry seemed to be snooping around the house. 'Seemed as if he was up to something, Alice.'

'Yes, Mum. We must keep news of the box to ourselves. That's worth something. We still have to get it valued.' She finally took off her coat and looked at the table, 'Oh Tom, you've prepared some tea. Salad would be nice, dear. I'll show you how to cook chicken fillets.'

*

After Mum left for work the next day and Gran went shopping, I heard a car pull up. I rushed to the window and saw George's dad dropping him off and then drive off.

I opened the door. 'How have you managed to allow your dad to bring you here when we have been suspended? Thought you might be locked in your bedroom.'

'Ha, no way. I said we had a project and the teacher had told us to get on with it and finish it. Dad's getting fed up with me around any road and boredom was driving me slowly mad, Tom.'

'Hey, it's lucky no one is in. Come in.'

It wasn't long, however, before Gran came home.

When she saw George, I think she assumed we were up to our old tricks.

'Aye aye, what have you been up to? You're suspended from school you know, you're not supposed to be having fun.'

'I know. It's great, eh, Tom?' George laughed cheekily. Gran usually had a good sense of humour but occasionally it had to be teased out. We both studied her face as we chuckled. She looked serious but then shook her head and grinned. We all giggled, but the sound of banging on the front door ended our bit of fun.

Gran went to open it. Then she came back to the kitchen, looking gloomy and worried.

'What's the matter Gran? Who's at the door?'

'School inspectors,' she said, sighing. 'You two are in deep trouble.'

We looked at one another with raised eyebrows, ready to scarper.

'C'mon in chaps…they're in here.'

Strange way for Gran to talk to school inspectors.

Then two workman entered.

'It's the men come to put the new oven in.'

'Gran, that wasn't fair.'

The two men were shown into the kitchen. One stopped and stared at George.

'Aren't you Arthur Howard's lad? I've worked with your dad. We were at a Christmas party together. You won't remember me, though. I often have a few drinks with your dad in The Old Gatehouse.'

George looked puzzled.

'I'm Sydney Fielding; just remember me to your dad, eh? I'll be in The Gatehouse next week, tell him, for a chat.' Then he introduced his workmate. 'This is Pete, by the way.'

George simply nodded, so I did the same. It was unlike him not to babble on. Strange.

We went up to my room to discuss our project, but it wasn't long until the banging from the kitchen was unbearable.

George asked for one of Gran's sweets. He'd seen them in a jar in the kitchen. He recalled the tale I told him when we first met, about the disappearing sweet.

'Where did it end up, I wonder? Show me again where it disappeared.'

I showed him.

'What if I drop another down this hole and we listen to it drop, then go down and try and find it. The workmen are right below us. It could be a good opportunity.'

I didn't disagree, so he dropped it.

Clunk. There was a distinct sound of the sweet hitting metal, several feet below. The voice of one of the workmen echoed to the fireplace in my room. 'What the bloody hell was that?'

George rushed out of the room. 'C'mon.'

In the kitchen, Gran was looking horrified. The men had used pickaxes to clear away most of the bricks from the fireplace where the old range had been. There was a big dust cloud billowing through the kitchen.

'Oh my God,' she said. 'Your mum only painted the walls a few weeks back.' Chipped bricks and mounds of mortar were strewn all over the floor.

'Did you see anything drop?' George asked Sydney.

'I heard something, don't know how with the racket, but something at that side.' He pointed to the right side of the fireplace.

'Isn't it time you had a break? You should go and have a breather.' I knew George wanted them out of the way.

'Ha, cheek of the urchin! Are you our boss? We've got to finish this, lad.' They exchanged glances. 'But if you insist, we'll have a walk out. Ere, don't get touching any of this lot, you'll hurt yourselves. We will have a break though, eh, Pete? I could do with a fag.'

'Go and drop another one, George. Quick!'

George bumped into Gran coming in the kitchen. For once, lost for words, he continued to rush past her and up the stairs.

She looked at me.

'Go and drop another what, Tom?

'I'll explain later, Gran. Honest.'

Within a short time, another *'clunk'* alerted me to the location of the sweet dropping. It struck something hard.

'What's going on?' she asked, her arms akimbo.

'I'll tell you in a bit, Gran. It's a kind of experiment.'

George came rushing back, just as I had picked a hammer from the workmen's tool box. He went over to the fireplace, climbing over bits of rubble.

'It's about here, somewhere.'

Dust has a way of hitting the back of your throat and coating it. I squirmed. The only way to get rid of it is to swallow it. We spotted a wobbly stone and managed to ease it away to get a better look at what was behind it. Yes…a metal container.

'Oh, God, what's that? Mind your toes!' Gran warned.

We pulled out a large metal chest, about two feet long by eighteen inches and a foot deep. We blew off a thick covering of dust just as the workmen returned.

'What ye got there? 'Ere, you took my hammer. I told you, no tools.'

'Sorry,' I said, but I wasn't sorry at all.

Pete, seeing us struggling to open the chest and curious himself, placed a large scraper under the rim in several places. Exerting pressure, he used it as a lever to prise open the lid.

George and I removed several layers of dark cloth, the eyes of the workmen eagerly focused on the contents.

What was underneath the cloth stunned us all. Silver candlesticks, robes embroidered with gold and silver thread, chalices, plates and gold and silver coins.

'Blimey!' exclaimed the man.

'The priest's vestments and coins, lots of them,' I was whispering, for some silly reason.

'That's some find, lad. Bloody hell.'

'Err, kindly refrain from that language in front of young boys, eh?'

'Sorry, missus.'

Then, to our horror, Gran, said, 'It's not the only thing. They've found stuff down a tunnel, near the summer house.'

'Gran!' I yelled and she winced, realising her mistake. I kind of tutted until a sudden crack at the kitchen window distracted us.

The raven had flown onto the kitchen window ledge outside and amazingly splintered the glass with his beak. His blackcurrant eyes surveyed the scene in the kitchen menacingly, until they came to rest on the chest of artefacts. The men jumped back in astonishment.

'What is it with that raven?' Gran shouted, 'Now we have to pay for a new window. Be off with you… Shoo!' It stayed put, walking one way then the other but constantly peering in.

The men were spooked, but amused. 'God, we haven't had a job like this one for before, have we Pete?' grinned Sydney.

'Not at all. But looking at that fella outside, I'm glad that window's not open. C'mon, we need to get on with this oven.'

When they had finally gone, saying the plaster work around the oven needed to dry naturally, Gran asked us to help her get the chest into my bedroom.

'This sort of thing can't stop down here, especially with a cracked window. I wish we'd not found it when those workmen were here; and yes, I'm sorry I mentioned the tunnel.' She slapped her hand in jest.

'Oh, don't worry, Gran. Who would want to steal from us anyway? Besides if it went tonight, we have those workmen to blame straight away.'

George then disclosed some scandal about Sydney Fielding. 'He was in the nick for armed robbery once. Mum doesn't like Dad meeting up him. Says he's always scheming, like finding ways to get rich quick.'

Hmm, typical that he should visit here and see those artefacts and hear of treasure in the tunnel, but it was done now.

George couldn't resist rummaging through the new treasure box, fascinated by the relics.

'Think about it, Tom. That priest would have had his hands on this very candlestick and these robes will have been worn by him…'

*

I was too restless to sleep. I stared at the chest. The find excited me.

The priest had collected some beautiful things, but why did the raven become so frenzied every time we found treasure? He could well be the spirit of the old priest, it was looking more likely.

In the still darkness of the early hours, I awoke, sweating like a cooking chicken, but paralysed as one is in a deep sleep. Although I felt hot, the room was icy cold.

The hooded man hovered above me. I heard the slow and deliberate words of an old man:

'Misery will haunt thee, brother, in this life and the next. I curse thee with claws, corvus, so thou can never grasp the treasures thou covets.'

Then, a soft childlike voice, *'Father, Father.'*

I opened my eyes to look round the room. I had been dreaming, probably caused by overactive thoughts since the new find of the priest's belongings. I turned over towards the fireplace to try and get back to sleep.

That was when I saw a boy standing close by, staring at me.

Chapter Twenty-Five

June 23rd 1598

The late evening sky was tinted with pink and shades of dark blue and purple. The air was still, not with calm, but more a sense of doom. After Father Peters and the children had departed from Father Morley's cottage, the latter stood at his fence, watching horses approach. About twelve or thirteen men slowed their horses from a gallop to a canter, and now the horses were whinnying as they came to an abrupt halt outside Father Morley's cottage.

The priest was dressed simply. A plain, dark robe was hitched up by a broad rope around his plump waist so most of the coarse cloth hung in folds over his belly. His keys and other small items for kitchen or garden use jangled from the rope as walked.

He greeted the men but did not like the look of them.

'What brings you in such a hurry to my humble abode?' he asked the first man, who had dismounted from his horse. He seemed to be the leader.

'We are looking for a priest, with two children. Have you seen them pass by?'

'Nay, I haven't. Why are you looking for these people?'

'No business of yours, but it is by order of the Queen that they are found. They are to be charged.'

'For what crime?' Father Morley sounded calm, but he was

tense with nerves. He must stall them.

'As I said, good man: no business of yours.'

'I am a farmer, still trying to keep my crops. I had my land reduced due to the wretched enclosures. Perhaps you can tell me if this is to stop, sir, now that you are here?'

'We are not here to discuss crops, sir. If you see them and do not report this, you too will be judged, heed my words! There remain some Jesuit priests among us, trying to convert good people to the old faith. As you know, this is an act of treason. You look a wise man, sir. You wouldn't be hiding anything from us, would you?'

Francis Morley was given another opportunity to stall them. He swallowed hard. The man gave him a steely glare which made him feel uncomfortable. Francis paused for a short time until he noted signs of irritation in the men, then he continued before his nerves got the better of him.

'Ah…my thoughts have returned to me. I remember a disturbance, early this morning.' He waited again for a response, praying that Father Peters and the children could gain a lengthy distance from these priest or witch hunters.

With further irritation, the man stepped closer to Francis. 'Well, speak up, man. What disturbance are you referring to?'

Francis hesitated.

'I cannot be hurried, sir. I am old now and slow of mind. Age is wearying, as one day you too will discover.' He rubbed his chin as if to indicate deep thought, ignoring the man's deep sighing and threatening gestures.

'Ah, yes, I remember…there were voices, early on. Somewhere over there behind the trees.' He pointed in the opposite direction to the track that Father Peters had taken. 'They must have gone on their way through the woods.'

Looking suspicious, the man mounted his horse.

'They are on foot. If we do not find them, we will come back, old man!' The last words were vindictively expressed.

Father Morley crossed himself, looked up to the sky and muttered to the Lord, asking for forgiveness. All his life, lying had never come easy. But the men would return.

*

Father Peters was making headway along the rough track to the back of Becton Manor. Father Morley was right. The track was treacherous in parts; large fallen tree trunks and heavy branches had blocked their progress. The horse had reared up in protest a few times and Jack and Ruth were thrown violently across the floor of the wagon, clutching each other to buffer the impact. Father Peters had to stop each time to check on them and cover them again with the sacking, straw and vegetables.

It was dark. He was about to light his lantern using the flint to ignite sparks in the tinder box, when he heard horses in the distance somewhere behind him. He tried to steer the horse and wagon speedily behind some trees and cover it with branches still laden with evergreen leaves. The horsemen had gathered pace however and had seen him.

They approached the wagon. Father Peters could smell ale on their breath.

'Where are you off to in the dark, old man?'

Father Peters was glad that he was dressed as a simple farmer.

'I am setting off early to market. Tomorrow is a good day for me. Midsummer Day's festival should yield a healthy profit. I want the best spot.'

'Why hide your wares, old man?'

'There are robbers on this road. When I heard you I thought I was going to have my fruit and vegetables stolen.'

One of them looked in the back of the wagon. Father Peters tried not to show the tension that he felt in his body. He prayed that Jack and Ruth would remain still and quiet.

'Plentiful strawberries, my man.' He picked a few, giving some to his friend. 'Ah, these are full of flavour. You are a good farmer, but why do you take this rugged and rocky track, especially with your fear of robbers? The lower road is better for you.' They didn't seem interested in an answer, more in the strawberries.

Father Peters knew he must remain composed, but he badly needed to get rid of these men. While they were sampling the fruit at the back of the wagon, he furtively placed some of his toxic powders into two flagons of ale and replaced the corks. As he put them down carefully, he was aware of them walking back to him.

'We are trailing behind the rest of our men, old farmer. Getting bored of looking for a priest and two children, so we sought nourishment from another farmer. We think he knew the whereabouts of the priest we are looking for, but he lied to us. Unfortunately, now…' the man stared threateningly at Father Peters, 'he will have no further need of his crops. You wouldn't lie to us, would you?'

'Why should I see children here, in the dark?' answered Father Peters, his stomach sinking hard as if he had been punched. What had happened to his good friend? He could not enquire.

The men strode to the back of the wagon again. Jack and Ruth gripped one another's hands tightly.

Father Peters held his breath. Then, he seized his chance. He turned round quickly and offered the men ale. 'This includes the spices of the New World. I hope to sell lots at the market.' Already drunk, the men were in the mood to try a different ale. One of them almost threw it down his throat.

His eyebrows shot upwards and he looked surprised. 'Strange ale you brew, farmer.' He still downed another large slug. The second man did the same.

'I must be on my way, good sirs. As I said, I need a good spot. Keep the flagons.'

The men started to laugh and joke as they continued to tip their heads back and let the ale wash down their necks. They were now unconcerned at Father Peters' departure.

'Adieu,' they echoed.

Father Peters clicked his tongue and sharply struck his horse to make headway, but also intended to make the men's horses jittery. It worked. The nervous horses scampered away.

The men jeered and stopped drinking but, as Father Peters glanced over his shoulder, he saw them staggering. Very soon, their vision would deceive them and the contents of their bowels and stomach would be ejected. He could not wait for this to happen. He had to make haste.

Ahead, Becton Manor was emerging as a dark silhouette. There were a few bonfires around; of course this was Midsummer's when bonfires were lit to protect from evil spirits.

But, as Father Peters looked across to the field just beyond the Hall, he spotted a crowd of people milling about and shouting. It was a disturbing, frenzied scene. He whipped the horse to accelerate his speed then, near to Becton, he spotted the edge of a precipice.

It gave him a good vantage point. Quickly dismounting and running to the edge, he saw a myriad of red sparks before his eyes.

Then...the huge bonfire. He heard the shout of an old woman that stilled his heart.

'She is innocent! This woman should not burn!'

Father Peters knew the woman on the stake was Kathleen. She had had no trial. This was an unlawful procedure. He wanted to run down the hill as fast as his legs could take him, but he looked back at the wagon. He made the sign of the cross.

How could the good Lord challenge him with such diverse loyalties? He would have to leave the children to save Kathleen and, by doing so, he would be admitting to his 'union' with a witch. The children would be found, and they would suffer, from the poverty heaped upon them by being orphaned, or worse, by death, as conspirators with their mother. What choice did he have?

He looked again at the roaring fire casting a halo of bright orange light in the dark sky. He heard the milling mob. There were supporting calls for her release but the flames grew higher and the timber broke and crackled, drowning out the protests. He knew she would not scream, but in the light of the fire, he saw wisps of her hair and he felt her pain.

Chapter Twenty Six

June 23rd 1598

There remained a strong smell of wood smoke in the field near Becton Manor later that night, on the eve of Midsummer's Day. It had been a long evening, a celebration evening to encourage a strong sun and to purge the land of evil spirits. Kathleen Melton had been deemed an evil spirit when she was convicted of being a witch.

Now, almost at the turn of the day into Midsummer's Day, bone ends protruded from glowing embers and white ash, soft dust particles mixed with orange sparks floated in the air. An odd sense of serenity hung over the field. A few other fires had brightened the night sky, while villagers sang, chanted and danced. Kathleen's flesh had long gone but her spirit had risen. A couple of hours later, the once noisy crowd had all but departed.

From his viewpoint at the top of the small bank, about a two hundred yards from Becton Manor, Father Peters was angry with them all. No one had tried to halt the burning. No one had protected her, including himself.

His misery was intolerable. With tears spontaneously running down his cheeks, he bent over to clutch his wretched body, contorted in pain. He could not wail but as he looked up to the heavens, crossing himself several times, he lost his resolve and his face crumpled into a hundred weary wrinkles. With a brief shake of his head, he gently sobbed.

'Why, Lord, why?'

He looked back at the wagon. There was no movement. The children must be asleep. He must compose himself. He needed to complete his journey and wake them.

*

Anne Sawyer and Edward Griffin were still standing near the edge of the field below, watching the embers and the departing crowd.

An unbearable sense of wretched disgrace and shame gripped the former governess. Every time she closed her eyes she saw the blazing fire gripping Kathleen's bound body, roaring like a wild animal, ready to devour her.

Dear Kathleen, what have we done to you? She had never moved; just her singeing wispy hair escaping as tiny sparkling fragments floated towards Heaven in the darkness of the smoke. She had looked like an effigy, but, no…she was an angel, just an angel, fading from their grasp. *Prepare for her, Holy Father. She will be a good angel for you.*

Anne felt hot, faint and dizzy. Griffin heard Anne's sudden raspy breathing and watched her bend over, violently ejecting her stomach contents onto the muddy earth below. There was no sympathy shown by him.

'Get up, woman. It was not my doing. I tried to save her. She should have paid me the money that I was owed by the priest and at least given me her box. She may have even taken my money box; it was stolen from the house. I would have defended her when the horsemen came. I did not know they were coming. You will do well to remember that she almost ruined my life: she and that priest of hers. We can be wealthy, Anne, in our own right, but you have to do as I say. Tonight we have to leave.'

He did not speak of searching for Kathleen's herb box or hitting her hard across the face when she would not tell him of its whereabouts. She had fallen and banged her head on the stone floor. Then men on horseback had arrived at the cottage. They had orders to take her away for a trial for murder by the means of witchcraft. In a few days she may have confessed when her body was pricked for signs of the devil, then tied to a chair before being ducked into the river. He knew she would not escape.

News travels fast of an angry mob wanting the demise of an accused witch who had poisoned an earl, his daughter and a local girl. Griffin had made sure it did.

Griffin told the men that the witch was unconscious due to ale and the herbs she used. He'd persuaded them they should burn her that night, as part of the Midsummer's Eve purging of witches and pagans. It would be humane. She would not feel the pain of the flames. There was a feverish animated mob outside, baying for her blood to be spilled. They were like a pack of animals, ready for the kill.

Suspicious of the horsemen, the villagers bustled around them. Vigilantes disliked the interference of outsiders who, with the increasing tension, were afraid to dismount, their horses whinnying, nervous and fidgety.

Several of them, eager for the bonfire, began to shout. One man was heard above the others.

'We are taking her now. The assizes takes too long.' There was a chorus of 'Aye, aye.'

The men looked at one another. The horses were agitated. Griffin had recalled a man once say to him that vigilante groups take the law into their own hands. It was never stopped. He had taken advantage of the moment by reminding the hesitant horsemen of this fact. They had listened.

'Why should it now be any different?' he had heard one of the men say to another. 'We won't get away from here easily it seems, looking at this lot.' So be it.

A limp Kathleen Melton was carried outside to the jeering crowd. They started to fasten her slight body to the stake. While they were tying her, Griffin had slipped inside to look for the herb box. In the frenzy of his search he'd knocked over a candle, which had started the fire. He had quickly opened every cupboard and drawer to no avail.

As the increasing heat and flames overpowered him, Griffin ran out, cursing the herb woman.

Somewhere, the priest and those children were in hiding, and they had his money. He was also nervous of the return of the earl's brother. Gilbert Harrison would scrutinise him and leave no stone unturned in the quest to blame him for the murder of his niece and brother.

*

He gripped Anne's arm tightly. She tugged it free and turned away, wanting to escape from him and the scene she would never forget. He grabbed her again. She smelled his sickly breath and was held by the steely glare that revealed his sheer dominance.

He spoke directly into her startled face.

'You must harden your resolve, madam. Listen to me. You must meet me at four o'clock in the morning at the stables. Ged arrives at five o'clock and we need those horses. We will travel to Lancashire, where I can allow my wool business to grow. We need to leave before daylight. Hark, madam. Do you understand?'

Tears surged down her crumpled face. 'Yes, I can hear you.'

Her head low, she crossed herself. She knew the Holy Father would never forgive her. She made her way back to the house of Margaret's ageing mother, where she had been made welcome since her dismissal from Becton Manor.

There was barely enough room. The house was tiny but clean, and at least it was a shelter until she would marry Edward Griffin. She didn't smile about the prospect of that now, just felt trepidation.

Griffin left for the inn to drink some ale. He listened hard to the rowdy 'witch-hunters', downing one tankard after another. There was always a buzz in the ale house whenever it was Midsummer's Night's Eve.

Griffin felt proud that his actions had saved Kathleen Melton from the pain of the searing flames. He could not afford to get drunk; he had to ensure his escape plan did not fail. The loud words of one broad shouldered 'searcher' however caught his attention.

'He had good strawberries all right, but the ale was evil stuff. What farmer would carry such ale or even strawberries at that time of night in a small wagon on a rough track? That one leading to the old earl's house…God rest his soul…that is the worse track I've ever come across!'

He downed another tankard of ale, then spat onto the reed strewn floor. Others laughed, too drunk to further question his comments. But another comment suddenly alerted Griffin.

'Our deed is done, lads. Now let's drink to the searchers up at Becton Manor finding the priest. Drink up, lads!'

Griffin hung his head in deep thought. He didn't think that the searchers would come on the same night as the burning. So the farmer—or was it the priest?—who had been seen heading for Becton Manor? Pleased he was dressed all in black, he hastily downed the dregs of his ale and left the inn.

Every few steps he looked around. He did not want to be followed. He needed his money casket and the herb box, or his future plans would founder.

He saw the Hall, as a black silhouette against a dark night sky; the moon was a mere slither and the light from bonfires had long ceased.

There were a few dim lights from lanterns within. Could his money still be inside? Would Frances let him in? If necessary, he would have to use force. The story of the farmer in the wagon was going round and round his head.

It must be him. He was desperate to get his money. If Father Peters was at the Hall, he would force him to hand it over. The jewelled box could not be found at the cottage, so the priest probably had that too.

He stopped to listen. The sound of hooves on stone and the barking of dogs was followed by the opening of the front door and a very nervous Frances speaking, but her words were short and muffled. Boisterous searchers forced their way in, one of them yelling orders to search everywhere. He was too late. *How can I get my money now?*

*

Inside the Hall, Frances protested to the searchers.

'You cannot come here without Lady Charlotte's permission, or the earl's brother, Gilbert Harrison. You are breaching the law!'

Her protests made no difference to the rampaging men. A large burly man with a toothless grin and scruffy beard pushed her to one side.

She steadied herself and ran quickly up the stairs. She did not know what had happened to Father Peters or Jack and Ruth, nor did she know when Gilbert Harrison would return.

He'd told her he had urgent matters with the court, referring to Master Griffin's conduct. Thank the Lord he would, at last, be accused and would hopefully hang, she thought. But for now, she had to ensure Father Peter's hiding places were secure.

She ran into the bedroom with the secret panel and placed her rocking chair against it. She sat firmly in it and put her head in her hands. She could hear wood being stripped from the walls, pots and pans being thrown around wildly below in the scullery, then the dining room chairs scraping the floor and doors and windows banging. The sound of thunderous heavy boots now marched across the landing. They were quickly getting closer.

'Ah, you...wench. Whither the priest doth hide? Tell me now!'

'There's no one here, no one. It's a closed house since my mistress went to London. There is no one here.'

The big man strode up frighteningly close to her face. He had a thick, scruffy beard and smelled of ale and a body unwashed in weeks. Frances gasped in alarm as he pulled off her coif, rose his fat fist in the air and then swung his knuckles down in a powerful strike across her face. She fell to the floor and hid her face with her arms, yelling.

'There's no one here, I tell you. No one.'

'You lie!' He struck her again, hard, and she slumped to one side. She lay still. Soon, blood began to ooze from her ear.

At that moment, more horses were heard on the gravel outside. The burly man marched out of the room and down the stairs. Gilbert Harrison quickly entered the Hall with his own group of men, demanding answers and ordering them to stop immediately or face charges from the Sovereign.

The big, burly leader gathered the men and faced Gilbert Harrison.

'We have orders to search this property for the recusant priest. You have no right to stop us.'

'Indeed I have. This is my house and I am a Protestant, a member of the Queen's Parliament and of higher rank than you, sir. The man you should be looking for is Master Edward Griffin. He is the murderer of my brother and my niece and is accused of the fraudulent handling of my brother's accounts. He is out there, in hiding. Find him or face the gibbet yourself.' He looked at the other men. 'That means all of you!'

The men hesitated, looking at their disgruntled leader, obviously infuriated by this sudden unexpected intrusion. He had his orders and now it appeared he was to obey someone else. He wasn't giving up easily. 'I have my commands, sir!'

'Well, I am overriding them. Get out of here or suffer the consequences.'

Some of the men, prompted by the uncertainty of their leader, began to leave. They didn't want to end up on the gallows.

'You will hear more of this.' The burly man said, intent on having the last word.

Gilbert Harrison simply grunted. He shouted for Frances but there was no reply. He took a cursory glance at the damage to the house. How did things get this far, he thought? Frances would have to wait. In the courtyard, he mounted his own horse and nodded to his men to do the same. He wanted to find Griffin.

'Split up and look everywhere. Meet at the inn at noon. One of you at least should have him! I want him captured but alive, and I have no care how you detain him.'

Edward Griffin crouched outside a window, listening to it all. He looked around him. He must get to the horses, meet with Anne and be on his way, but his money was still inside the house. He must deal with Frances.

In the darkness, he crept stealthily to the back of the house to enter by the scullery. He was dismayed to hear the dogs barking, but thankfully they were tethered. It was just that their din could affect his escape. He recalled the tale of the man in a wagon and hastily looked for signs of it, but he could see nothing. It would soon be dawn; he would need to hurry.

He tried the door. Luckily, it was open. He crept in slowly, looking all around him and listening hard. Planks of split wood were strewn across the hall and some of the stairs had been ripped apart so there were great gaps. He stepped carefully across them. Where was Frances? The door to the schoolroom was open, the chairs and tables askew or fallen. The searchers had been thorough. He thought the priest might be in hiding with Frances, but all he wanted was his money. He thumped an upturned table hard.

The dogs were still ferociously barking and the darkness of night was quickly lifting into a hazy dawn. There was no time to waste. He ran to check the other rooms. The priest and Frances had to be somewhere.

As he looked into the third bedroom on the left of the galleried landing, he saw Frances slumped on the floor. Blood had pooled around her head and was now soaking into the floor. Her eyes were open and fixed.

He ran down the stairs and rushed out of the scullery door... then stopped abruptly, crouching to hide behind a bush. There was a shimmering light behind the stables. He could see the back of a wagon and a flicker of movement.

He muttered under his breath. 'The priest.'

Chapter Twenty-Seven

June 22nd 1958

I could hardly breathe. The air in my room was freezing. I shivered, wanting to bolt downstairs but some invisible force held me rigid in my bed. The boy, about eight or nine maybe, stood only a couple of feet away, staring at me.

Dressed strangely in a sort of tunic and baggy trousers, he came nearer, bending over me so that his face was visible but appeared veiled: white, gaunt and pointed. I remembered the face at the window of my room, when we had first looked round the manor house. This was that face, I was certain. Wide eyes studied me without blinking. I knew my mouth was wide open but I couldn't make a sound.

He spoke, 'Oliver?'

'No...no, I'm not Oliver.' I was so shocked I could not even swallow.

Then the form melted away. I closed my eyes and opened them again to check if he was still there. I was more disappointed than relieved that he had gone, in whatever form he was.

*

I couldn't wait to see George at school. Before lessons began, I told him what I'd seen and heard the night before, including the weird dream of an old man saying, *'I curse thee with the claws of corvus.'*

George was grinning. 'You're beginning to sound like me, Tom.'

I didn't care whether I did or not. I felt like we were getting closer to solving the mystery of my house.

At lunchtime, George delved into his pocket. 'I've been to the school library and got this book out.'

'Raven mythology?'

'Yes, it says they can represent evil and some people believe they can actually possess the soul of a wicked person. So who do you think that might be, the priest? Think of it, Tom. That bird has been flying around, hopelessly, wanting something he cannot get for perhaps centuries and never dies, because he has been cursed!'

'Ugh. Imagine how that must feel.' I was starting to feel sorry for the raven. That was a turn up for the books.

'So what do we do with a four-hundred-year-old demented and cursed raven?' asked George.

'I don't know. Tonight we're all going to the hospital to see Dad. Wish I could tell him everything.'

George looked thoughtful. 'There's something else you should think about Tom. Remember, you said the boy in your room wore a thick doublet and breeches; quite posh clothes, would you say?'

'I suppose so, why?'

'Well, sounds to me like that was more likely to be Oliver, the son of the Earl of Becton. So the other bones must belong to his sister, Mary.'

'Hmm… Nice try, George, but why did the boy ask me if I was Oliver, if he was Oliver?'

*

At the hospital, Dad was maintaining his own respiration well and had started with rehab. Because of this progress, he was moved onto a general ward.

It was a long, narrow room with high ceilings, huge windows

and a big Victorian fireplace in the centre of the far wall. A few vases of flowers were displayed on the mantelpiece. Several beds were placed in two rows, facing each other. Each had a bedside table and was surrounded by a rail which held cream-coloured curtains to use as screens. The sister's office was tucked in the corner and was the first room on the left as we entered the ward.

The nurses said he had been continually asking to go home, but soon got anxious. We were asked not to tire him at this stage, reminding us that head injuries took quite a while to heal and that he may say or do things out of character.

I laughed. 'He's been like that for years.'

Mum did not find it amusing and Gran gave me a look of warning.

He was very pleased to see us and fidgeted to ensure we had a space to sit down. His voice was still a bit raspy, but we were told that this was caused by the tube that had been in his windpipe for so long. It would improve. 'I keep on asking, Alice, when I can go home. Feel like I'm in a prison now. I don't get much sleep. Don't look now, but that chap over in the corner bed starts snoring so loudly the walls rumble. Then, there's the meals. Oh Alice, nothing like yours. Or yours, Dorothy. Spuds are always bloody cold.'

'Shh…Albert, they'll hear you.'

'Well, it might make 'em glad to get rid o' me then. 'Ere, Tom, don't get inviting George's dad in the house will you? I've got my suspicions about him. Don't ask me why, but somat ain't right. And another thing, take this stuff back with you.' He leaned over to his bedside cupboard and took out the box and the chalice. They're bobby dazzlers Tom, well done…but they ain't safe here, lad.'

*

It was dark when we travelled home. Mum was pleased we had a car again; the insurance had finally paid out and we could afford another one. It made travel to the hospital much easier. We were all in good spirits now Dad seemed almost back to himself. Mum was worried that he would be permanently suspicious of people thanks to the head injury. I just hoped it wouldn't make his leg worse or that he might be grumpier.

As we neared the house, we could hear Mickey barking. Mum drew up sharply on the gravel drive. Something was wrong. She threw me the house keys and in the dark I fumbled to open the front door.

Mickey shot out barking, not even bothering to greet us. He ran to the back garden. Annabel and I hurriedly followed him. He stopped when he reached the summer house, near the entrance to the tunnel, excitedly circling and sniffing.

When we caught up, we saw that the corrugated iron sheet over the tunnel entrance had been removed. There was a sound of someone coming up the steps of the tunnel. Surely the priest wouldn't make that noise? I watched with interest.

George.

'George? What's happening? Why are you here?'

Before he could answer, another figure scrambled out, desperate to get away. Mike Thompson!

George was sharp. He immediately thrust his leg in front of Mike, tripping him up so he fell on top of the iron sheet. Annabel helped George to keep him pinned, but George was yelling and pointing towards the cess pit.

'Get them, they're who you need!' Mickey was already barking and on the heels of the shadowy forms of two men. One of them was helping a third climb out of the cesspit. Mickey, barking then growling, was ready to pounce. The man promptly let his companion slide back into the slimy water and started to run. I ran after him and lunged at his legs, bringing him down. Mickey took over, guarding him.

Looking over to George, I could see he and Annabel were still tussling with Mike who, by thumping Annabel in the face, got away from them. He scurried off like a timid rabbit, with Annabel in rapid pursuit.

'I'll get him!' She was a good runner, always winning prizes at school sports events, and because he'd been hurt by the fall on the iron sheet he was slower than usual.

In the darkness, I could just about make out that Annabel had grabbed him again and, I suppose because of sheer anger at the punch she'd received, was hysterical.

She thumped and kicked him endlessly and even reached for a nearby stick to beat him. She was continually screeching, like a banshee. He was forced to the ground, bringing his knees towards his chest and covering his face.

'Who said sisters were a nuisance?' George had joined me but our attention had to be on the escaping men and the one in the cesspit. Mickey had the one on the ground under control but the other was still running, although by the style and speed of his pace, he wasn't a young man.

'Quick, we mustn't let him get away!' I yelled.

We both ran after him and soon narrowed the gap. The man's legs were not strong. He was panting. As we got nearer, I could see he was wearing a dark balaclava, but all of a sudden a wild whoosh of water pushed him over.

Gran was pointing the outside water hose full pelt on the escaping man.

It bought us time to help Annabel, who was yelling for assistance. Mike Thompson was thrashing again.

George came to her rescue with the rope that luckily was always hanging on a hook outside the house. I went to help, glancing over to check that Mickey was all right. It was then I saw Mum. She was standing nervously, wielding a pitch fork, pointing to the cess pit where a figure doused in thick, slimy excrement was attempting to crawl out. It reminded me of the film *'The Creature from the Black Lagoon.'*

'Oh, my God!' Mum cried out in horror at the sight and the smell of him slithering closer, with the pitch fork swinging in her hand, but tentatively poking him.

After checking that Mike Thompson was securely tied up with

the rope, I went to help Mum. The man started to cross the garden to escape but the slurry that entrapped his body forced him to fall. Gran, satisfied the man in the balaclava was immobilised, relentlessly attacked the lumpy creature with the hose pipe until he looked more human.

She finally clamped off the hose. I could see that she had thoroughly enjoyed that exercise. Using the good torch that she had quickly pulled out from her coat pocket, the men could be now be identified. I called Mickey to heel and all three men were more or less together, facing us.

'Dad?' George was shocked. There stood Arthur, with Harry the electrician by his side.

Mum prodded the lumpy man to stand a bit closer to his 'comrades'. It felt like the preparation for an execution; rather worryingly, at that particular moment I could have shot them all. The third man was revealed to be the man who had installed our new oven, Sydney Fielding.

Arthur looked at his son.

'I'm sorry, lad. Sydney said there was a heap of buried treasure down there. We couldn't resist taking a look, that's all: human nature, like. You know your mam would like more for you. It was all for you lad, all for you.'

Gran couldn't keep quiet. 'Huh, human nature, my…arse…'

'Mum!'

Gran persisted, 'You were all up to no good. Plain stealing, that's what it is! You knew we were all at the hospital, didn't you?'

'These put me up to it.' Arthur nodded towards his accomplices. The builder just stood pitifully, some of the foul-smelling sludgy excrement still stuck to him. There was no chance of him running away in that state.

Harry, however protested. 'Hey, just a minute. You had a lot to say about it all. It was your idea, knowing what your lad brought out of that tunnel. You never told us it was so spooked, though, did you?'

Gran frowned. 'Spooked?'

'Yeah…we were pelted with stones and this big black thing threw Arthur to one side like a sack of spuds.'

Gran looked at me. 'Well Tom, you know, I never thought that being haunted was actually a good burglar deterrent, eh? How things turn themselves around.'

'How you put up with all that in your back garden, missus, amazes me.' Harry continued.

Mum was furious as she faced Arthur.

'If you weren't George's dad, I would call the police.'

I could see George holding back tears before he turned and ran into the house. Just then, Annabel yelled for help, unable to contain Mike Thompson anymore. The rope was loosening. Poor Annabel. Dorothy reached for her favourite weapon and directed the hose on him as well, until the water forced him back to the ground. I pulled him up and brought him to where the men were standing sheepishly. Mum, also taking a liking to her weapon, prodded him with the pitch fork that she still held in her hand.

'So this is the beast who bullies my son, is it?'

'It was a just bit of a lark. Let me go, let me go, missus!'

Gran chipped in, 'I can give you a bit of a lark if that's what you want, lad!'

Arthur looked sheepishly at Gran. 'Look, we've had hard times this year. His mother worries all the time about money coming in and keeping the bills paid. Why shouldn't he have a share of all this treasure anyway? He helped to find it, after all.'

'Stealing is never the answer though is it, Arthur? What is that teaching George? You could have come and spoken to us if you were struggling and we would have worked something out, as friends do.'

Arthur, Harry and Sydney knew they were beaten.

'How did you get here?' Gran asked.

'We have a car waiting, parked down the track,' Harry muttered.

Of course, we came in the opposite way from the hospital. Arthur would have known that. The car was parked twenty or so yards away, well into the hedge.

Gran and I escorted the men to the car. There was a man sitting behind the wheel. I went to open the door.

'Be careful, Tom,' Gran said.

The man swung his body round in a panic. 'What the...?' It was Mr Haslam from the newspaper shop.

'Oh, you're in this game as well are you? Of course. You must have been itching to get your hands on treasure for years.'

He ignored me but yelled at the others as they approached the car.

'How the hell did the three of you foul up against an old woman and a boy? What went bloody wrong? Christ, you stink!'

They said nothing, but got in the car.

Before Gran slammed the back door, she warned them, 'It's only because of poor George that I am not ringing the police. But we know all your names so when we can think of a suitable payback, we will let you know. Don't go back thinking you've got away with it.'

I was impressed with Gran's tactics. Been watching mafia films obviously.

We went back to where Annabel and Mum were guarding Mike Thompson, the pitch fork threatening him to keep still.

'What were you doing here, Thompson?' I asked. George had come out of the house now that his father had left. He had been crying but I said nothing. Mike Thompson wouldn't answer me, but George, regaining his composure, spoke.

'I'll tell you how he got here. Sally lives not far from me and she came to tell me that Thompson and his cronies were coming to your house as soon as it got dark to find the tunnel. It's my fault. I told her you were all going to see your dad, but then she bumped into Mike and told him that nobody would be at your house. When he said he was going to get his mates, she put two and two together.

'He's talked about trying to find the tunnel for months. Anyway, she felt guilty, so she came to my house. I had already told Dad the day before, so I guessed he was meeting up with his mates. So

221

I rushed to get here first. Took me ages to shift that corrugated sheet, but I did it then waited for them in the smaller tunnel. I heard footsteps, then a man's voice. I thought I recognised it but I wasn't sure who it was, then I realised it was the builder—that man I don't like—Sydney Fielding. He's been in the nick before for robbery, I told you. Then I heard Harry and the pair of them were talking and laughing loudly, really excited they were. I didn't hear my dad, because of a sudden rush of stones, grit, gravel, dust, everything. Nothing like we experienced, Tom. It was deafening.

'The men were spooked, but something odd happened. As they were shielding their faces, Harry yelled. Behind him was a great bulk of black. Not sure if he was the priest, but the men couldn't scramble out quick enough. It scared me frozen, but something else was out there.

'I heard a splash, followed by a groan, then more footsteps, coming towards the tunnel.

'Mike Thompson and his two cronies were climbing down the steps. I threw some stones at the walls to scare them, but the sound seemed to cause an avalanche, made worse by the echoes.

'I did find it funny to see their backsides in competition for the way out. Mike was last and fell backwards on the steps, so I jumped out and grabbed him by the ankles and dragged him down into the tunnel again. He banged his head and, what do you know? The big class bully started to cry. Then you lot arrived and you know the rest.'

'Great stuff George, for a little 'un.'

'Yes,' smiled Gran, 'we are very proud of you, George.'

George looked chuffed. I turned to Mike Thompson. 'Got anything to say then, have you?'

I thought he was going to vomit. He gulped a few times but shook his head.

'I know it's dark, lad,' Gran said, 'and you're very wet and you don't have a torch, but…it seems you were wanting to steal as well and that's a matter for the police. They can see to you now.'

'No, missus. My dad will go mad.'

'Well, I can only suggest you start walking home then. One more thing…do you promise, with hands over your heart, never to bully anyone else again?'

There was a silence before she demanded.

'Well? Should I call the police then?'

'No, I promise…'

'With my hand on my heart…' Gran interrupted.

'With my hand on my heart…to never bully anyone again.'

Gran nodded. 'Or you will surely find the police at your door. Go on, be off with you.'

'Gran,' I said. 'He has to walk about three miles.'

Annabel had her say. 'So what? It'll do him good.' She glared at him and, taking the fork from her mum, prodded him.

'He's had his warning,' Gran cautioned her. They watched him hobble away.

'Aren't we giving him a torch?'

'No! Don't be soft, Tom.' Annabel was turning into a hard nut. 'Anyway, the men will be walking by now.'

'Why?'

'While you were talking to them at the car, I used a knife to slash the tyres.'

'Annabel!'

Surprisingly, Gran laughed out loud, and Mum joined in. She had surprises up her sleeve, my sister. We turned towards the house. 'C'mon, it's getting late. But whether any of us will sleep is another matter.'

We went into the house and Mum put the kettle on.

'Oh, come on, Alice. After all that's happened, isn't there any whisky?' Gran asked.

I slapped Annabel gently on the back.

'You were a bit cruel back there, sis, but well done.' She gave a proud smile.

We sat at the table and watched Gran pour a whisky and then Mum do the same. We laughed. What a day!

George didn't want to go home. 'There is a sleeping bag George,' said Mum. 'At least your dad knows where you are. You stay here, love. I'm sorry about what's happened'.

George said nothing but nodded.

Mum changed the subject. 'This house is full of surprises, eh? Oh, hope it won't do any harm, leaving that iron sheeting off that hole tonight?'

'It'll be fine, Mum. I doubt we will get more burglars tonight.'

Annabel and I smirked. There was an unspoken knowledge of what we would be up to tomorrow morning. Exploring the tunnel without having to remove the iron sheeting was a great start.

Chapter Twenty Eight

June 1958

G ran was right: sleep did not come easy following the bungled robbery. There were so many thoughts running amok in my head. I was so impatient to get to the truth; well, as much truth as I could muster after four hundred years.

George in the sleeping bag was also fidgety, so I persuaded him to have another go at trying to open the jewelled box, but nothing happened. He gave up, still looking sad and being quiet. His dad's attempt to steal from us shocked him. I tried again.

'Oh leave it, Tom. We'll try it tomorrow. If we force it, we'll damage it.' He snuggled down in his sleeping bag, eager to shut out the day's events.

Before closing my eyes I looked towards the fireplace. I thought of the boy in the tunic, but I was far too tired to dwell on him.

*

The next morning, a Saturday, Gran and Mum were debating what to use to clean the box. Mum said to use alcohol and we only had whisky, but Gran's face dropped.

'Oh no, Alice. You can't possibly be thinking of using my whisky to clean something. What sacrilege! We'll use baking soda and hot water to make a paste. Works wonders: abrasive but not harmful.'

Mum was not convinced.

George was still a bit quiet at breakfast. His face usually lit up at food, but today he was subdued. We all noticed and Mum offered to drive him home to see his mum and dad. They needed to talk, but he refused. She didn't push him.

It was odd, like a part of his life had been snuffed, perhaps like someone who had undergone one of those lobotomies where they take out the frontal lobe and leave you without emotion. The babbling used to irritate me so much…and now, surprisingly, I was missing it.

Meanwhile, Gran laid out some newspaper and began to clean the box with the baking soda paste. She rubbed hard.

'Don't scratch it, Gran,' I warned, but she puffed, saying it had been scratched umpteen times over three and a half centuries.

I quizzed them about when they were going out. George and Annabel kept looking at me, their eyes begging me to persuade them to leave the house.

By late morning, Gran was pleased with her efforts in cleaning and polishing the box. I didn't know much about precious stones, but around the perimeter of a beautifully inlaid gold cross was a pattern of alternating coloured stones. The pattern was repeated around a square set in the axis. The stones looked like emeralds, rubies, sapphires and diamonds. Some were rounded and others like the diamonds were cut to a point. It was exquisite.

The cross itself was in the middle of the now shiny metallic box, the surface adorned with gold-coloured swirls. There were some patches of tarnished metal but not many. Gran had done a good job. The box measured eight inches by six inches, with a depth of about five inches. This, I was sure, was much more valuable than the chalice.

I praised my mum. 'Wow, Mum, you've done a great job there. It looks beautiful.'

George quietly nodded.

There was a knocking sound on glass in the hall. We all looked at each other, a bit shocked.

'Cover it, quick,' Mum said.

Gran frowned. 'Alice, we can't go on suspecting that everyone is a thief, dear.'

Nevertheless, Mum got a tea towel and flung it over the box before going to investigate the knocking.

She came back in, exasperated. 'That raven is perched on the window sill of the little window in the entrance hall. He's such a nuisance and looks really evil. We'll have to do something about it.'

'I know,' Gran said. 'Make sure he never gets in the house I suppose…God, that really is a possibility. He could harm us, I'm darn certain of that, but now, Alice, we must go to the hospital.'

'Yes what a good idea!' I was almost too enthusiastic. 'You can both catch early visiting then you won't tire Dad so much. Evening visiting has tired him out.'

Gran gave me that *'You're up to something'* look. As they put on their coats, she remembered something. 'Oh Tom, your mum and I will take the box because, as well as showing it to your dad, we have made an appointment to value it at the antiques place near the hospital.'

We three kids gaped with excitement. Soon, we will know how much the box is worth.

*

Gran and Mum left for the hospital.

Annabel, George and me simply climbed down the steps into the vault, each with a torch. The last bit of the puzzle remained, the little tunnel off to the left. We were all a bit nervous, now that we knew the dark mass or priest may in fact be threatening and there was a possibility of an onslaught of grit and stones. I had asked George what he thought caused this and hoped he would show some interest. He did. 'Apparently any noisy disturbance sets it off. Pure observation, I haven't read it anywhere.'

'Well observed, George. Shows you can learn things by other ways, rather than reading, eh?'

'Hmm...'

I told Annabel to wait with George while I investigated the small tunnel, as quietly as possible. The entrance was about three feet from the ground. George had the impression from when he was hiding there that it could be quite long.

As I crawled along the narrow passage, through rough gravel and ample dust, I could smell the stench of mould and decay. Woodlice scurried away from my torchlight and spiders' cobwebs stuck to my hair and face. *Ugh.* I wiped them quickly away and licked the dust from my lips.

Shining my torch ahead, I could see that the narrow passage bent slightly to the left. It was so small that I was practically crawling on my belly. I glanced behind me to see debris starting to fall from above. My nerve started to falter. I had visions of being buried alive and realised how people with claustrophobia suffered. I had to carry on.

The smell was now more like the cess pit. Of course: it must be close. I wondered if I'd be able to get out into the garden again by yet another route. The air had become so dank, thick and nauseating.

I reached another tiny vault just to the right and, focusing the torchlight slowly from left to right, the sight before me was breathtaking.

Nestled in the middle of the chamber, was a pile of blackened bones and two small skulls, obviously human bones. Huddled together...starvation maybe? Could these be the bones of the whispering children? But why were they buried down here? Were they trapped by accident, or had they been left here deliberately? Before death or afterwards?

I shouted George and Annabel. 'Come quick, come here.'

The bloody echo: *'Come here, quick.' quick...quick.'*

Forgetting the assumption that loud noises caused a swirl of grit, I cursed. The walls seemed to vibrate, but it wasn't just the grit flying everywhere. The sound of voices bounced off the walls resonating through the entire tunnel, which I imagined collapsing with the cacophony. Latin voices, the echo almost unbearable as it was so repetitive:

'*Libera nos, Sancta Pater...libera nos...Sancta Pater...libera nos...*'

Gritty debris was swirled upwards by force, just as a tornado does.

'STOP' I yelled, my hands covering my ears. 'STOP! STOP!'

I shielded my face from the sharpness of the pelts, gave a last look at the bones, and then headed down the passageway at full speed. My knees stinging from the bleeding of sharp grazes, I could only open my eyes for short flickers as grit continued to bombard me.

Almost like a miracle, immediately after the echo, the menacing Latin ceased and there was an uncanny calm.

I aimed the torch ahead but then I stopped, sharp. The beam of light revealed a dark shape hovering. The priest. I understood how the ancient gladiators felt when they entered the arena.

George's description of a poltergeist came to mind: '*A supernatural being supposedly responsible for physical disturbances such as loud noises and objects being moved around, even levitation. They can punch and kick and really hurt someone, if they want to, I've read it somewhere...*'

I had hated the racket in the tunnel, now I hated the silence. I crouched stiffly. So still, like a timid rabbit. Petrified. Then, slowly crawling towards the large chamber, I prepared myself to come face to face with the priest. The bombardment of dust and grit had blurred my vision, my eyes felt painfully sore. A muffled shout. It was repeated. There was a shaft of light ahead.

'Tom...why don't you answer us?'

Oh God, thank the Lord. It was George.

'Help me out of here. Quick!'

He and Annabel pulled me out of the tunnel and helped me climb the steps.

It was only when we got to the kitchen that I started shaking uncontrollably.

'Take some deep breaths, Tom. I know what it is: it's shock.'

At least that made me chuckle. 'I know, you read it somewhere.'

'Yeah…I did some first aid when Mum took me to the boy scouts. Everybody should learn it, but I wouldn't want to find anybody not breathing, 'cos you have to seal your mouth on theirs and keep blowing. Ugh, didn't like the sound o' that.'

'For a change, George, your babbling is making me feel better. Ha!'

Annabel got warm water and put some salt in it for my knee wounds. The trousers were rags, I had crawled that quickly.

When the shivering had stopped, I told them all about it.

'Two skulls, you say?' queried George. 'But they may not be of Tudor origin you know. How can you be sure they're not the bones of Victorian children, or even earlier this century?'

'Yeah, I had thought about that, but ask yourself, why would Victorian children whisper in Latin? Those are the bones of the children wanting to be let out. They wanted to escape and they were either deliberately buried there, or hidden there and no-one let them out. There was shouting, in Latin, *Libera Nos*, then the sancta pater bit, meaning "Free us, Holy Father".'

It's the spirits of those children and the priest was trying to get them out, Tom.'

Annabel offered her thoughts. 'Or maybe he imprisoned them down in the tunnel in the first place.'

'Well, whatever…but you do have to report the bones, Tom, otherwise you are breaking the law… I've…'

'I know: you've read it somewhere.'

At last he laughed.

Chapter Twenty-Nine

June 23rd 1958

Mum and Gran came home that evening about five pm.
I kept wincing with the sore knees, elbows and red eyes. I found some clean trousers and sweater to wear and hoped I looked okay. It didn't work.

'Tom, what happened to your eyes?'

'Just dust, Mum. They'll be better in the morning when I've slept. Don't fuss.'

She didn't keep on.

'How's Dad?'

'He's so much better. His memory is improving all the time and he seems more with it. He said tonight he was worried about the young lady and when I asked what young lady, he answered, *"The one I hit, Alice. She ran in front of the car. Really long haired woman. Did I kill her?"*

'We were amazed. But poor man, worrying himself about a woman who didn't even exist. We tried to explain he simply hit a tree because of the storm and missing the bend. Didn't like to say he was drunk.'

'Did he settle down?'

Mum shrugged. 'I think so. Difficult to tell. He badly wants to come home, but his mind is still a bit confused. Was a bit worried though about this young woman, but if there had really been one, surely the police would have found a body. No…he was just hallucinating.'

The really long hair bit made me think. It might well have been the same woman I saw above the flames on Bonfire night, but no way was I going to start something else, so I changed the subject. 'And what about the antique place, the evaluation?'

'Ooh, now that was interesting.'

Gran was lifting the box from her bag. We were all ears. 'Look' she demanded, 'This is how it opens; a small sliding compartment underneath shows a hidden catch. Hey presto. The antique dealer had seen something similar so knew what to do.'

We bent over the open box. Gran and Mum were smiling, in fact they were ecstatic. Gran's eyebrows were arched into her forehead as she asked, 'Enough for a good Christmas?'

Inside the box was dozens of coins, gold and silver among lots of tiny threads and fragments of cloth. Below these, it seemed, was a pile of dusty particles. Very puzzling. Below that were thin papers, but rolled up tightly.

Gran continued, 'The antique dealer had to wear gloves before carefully unrolling what she called parchments. The writing was tiny.'

Gran gave us a piece of paper. 'These are the words, in English too. They had a piece of equipment there which magnified the writing, making it easier to decipher. Read it Tom. Read it out loud.'

I took the paper from her and squinted as I read:

'I declare this chest is the sole property of Kathleen Melton and this is a true accounte of my work and sole duties as the healing woman for the Earl of Becton and his family. I have been a trusted servant for the last twelve years and to the villagers of Becton. I feel I have to defend my faith in my work as one man doth accuse me of ill doing.

'My heart doth ache with Mary's death. I do with honesty suspectt ceruse may be of a poisonous nature over time, but this was not known to me. Ye feverfew & lavender – 2-4 drops was of little use. Purging

& vinegar-solution – 4-5 drank with Ague & sourapples & berries & warm clarysage was of no benefit. Father Robert is partisan to my beliefs. It did not pleaseth me that this harmed Lady Mary. I cannot deny my duty failed, but of no foul intent to harm.

'*Ye Earl was poisoned by belladonna, plentiful in ye hedgerow. I could not save him.*

'*I fear my medicines will be my doom, my sin. This may have been a folly that Master Edward Griffin has indeed, upon my word, accused me thereof and to see me hang. It is he who is guilty of administering this poison. I can only pray to ye Holy Father, for those who stand in judgement may believe me.*

'*I have just done my humble duty. My children are innocent. Father Robert is innocent.*'

Gran said they had told the antique dealer about the treasures found in the house and the notes in the library book. Apparently the expert as Mum referred to her, had her own large books there, all about 'historical records and such'.

'She was very knowledgeable, Tom. She said Kathleen Melton was the accused witch. She had been afraid, but wanted to state her innocence to whoever found the box. All her medicine samples were once, hundreds of years ago, in that very box. The question she asked, though, was why was the box in the tunnel and filled with money?'

George now had a question. 'And what was ceruse and belladonna? I must admit I haven't read about those anywhere.'

That sounded very mature for George, admitting that he hadn't read something, but there were other things yet to discuss. The bones in the tiny chamber and the value of the so called medicine chest.

'So…did this expert give a figure on the worth of this medicine chest of Kathleen Melton?'

There was a pause, before Mum grinned. 'Wondered how long it would be before you got round to that. Well…' she paused again, this time to tease.

'Oh come on Mum, tell us.'

Yes, tell us!' yelled Annabel.

'Guess.'

'Oh no…£3,000?'

'Guess again.'

I grunted. 'Higher or lower?'

'Higher.'

Gran was giggling.

'Okay, £4,000?'

'All right, close. Its approximate value is something around £5,000 and the artefacts in the chest found in the kitchen would be about £2,000.'

'Ye Gods!' 'Blimey!' 'Ooh!' were our combined responses, all at once.

'I can't believe it.' I shook my head.

'Gran took photos of all that stuff and had the film developed last week. The antique dealer listed the items, but she said they would need to be seen before proper evaluations could be carried out. Anyway, this is the list:

'Discovered at Becton Manor, of Tudor origin, the following items were discovered in a large metal chest hidden behind a fireplace:

'Wrapped tightly in dark coarse cloth: priest's vestments and artefacts:

One long robe of heavy white material, lavishly decorated with gold and silver thread

One cape, in the colours red, purple and green, elaborately embroidered.

Two candlesticks,

One chalice,

One ciborium,

One paten,

Two flagons or cruets, one for the wine, the other for the water,

One monstrance,

One sanctuary lamp,

One tabernacle

One small plate.

Three embroidered cloths: a small square one (a pall for the purpose of covering the chalice or the ciborium during Holy Communion).

The second cloth was long and narrow—an altar cloth

The third was a rectangular piece of linen, not too big, for purification purposes.

At the very bottom of the long chest was a magnificent gold-coloured processional cross.

'We were advised not to handle the linens and robes as they will be delicate and thin in places, and to keep a black sheet wrapped tightly around them to exclude the air. In fact, one corner of the white robe was stained very yellow. Gran said it was probably the damp; perhaps that's why its hiding place was next to the large fireplace in the kitchen.'

'No-one better try and steal any of that stuff,' Gran declared. 'Or I'll chop off their fingers myself.'

'Now that does sound medieval, Gran.' Annabel grinned, 'but I have to say, I've never heard of those items and wouldn't have a clue, what they are used for.'

Of course, George offered some ideas, but floundered.

'Ha! You'll just have to read it somewhere George, then come back and tell us.'

'Very funny…but the bones?'

'Bones?' Mum repeated and Gran looked puzzled.

'Err, yes, Mum. My eyes are red because we went in the tunnel— one last time of course—and this time we found an extended bit, which led to a chamber. Well…in this little chamber, were the remains of two children: definitely two small skulls close together, as if hugging each other. Was really weird, especially to think they lived here.'

'Oh Tom.'

'We need to call the police, Alice,' a worried looking Gran said.

'The sooner, the better.'

'What, now? At this time of night?'

'Well, I think they may ask why we waited. Even though they must have been there some years, the police don't know that, do they? There will be investigations.'

'Ugh… imagine being buried alive.'

'But we don't know if they were actually buried alive.' I said.

'Tom, can you and George run down to the telephone box and ring the police? The number is on the wall in front of you. Here, take four pennies, you'll need them for the slot.'

Gran interrupted, 'Won't it be a 999, Alice? The bones could be the result of murder and as I said, nobody really knows how long they have been there. In which case Tom, you don't need those four pennies, just dial 999 and say you want the police, then tell them what you found.'

*

At first, because I was a kid I suppose, the police thought I was joking. They asked all sorts of details and checked them again and again. Another man came on the phone and said he was a sergeant. I had to start the story all over again. I remember thinking what would it have been like if anyone was actually being murdered at that very time. They wouldn't stand a chance of making it alive by Christmas, with all this questioning. I was rude. 'Well, are you coming or not, to see these bones?'

'Don't get cheeky, lad. We have details to take, it's our job.'

'So when are you coming?'

'Go back home lad and we'll send two policemen. You say these are ancient remains. Are you sure?'

'Oh, for God's sake.'

'Excuse me?'

'Never mind, we'll go back and wait for the policeman, thank you…very much.'

I put the receiver down and shook my head. 'That was a palaver,

George.'

*

It was way gone midnight when we heard the police car pull up. We all stayed up. It was pretty useless really, because the men just took more notes and decided they needed to come back when it was daylight, seeing as the bones were in a tunnel.

I told them to come back with someone small as a big person wouldn't get through the shaft. They at least left with the impression we didn't look like murderers. They did a lot of looking around however and asked us not to go out anywhere…as if.

Chapter Thirty

June 23rd 1598

Father Peters sighed with relief to finally arrive at the stables. Dawn would be upon them soon, but he could hear a rumpus from within the house. Jack and Ruth were still in the wagon.

He kept out of sight but peered through the bushes next to the stables and listened. He could hear the raucous shouting of lots of men amid loud bangs and the cracking of wood. Searchers. Griffin must have claimed that a priest was in hiding at the manor house. The scoundrel wanted no stone unturned; the man was obsessed with the devil.

He badly wanted to speak with Frances to tell her of his plan, but could not venture to the house.

He would need to stay hidden, but he woke the children and ushered them into the chapel, his finger on tightly sealed lips.

The secret chapel was a tiny room, about twelve feet by nine feet. It was carefully concealed behind the far wall of the stables, the wall being adorned with rope, saddles, bits, garden tools and old cloths.

The entry door was hidden behind one of the saddles and several cloths, and designed to blend in with the wall. It was well disguised. Father Peters knew exactly where the hinges were.

Nothing had to be removed in order to open it. Once they were safely inside the chapel, he heaved the altar to one side.

He removed the large carpet. Underneath was a trapdoor with a big metal hook. He took his staff and lifted the heavy slab. Still with his finger to his lips, he gestured to a dazed Jack and Ruth to quickly but quietly go down the steps into the tunnel. He gave the herb box to Jack.

'Look after it well.' He gave Ruth a lantern, but Jack was anxious.

'Father, what is that noise?'

'Searchers are inside the house, looking for me. Listen carefully...I will come for you. Stay put and stay quiet. If I am not here by tomorrow evening, follow the tunnel. There is a shaft at the far end with struts. Climb it. At the top, turn to your right into a tiny passage. Crawl to where the passage drops. The space is tiny but there is a metal pin near the floor. Slide it and then pull the wooden panel as hard as you can towards you. It's next to the fireplace in Oliver's bedroom at the end of the landing. If you can't open it, go back into the passage. It also leads to the front bedroom, the one Lady Charlotte keeps for guests. There is a metal trapdoor on the floor of the passage. Pull it hard. You will drop down into this bedroom. Frances will know about you. I will tell her when I get inside the house, when the searchers leave. She will look out for you. Do you understand?'

They nodded, but Jack was eager for news of his mother. The question Father Peters was dreading.

'There is no time, Jack, to explain it to you. You must go quickly. I will explain it all to you both tomorrow. Make haste, lad.'

Father Peters hugged them close and kissed them, then closed the trapdoor behind them, replacing the rug and the altar, but he was disturbed by a sudden thud in the near distance. Stopping to listen, he heard footsteps.

The horses were whinnying. It was still dark, but Father Peters dared not give himself any light. He hastily hid in the darkest corner; whoever it was, they were very near. He stood very still, waiting. For a few minutes, there was no sound. He knew he had closed the door of the chapel behind him, or at least he thought he had. He gingerly came out of the dark shadows. The door was slightly ajar. He had been careless. He started to close it slowly but as it scraped the stone floor he cringed and the door was flung back into his face with an almighty thud. Broad hands grabbed his throat and a deep, gruff voice growled into his left ear.

'So…this is where you heretics conduct your clandestine meetings, is it?'

Father Peters twisted his body and ducked sharply to free himself from the clutches of Edward Griffin. He tried to reach his staff, but Griffin grabbed his cloak and viciously pulled him close till their noses were almost touching. Griffin's eyes pierced those of Father Peters.

'Where is my money, you charlatan? You stole from me at the inn, and you have my money chest that was kept in my room at the Hall. I know you are scheming to pin the Lady Mary's death and that of the earl on me…to ruin me. Why after all would you protect the witch with whom you lived?'

Father Peters summoned all his spirit to give him new strength to fight this demon, but the journey had exhausted him. Nevertheless, he held his chin high. 'I do not have your money. Which in any case is the earl's money, money that you stole from him… And yes, I believe you did poison him. Kathleen was innocent. You are consumed by greed.'

'Ha! You…you have the audacity to call me a thief.' Griffin spotted the jewelled candlestick and picked it up. 'Isn't this part of the spoils of the monasteries? Eh? The jewels here and on that wretched witch's box are not yours, but belong to the Queen! You are answerable for your deeds, old man. Your days of secrecy are over. You should have been burnt along with your accomplice, now in purgatory, begging your God for forgiveness. You are not fit to call yourself a holy man!'

The priest saw a rage in Griffin's black stony eyes unlike anything he'd ever seen before. The man was a devil. He had to act quickly.

He brought up his right arm in a brilliant riposte, knocking the candlestick from Griffin's grasp.

Griffin, with equal speed, struck him across the face with the back of his hand. Father Peters stumbled but rose immediately, punched Griffin hard in the stomach and kneed him in the groin.

As Griffin doubled up in pain, Father Peters made for the chapel door but Griffin, groaning, straightened up and dashed towards the priest. He threw himself on his back, bringing him to the floor again.

Father Peters dug his elbows hard into Griffin's body and rolled himself over in an attempt to face him. He was too weak. He saw his staff within reach. Grabbing it, he swung it with an almighty strength at Griffin's legs, knocking him flat to the stone floor. Griffin yelled but wriggled under the table, pulling down the altar tapestry.

Father Peters knew this fight would have to end in the death of one or the other of them. He could not allow the discovery of the secret passage. Then Griffin jumped up and, wrapping his large hands tightly around the priest's neck, he pressed his thumbs into his throat.

The priest dropped the staff but he grabbed the keys that were attached to his belt and, with his right hand, plunged them Griffin's left eye, then kneed him in the groin. Griffin doubled in pain as blood surged from his left eye. Father Peters picked up his staff again and, gripping it with both hands, brought it back behind him, ready to deliver a heavy blow to Griffin's head which was still bent low and facing the ground.

Before he wielded the staff, he looked down at Griffin, whose punctured eye was full of blood, squinting and demonic. Father Peters gave a beast-like roar before he cursed him:

'Misery will haunt thee, brother, in this life and the next. I curse thee with eternal claws, corvus; thou will never get thou hands on what belongs to me.'

As he finished the curse, he brought back the staff once more to wield it with force.

A soft voice from below ground distracted him.

'Father?'

Griffin, with his one good eye, noticed the hesitation and the slight fall of the staff. He grabbed the priest's ankles, knocking him over towards the stone altar.

A cracking sound from the ground could be heard just before the altar began to tip over. Griffin had dodged the striking staff and he rolled quickly out from beneath the collapsing table. Father Peters was slumped across it, blood pouring from his head.

Shielding his bloody eye, Griffin looked up. There in the darkness was Anne, her arms shaking. She was stood with the heavy candlestick in both hands, high above her head, as if ready to strike a second time. She stared wildly at the priest's lifeless body, lying still on the crumpled tapestry.

She shook violently as she watched the fabric soak up the blood of the priest.

Griffin had no time for emotions. He cursed that he had not got his money and he cursed the commotions in the house, by the searchers. Just for a moment he wondered what had distracted the priest and thought he had heard a sound, but he had no time to investigate.

'Quick, get the horses!'

Anne remained in the same position, a stunned mute but shaking uncontrollably. 'Act, woman, act! For God's sake, we have to leave now!' He grabbed her. 'Listen to me! It needed to be done. I haven't got my money but we have to leave, now.'

'I killed…I killed the priest. I killed Father Peters. Oh Lord, forgive me. Forgive me!' she wailed.

Griffin was becoming impatient. 'Enough…enough of this hysteria! Quiet, woman. Fetch the horses, before that wretched Ged appears. And take the candlestick. Put it under your kirtle. Now, woman!' Anne could not stop whimpering and trembling but she did as she was told. She must not faint.

The searchers were still working in the house, but some sounds were those of men outside.

They had to hurry. The horses whinnied again. Griffin looked up at the house. A man appeared to be looking out of the window. There was candlelight in the room. As he calmed the horses, he gazed up at the window. He hoped and prayed that they could not be seen in the darkness. Anne also saw the man.

'Edward, Master Gilbert is in the house. He will see us.'

'Get on your horse. Now, now!' a frantic Edward Griffin was shouting to Anne. She obeyed. She would always have to obey, from here on.

Chapter Thirty-One

In the Early Hours of Midsummer's Day, 1958

Mum and Gran didn't mind George staying over again on that Saturday evening. It had been a long eventful day and we were surprised that neither his mum nor dad had come to collect him. I think they felt sorry for him since the botched burglary, following Arthur's behaviour and knowing his parents argued a lot. I don't know to this day if the lack of communication was worse for George than the knowledge of his dad scheming the theft. I wondered if the other men had told their wives what had happened that night, and imagined the after-affects in their homes.

At almost two o'clock on the Sunday morning, after the police had left, nobody cared about anything but getting to sleep. It was pretty nice though to think we were going to bed rich, after those evaluations.

Once under my bed covers, I frequently stared at the secret panel or imagined the boy in breeches might appear, but I was so tired this time and my eyes still very sore, that I went straight to sleep.

I heard heavy footsteps coming up the stairs and along the landing. I looked over at the door just as a tall, broad-shouldered man in a hat and huge boots appeared. He strode over towards the fireplace where a woman sat in a rocking chair: the same rocking chair that had so unsettled me on the first night I'd slept here.

'Where is he?' the man yelled.

The woman's voice cried out. 'I don't know, sir. There is no one here.' I watched in horror as the man raised his arm and struck her.

'NO!' I yelled, sitting bolt upright. I looked for the man and the woman: no one, just George in the room, stirring in his sleeping bag because of me yelling.

It must have been a dream.

It had been a muggy day and it was now followed by a bad storm.

A great bolt of lightning illuminated the bedroom. Then, as I was just sitting up in bed, a great roll of thunder rumbled above.

Rain lashed the window. We had never bothered to close the curtains, going to bed so late. Down by the summer house, I saw a light flicker. Who would be down there with a torch, this time of night, in this weather? Not another burglary, surely?

George picked up the torch. We always had one, in case we wanted to use the chamber pot at night. He opened the window of my room, flinching at the onslaught of rain belting him and bouncing off the window sill. The shaft of his torchlight scanned the garden from left to right. He saw no one. 'Are you still asleep and dreaming, Tom?'

'No, I am fully awake.'

The words had hardly left my mouth, when the sound of doors being opened and immediately slammed shut again, reverberated throughout the house. This was scarier than thunder. Someone or something was inside our house.

'What's happening?' a troubled Gran asked as she hobbled from her room, walking stick in hand, not yet focusing, as she stood in the bedroom doorway.

As we went along the landing, we could hear pots, pans and plates being smashed in the kitchen. Mickey was barking furiously. *Please don't hurt Mickey*, I thought. By now, Mum and Annabel had come rushing out of their rooms.

The thunderstorm outside was relentless.

What was happening within our walls was worse.

'There must be some windows open somewhere,' Mum shouted as she followed us down the stairs, but this was caused by much more than an open window. A storm of a very different nature was at full throttle inside our house.

Annabel hovered on the landing, panic-stricken. 'Oh no! Is it burglars again?'

Outside, the rain was ferocious, but it was difficult to distinguish the sound of it on the windows and the sound of continuous smashing of objects, doors slamming on the inside and constant banging that panicked us.

The scene became horrendous when the kitchen door flew open and a multitude of pots and pans whizzed through the air by some unbelievable, sinister force.

'Oh my God, Oh my God! Get back, get back up the stairs!' Gran yelled, but not being able to run she held on to the table in the hall. Despite her instructions, we all came downstairs by holding tightly onto the banister. Gran's support table flew off her hand and into the air. She grabbed the spindles.

'Poltergeists!' yelled George.

It wasn't just pots and pans, but buckets, brooms, cups and plates from the Welsh dresser, coats and umbrellas and smaller items like notepaper and pens. They flew through the air, propelled by this remorseless strength.

Some china smashed against the walls of the hallway, crashing to the floor or even into each other, landing in hundreds of shattered pieces. The debris was now suddenly illuminated by another flash of lightning.

Annabel was crouching low, still on the landing. Mum was holding onto Gran and I was trying to get across to the kitchen. I couldn't see Mickey. I called him several times until finally he appeared but ran back into the dining room, to seek refuge under the big table. At least that wasn't moving. Annabel was shouting, but was hardly audible.

It lasted about five agonising minutes. Everything that sailed in the air, dropped to the floor. Complete and unbelievable silence. We crept out one by one and beckoned each other to safety.

Mum hugged Gran tightly, 'Are you okay, Mum?'

'Yes, dear. But you know what? It's that day isn't it? The reason for other families leaving this house. The reason Uncle Charles said *"strange things happened"*. It's the eve of Midsummer's Day. We forgot about the folklore.'

Mum, surveying the damage and strewn objects, was in tears. 'We chose not to believe silly legends. Why? Why?'

No one could answer her.

The only thing moving was dust, lots of it. It was horrific.

'This is like the blitz again,' said Gran. 'Alice, don't tread on that broken glass with bare feet.' Mum shed inconsolable tears, covering her face with her hands.

I think we all had bare feet that night. Tiptoeing gingerly to the far end of the kitchen, I spotted more glass all over the floor. The weak panes in the French doors had all collapsed.

I looked out. It wasn't that clear, but it looked like a hooded figure by the summer house. I was about to shout something, when I heard mum's heartbroken cries and decided to keep the vision to myself, but it didn't stop me going out of the still rickety French doors towards the figure. It faced me, and I told myself it was just a big shrub, until it glided. The priest.

'It's not your doing. They will have a proper Catholic burial, you'll see.'

An eerie silence. Midsummer Night's eve. I went back in the house.

George was sweeping. What a task. There were thousands of pieces of broken crockery, frying pans, saucepans and kitchen utensils: all had been mercilessly strewn and dumped.

It reminded me of the aftermath of a tidal wave.

Now, having located something to put on our feet, we all picked things up; Annabel had brought some rubbish bags. It would take forever. Gran had managed to boil water and make Mum some tea in an unbroken cup. No doubt Gran had searched for the whisky.

I hoped the bottle had escaped being chucked and smashed on the floor. They were sitting on chairs that they had to turn the right way up and just taking it all in, unable to speak, while we cleaned up. Mickey was let outside, to save his paws from being cut. He had been terrified.

Mum said she hated the house and nothing had gone right since we had arrived. I'd hated the house too, last summer, but now I never wanted to leave, in spite of all this.

Mum rose from the chair wearily and paced slowly around the rooms, touching things she'd valued, things she'd asked the delivery men almost a year ago to be so careful with, now all broken.

I worried for her. She had been through such a lot, with Dad and everything.

'I'm not sure if Dad renewed the insurance policy,' she said softly to herself as she surveyed the damage.

Mum watched Gran bag some treasured pieces of plates, cups and saucers from a set she and Dad had been given as a wedding present. Tears trickled from under her dark lashes and I suddenly recalled the excitement she felt when she first saw Becton Manor, almost skipping around it, like a little girl.

Gran, practical as ever, comforted her.

'Look…they're just things. We have the money now, if we sell the chalice alone, to buy an even posher set. What matters is not material things, Alice, but that we're all safe. And soon Albert will be completely well again and able to come home. We will get over this. We are a stoic lot: we all learned how to be during the war.'

It did the trick. Mum nodded, 'Yes, you're right, no reason to be miserable. But I can't face that again.' She fixed her gaze on Gran, 'Not one more night like that. Besides, if we bought a new set, come next June, it would just get smashed. We must be stupid to live here, Mum, absolutely stupid.'

Chapter Thirty-Two

June 24th 1958

Dawn was breaking. A beautiful hazy sunshine filtered through the windows on that Sunday morning. It was a relief it was June and not January, with every pane of glass shattered from the effects of the 'poltergeist'. More likely it was the work of several of them, looking at the state of the rooms. We were still sweeping and bagging up broken glass, crockery and other things, all now deemed as rubbish. Mum had calmed down but the look of disgust and hatred for the house was evident.

Two constables and another man in a suit came to the house early, about nine o'clock. One of the constables was a petite woman. She would probably fit in the tunnel, but assessing whether she would crawl on her hands and knees was another question.

We hadn't been back to bed, so we were all sleep-deprived and, by the look on their faces, they noticed.

After formal introductions, they took pens and paper from their bags. The policeman was called PC Andrews, the woman PC Wilcox, and the man in the suit was a forensic archaeologist called Marcus Sampson. He was about thirty and a 'know-all.'

They were astonished at the state of the house and the broken windows. When we related all that had happened, PC Andrews had so many pages of notes that his pen ran dry.

We had a job to find him another. Pens could have landed anywhere. Upstairs was nowhere near as bad, however, and Annabel brought him one from her school satchel. He drank no less than three cups of tea, by which time, he was looking flustered, his paperwork was so disorganised.

George had been studying him and now said he wasn't going to be a copper when he left school: far too much writing.

The three of them occasionally had little chats that obviously weren't for our ears, but then one or the other would turn to us and summarise what they had been discussing.

Marcus Sampson explained that the bones, although apparently bones of antiquity, still presented a case for a criminal investigation. Mum's eyebrows were raised when he further mentioned that murder had to be ruled out.

They had brought photographic equipment, wanting to photograph the bones and the area. As they were quite smartly dressed in dark suits, the image of them crawling through the shaft amused me no end.

When at last Marcus Sampson was satisfied that he had obtained sufficient data, he explained to us that all discovered human remains have to be reported to the coroner's office.

Of course, it was necessary to liaise with the criminal team, just to rule out a murder…and that was the reason for PC Andrews's presence. But he emphasised, noticing Mum and Gran's concern, 'I'm sure they are simply bones of antiquity. There are ways of establishing the age of bones and we also take samples of the surrounding soil or debris. It's a balance of scientific and contextual evidence.'

Mum, Gran and Annabel nodded, but I was unsure how much of that had sunk in. Then they asked for somewhere they could get changed. It would just be PC Wilcox and himself. Ah, I was beginning to be impressed.

We went to the iron sheeting. It was only loosely placed now. I offered to show them the way into the far chamber but they wanted to go it alone, muttering something about safety. Yeah, tell me about it.

I had warned them not to talk while down there, lest they cause the release of grit and stones by vibration. I didn't mention spirits.

They didn't listen. Marcus Sampson got stuck and started shouting to PC Wilcox, to go back. It was too late.

Swirls of grit and other debris erupted from the tunnel. Why was I grinning? PC Wilcox was shaking as she emerged: normally a brunette, she was now a dusty grey. Marcus Sampson was demonstrating being flustered on the job.

Gasping, he managed to say how tiny it was down there, how he had forgotten his claustrophobic tendencies and how he never realised the extent to which vibrations could cause a potential collapse of a tunnel.

Well, I did say. After checking his photographic equipment, he was pleased it wasn't damaged. 'We will have to come back, I'm afraid.'

You don't say.

Mum apologised we didn't have a bathroom.

'It doesn't matter,' smiled PC Wilcox, but I think it did.

When they were back in their own clean clothes, Marcus Sampson said he would send a letter to us with the date of the next visit and be much more prepared.

Later on that day, George's mum came to take George home. He reluctantly left. She had said sorry about 'the incident' but declined to come in for tea.

It was all a bit quick and impersonal after all we had been through.

We all missed him. He was like part of the family. But there was so much to do in terms of tidying up and arranging for somebody to repair all the damaged windows.

Mum mentioned that we should talk to the local Catholic priest. She thought it was a good idea for a blessing. It might help prevent future turmoil.

So she donned her best hat—whatever for, I don't know—and she and Gran visited Father Terence Henderson. He understood, agreed, and said he would phone the police to arrange a suitable Sunday. Being a religious figure, he had a phone, lucky man; he didn't have to run to a red box every time he wanted to reach someone quickly.

*

I didn't want to go to school on the Monday except to see George. His parents were going to get a divorce. It had been rough going for years but he didn't want to say much so I didn't push it, but to take his mind off his home troubles I got a library book out at lunchtime and, in Science, our project was simple.

I placed a large Science and Nature book over the top of an encyclopaedia, just in case Mr Pearson, the teacher caught us. Quiet research and project work all afternoon. Brilliant.

We searched the encyclopaedia for information on ceruse, white lead make-up and belladonna. We discovered the lead mixture over a period of time caused lead poisoning: the symptoms being weakness, mental confusion, and seizures. The worst-case scenario being death, especially for children.

'That's amazing. If this Mary wore that white stuff, she could have died from lead poisoning.' said George. 'Kathleen Melton had provided her with the powders and that's why she says her heart has broken. She blames her medicines and also her faith on her possible downfall, but also says this Edward Griffin is to blame.'

I was glad he referred to this information as amazing and hoped he was returning to normal. He began to search the index pages for belladonna. After he had read the few paragraphs, muttering under his breath, he offered his theory:

'It's a highly poisonous plant, growing in some hedgerows. Its other name is Deadly Nightshade. Very likely the plant that poisoned the Earl of Becton.'

Mr Pearson was looking at us.

George smiled, 'A good lesson sir, very interesting.' Mr Pearson frowned. We looked down and stifled giggles.

*

A letter arrived a few days later to say Marcus Sampson would visit again on Sunday July 27th to take away the bones. Permission to exhume with the purpose of a sacred burial was sanctioned.

He had received notification that, on the same afternoon, there would be a ceremony by the local priest, Terence Henderson to bless the house following the exhumation.

On Friday July 25th, the first day of our school holidays, PC Andrews came to the house, wielding a letter: or rather, a report.

'It's from the County Records Department in Matlock. They have a few parish records from the late sixteenth century. From 1597, a copy of all parish records had to be made and they were sent to the Bishop of Derby. Many, though, were chewed up by mice or rats or destroyed by the elements: mainly damp. You're lucky... Copies of the records for your house were kept almost pristine, in metal boxes.

'It seems a Father Robert Peters was murdered at this property: in the stables. He sustained a fatal head injury on the night of June 23rd, 1598. They never found the culprit, but about six years later a gardener by the name of Ged Connor, eager to go to Heaven and not hell, confessed on his deathbed that he had seen a man and a woman steal horses from the stable after killing the priest. He thought he heard children crying but he had dismissed it. He said nothing at the time because he was sure the man was the family tutor: a Master Edward Griffin. A man he was afraid of.

'It also states in the records that the Earl of Becton's brother wanted the tutor arrested for embezzlement, but he was never found. The earl's widow, Lady Charlotte, moved to London with her son Oliver, leaving this brother-in-law—Gilbert Harrison Esquire—to act as caretaker of the estate, but he died before the gardener's confession. Lady Charlotte died about two years after moving to London and there is no record of what happened to the son, Oliver. Which is strange, because Oliver would have inherited the house and land. It's assumed therefore that Oliver met his end, somehow.'

He paused to check if we were taking it all in. The silence confirmed that we were certainly doing a lot of thinking. I needed to summarise.

'Edward Griffin murdered Father Peters? And...the gardener thought he had heard children, but dismissed it. I don't think the boy ghost was Oliver because he went off to London with his mother and apparently never returned. Strange, I had a vivid dream that a boy dressed in Tudor style clothes ask me if I was Oliver. So...I think the boy ghost is Jack: the other bones belong to his sister.'

'I'm astounded.' Mum whispered, nodding her head.

'Perhaps that is all accurate, Tom. So you have quite a history here, Mrs Winchett ...once the bones have been analysed, Tom, you will know if you have a boy and a girl down there, won't you?'

'Yes, it seems so.'

'Oh those poor children.' Gran shook her head. 'Where will the bones be taken to?'

PC Andrews told us they would go to the mortuary, where they would have all sorts of tests on them to ascertain the age, gender, the approximate time of death, the cause of death, and so on. With such old bones, it may not be too easy because of decomposition, or scavengers.

Annabel was curious. 'Scavengers?'

'Yes,' he said. 'Insects down there, things that want to eat dead flesh.'

'Ugh.'

Gran was also curious.

'How do they find out the age and the sex?'

'Well, the state of the teeth are a giveaway. Young people's teeth are much better and they have more of them. Bones have joins in them and children may have fissures: that's little cracks that indicate more growing to do. Regarding gender, the pelvis on a female is bigger, the skulls would be different. The actual age of the bones can be measured by the mineral deposits in them, mostly carbon, I think, but I'm not the expert.'

'Hmm,' she said. 'Interesting stuff.'

'Yes,' said the policeman. 'I wanted to ask you if I could be at the service on Sunday when the forensic people take away the bones. I understand the priest has recommended a blessing. It's not a work request, I'm off duty. Just fascinated by your story.' He was smiling at Mum, eager for her response.

'Yes, the priest is coming to do a blessing. Seems appropriate, maybe a bit of insurance, to stop it happening again. Of course I don't mind if you attend.'

Annabel and I both asked if George could come and Mum agreed.

*

George was allowed to stay over. We didn't sleep much: excitement, I suppose, in anticipation of the following day's event.

When we arrived at our house, from picking up George, the smell of dinner was so welcoming. Gran had made a lovely shepherd's pie, to be followed by an apple pie. George never had home cooking and his expression of pleasure and appreciation always pleased Mum and Gran.

After dinner, we all talked and talked and talked about the last year at Becton Manor, about Dad's accident and recovery, the whisperings, the priest's holes and tunnels and the treasure.

We hadn't yet mentioned that to the police. We debated whether we needed to disclose everything that we had discovered. Mum thought that we should. I mooted giving up the herb box for burial with the bones and Annabel said we should at least hold it during the removal of the bones as a sign of respect, but she was adamant that we keep all the treasure.

'Well why not? It was all found on our property.'

Mum and Gran nodded. They then discussed whether we should sell the items. I really didn't want to, unless it became necessary…but, I did tell George he would be a beneficiary.

I couldn't quite decide whether the glee on his face was greater than when he knew he would be eating a grand supper. In any case, the old George seemed to be coming back.

*

Marcus Sampson and a female colleague, called Sally Barnes, arrived to remove the bones, as planned on the afternoon of Sunday, July 27th.

Sally was petite and athletic looking and I wondered if that's why she'd landed this job. She looked like she might be up for it. By this time, I could pretty much put my money on who would make it to the end of the tunnel and back. No one had ventured down the first way we found, climbing down that shaft from Gran's room and through the tunnel's foul water. This entrance had been a great find and I was proud of that.

Sally and Marcus were shown into different rooms to put on their overalls. We waited for Father Terence Henderson and PC Andrews to arrive. Mum was anxiously looking out of the window.

'The priest is here,' she announced. 'And he looks rather grand.' She excitedly walked to the front door. The priest did look grand. He was dressed in full white robes with a clerical collar of purple and green, a gently swaying beautiful gold pendant hanging around his neck.

He was accompanied by an assistant: a short, serious-looking man with a dark moustache and flat well-parted hair. I thought he looked like Adolf Hitler, but no…can't be.

My mum greeted them and they quickly entered, the priest shaking my mum's hand and that of my Gran. Then, surprisingly, I thought, he took notice of us, a broad smile on his face. He shook the hands of Annabel, George and I. At last, someone who had respect for young people.

Gran asked them to sit down and it was just at that point that PC Andrews arrived. He apologised for being late but was pleased to hear the explanation of the blessing procedure. 'Adolf' had all the equipment in a large leather bag. He proceeded to withdraw a thurible, a cross and a flagon of holy water.

I'm sure George was thinking what I was thinking: about the religious artefacts found in the chest near the kitchen fireplace.

The service, Father Henderson said, would not take long but would involve prayers of deliverance, to bless our house and the garden, with the intention of driving out demons.

There were more introductions, when the forensic archaeologists came out of their 'changing rooms' wearing their work overalls, Sally with her head covered. Marcus must have warned her.

Then, as if we were on a crusade, we all set off to the tunnel's entrance. A breeze was stirring but it was still quite warm, about four o'clock in the afternoon.

Marcus and Sally started their descent. We would wait until they returned with the bones.

I didn't like it. Something was amiss. The aura moment was too eerie. The skies went dark as if we were about to experience the biggest storm ever; it was more like the darkness of midnight rather than four o'clock.

A sudden gust of cold wind blew some dust and grit into the air. It caught our attention. Father Henderson said he hadn't thought it was going to rain this evening and he smiled. He was so calm. The way he spoke and his demeanour made you feel very peaceful.

Then…grit and gravel swirled upwards from the tunnel aperture, the way a tornado does and spread itself among us. A series of explosions were heard from below. Mum and Gran held one another.

PC Andrews was agitated. 'Get out of there, quickly!' he yelled, covering his face as he shouted down the hole to the forensic people.

We heard cries for help. Sally was screeching. She emerged, breathless, dishevelled, dirty and in total panic. She scrambled out, gasping, as she faced the policeman.

'There's something evil down there. It was awful. There are

more bones, but I was scared. Marcus is still there, trying to bag them up, but it's not good. It's so threatening and claustrophobic.'

Well, I thought, *what did you expect of an underground tunnel and vault?'*

PC Andrews yelled again into the tunnel.

No sign of Marcus. Although he wasn't supposed to be on duty, I guess he felt like he was at that moment. What could have happened to the forensic archaeologist?

George confirmed that he too, thought PC Andrews was in 'copper' mode.

George, Annabel and I looked at one another knowingly. 'I'll go,' I said.

'No, it's too dangerous for you,' PC Andrews said firmly.

Mum, having never seen the flying debris, was worried. 'He's right, Tom. You can't go down. It might cave in or something.'

Annabel and George added their support. 'He'll be fine, let him go.'

Amid the group's hesitation, I took a bag and gloves from Sally and climbed down. I chanted my learned Latin, repeating it all the way through the small tunnel. When I reached the end, Marcus was huddled, his arms covering his face. 'Does it ever stop?' he yelled, as he saw me approach.

I stopped chanting and looked at the bones, then in English, I said loudly, above the din: 'You can be free, Jack. Father Peters is waiting for you both.'

The silence that followed was surreal. Marcus stared at me. No swirling, no debris, nothing but calm. No dark shape, no eerie feelings. Just an odd sense of peace, an aura.

In the chamber, I put on the gloves and gently picked up the remaining bones. I couldn't stop tears falling. It was so unexpected an emotion, but now I felt I knew them.

*

Marcus joined me in carefully removing the bones. He was quite a sight, poor man. Covered in grey dust from head to toe, with red patches and traces of blood on his face; the bombardment of grit and debris had stripped him of any composure. He admitted to me that he had never experienced anything like that before, and he was fair trembling.

As we climbed out to meet the others, with the skeletons in our possession, the darkness was foreboding. All seemed visibly relieved to see us, however…with the exception of a new arrival… in flight. The raven.

The wingspan was daunting and I could see that Father Henderson was troubled by him, as the bird made his familiar *'prok'* sound and then, unbelievably, perched right on top of the herb box, which I had left on the ground. He pecked at the jewels.

Annabel went to scare it away but suddenly it pecked her face until blood appeared. 'Ouch,' she called out, wiping her cheek. Gran, Mum and George then ran at it, Mum waving a stick. It briefly flew upwards, but came back to swoop at all of us, trying to peck at anything that got near it.

Father Henderson lost his calm exterior and was now a flustered bag of nerves, trying to wave his cross at the bird, but going hopelessly dizzy. Marcus was protecting Sally, and George and Annabel were helping me to fight him off.

Gran offered Father Henderson her hip flask, expecting a refusal.

'Would you like some brandy?'

He took a large swig.

Corvus was relentless. We kept on ducking, but it was the herb box he was drawn to. Incredibly, the box lifted from the ground as Corvus shoved his beak under the lid. Father Henderson grabbed Gran's flask, taking another swig.

I approached it and pulled the box away. In a rage and squawking, he dived at my face. I wouldn't put the box down but he forced me to crouch over, in an attempt to protect the box and my face. He started to peck the back of my neck.

PC Andrews, wearing thick gloves, rushed forward and grabbed the bird. It turned on him but he managed to pin it down on the ground with a large stone, before thrashing it a couple of times. Then he flicked out a pen knife from his pocket and slit its throat. We all stood, stunned as blood spurted and feathers were scattered.

Gran couldn't help herself, 'Oh Jesus Christ.' Then gasped again as she realised her blasphemy and muttered, 'Sorry Father,'

I turned to the priest.

'Please hurry. Please complete the blessing.'

A speechless Father Henderson was gaping and quivering, 'Er...er...' He lifted the processional cross high in the air and began to conduct the blessing. His bottom lip quivered as he rushed through the prayer:

'We pray for deliverance...in the name of Jesus Christ. We.... pray that the demons who beset this house, will be cast out forever. We pray for God's blessing.'

He stopped to check that the bird was motionless before throwing holy water over the entrance to the tunnel. Then he spoke again, 'Peace be with you...eternal peace...and no more... suffering. Peace be...with the children who... are now...free. God...rest their souls. Peace in this house and in this garden.'

He looked again at the bird, before Adolf gave him the thurible, which contained the lit charcoal and now the burning of the incense. He chanted as he swung the thurible on its three delicate chains, scented smoke dispersing.

'May the blessing of our almighty God, the Father and the Son and the Holy Spirit be with you, for ever and ever.'

Again he looked at Corvus as if he expected the bird to rise at any moment. He then gulped and continued, 'Be damned, you of all evil intent, be gone from this world. God Bless those affected by your sins. Leave, in the name of Jesus Christ.'

He paused to look at the corpse of the bird, before repeating, 'Leave now, in the name of our Lord. Amen.' He kept crossing himself and muttering before he gasped deeply for breath. 'We will... say... the... Lord's Prayer.'

We did so, but it was difficult to keep our heads down, even though Corvus had been killed. The priest crossed himself again. 'Blessed be the name of the Lord. Amen.'

We repeated, 'Blessed be the name of the Lord, Amen.'

There was a calmness, a tranquillity that I had experienced briefly in the tunnel with the bones.

The darkness lifted, the air became warm. Gran squeezed Mum's hand and hugged her.

For me, those words heard in a dream resonated:

'Misery will haunt thee, brother, in this life and the next. I curse thee with the claws of the Corvus; thou will never get thy hands on what belongs to me.'

'It's all over, George. It couldn't have been done without you, babble bum!' I whispered after the prayers.

George laughed. 'You're welcome. I'll never forget all this Tom, ever. It's funny, but I feel different, sort of grown up.' There was a pause before he added, 'I didn't think Corvus was the priest. I thought he was Edward Griffin. I read somewhere…'

'Not now, George. I already worked it out…'

George smirked. 'Well, he didn't get away, did he? He had to live as a bird for nearly four hundred years, still wanting the treasure. But first he had to die, didn't he? So when did he die? I've read somewhere about reincarnation, it could be that…'

'Not now, George…'

After the blessing, Gran, with Mum and Annabel's help, made tea for everyone, Gran managing to keep her cup, laced with whisky, separate from the others.

Inside, there was a lot of discussion regarding where we went from here. The forensic archaeologists had made a good job of getting cleaned up and were back to normal. Marcus was pretty certain that the bones belonged to a young boy and a young girl. He then joked that he was going to ask for danger money the next time a similar assignment comes his way. I was thinking that sort of work, if well-paid, would be well-suited to me and George. We would make a good team.

PC Andrews was bragging about his 'kill'. 'He won't bother you anymore that's for sure.'

The body of the raven was still out there: fodder for something wild in the next few days, no doubt. Didn't fancy burying it.

Mum was looking forward to Dad being discharged from the hospital in the very near future. Some therapy needed, but almost as good as new.

I was thankful for the box still being with me. I had intended it to go with the bones; I hadn't decided.

When all the professionals had gone, there was an eerie silence. Another aura moment. I knew exactly what an aura was now. Not only had George matured, but I had. I had grown up in that year. I looked down at the box, still in my hand. Yes, I would keep it after all…

The next day, I looked for Corvus on the spot where he laid slain…nothing, not even a single black feather.

'Misery will haunt thee, brother,
in this life and the next.'

The End

Did You Enjoy This Book?

If so, you can make a HUGE difference

For any author, the single most important way we have of getting our books noticed is a really simple one—and one which you can help with.

Yes, you.

Us indie authors and publishers don't have the financial muscle of the big guys to take out full-page ads in the newspaper or put posters on the subway.

But we do have something much more powerful and effective than that, and it's something that those big publishers would kill to get their hands on.

A committed and loyal bunch of readers.

Honest reviews of our books help bring them to the attention of other readers.

If you've enjoyed this book I would be really grateful if you could spend just a couple of minutes leaving a review (it can be as short as you like) on this book's page on your favourite store and website.

Thank you so much—you're awesome, each and every one of you.

Warm regards

Patricia

Historical Notes

Although Queen Elizabeth 1st had tolerated the religious differences of the times, in her later years, it is well documented that she was nervous and fearful of the conspiracies against her by the Jesuits.

Richard Topcliffe was her chief of operations, who held the responsibility to seek out those conspirators, but he was a cruel and ruthless investigator.

Francis Walsingham was the chief secretary of state from 1573 to 1590. He was a devout Protestant and a cunning spymaster, to whom the Queen turned in times of threat and potential treason. In the end, however, it is documented that she felt trapped into condemning Catholics to their death and was mortified following the sentence to death of her cousin, Mary Queen of Scots.

Saint Nicholas Owen was a trained carpenter and joiner as well as a Jesuit priest and devised many of the hiding places in the larger Catholic households. Tortured to death in the Tower of London, he was honoured as a martyr by the Catholic Church and canonised by Pope Paul VI in 1970.

All other remaining characters are fictitious. Reference to practices, speech and lifestyle of the period are close to accuracy, having been thoroughly researched, but who can, hand on heart, determine what facts are one hundred percent true?

There is an abundance of literature pertaining to the division of social classes. The Sumptuary Laws, for example, reveal what the different social ranks could wear. Crown princes, Kings and Queens were in fact believed to be born privileged and second only to God.

With regard to the greed of Edward Griffin, there was indeed a new wave of higher status gentry achieving recognition from acquired wealth, particularly from sheep farming on the recent enclosures of arable land.

The Earl of Becton would no doubt have had a much larger staff than is documented in my story, but for the purpose of character building this was deliberately kept low.

The study of antidotes for suspected cases of poisoning was becoming popular in the late sixteenth century. Although toxic ingested substances were on the whole accidental, in political circles, cases of deliberate poisoning was still around as it had been since the Middle Ages and continued to be feared.

Wise women or 'Herb women' did indeed experiment with plants and herbs thought to cure common ailments. Witchcraft was an offence punishable by drowning or burning at the stake but unlike Kathleen Melton, the crime victim was likely to have been beaten unconscious or strangled before her body was burned. Scotland hosted most of the burnings of witches.

A Few Tudor Properties with Identified Priest Holes

Coughton Court in Warwickshire. The home of the Throckmorton family. The hole is disguised in the turret. (National Trust)

Harvington Hall in Worcestershire, contains about seven priest holes.

Oxburgh Hall, in Norfolk. Mary, Queen of Scots was once imprisoned there. (National Trust)

Baddesley Clinton in Warwickshire. The house was said to have held a secret Jesuit conference that was raided. (National Trust)

Other Tudor Houses to Visit

Hardwick Hall, Doe Lea, Derbyshire. The home of Bess of Hardwick. (National Trust)
Rufford Old Hall, Lancashire (National Trust)
Hampton Court Palace, London
Anne Hathaway's Cottage, Stratford
Bradley, Newton Abbot, Devon (National Trust)
The Old Manor, Ashbourne, Derbyshire (National Trust)
Sudbury Hall, Ashbourne, Derbyshire (National Trust)
Greys Court, Oxfordshire (National Trust)
Cotehele, Cornwall (National Trust)
Trerice, Cornwall (National Trust)
Montacute House, Somerset (National Trust).
Longleat House, Wiltshire
Burghley House, Peterborough
Moreton Corbet Castle, Shropshire (English Heritage)
Old Gorhambury House, (remains of), Hertfordshire (English Heritage)
Kenilworth Castle, Warwickshire. (English Heritage)
Kirby Hall, Northamptonshire. (English Heritage)
Lyddington Bede House, Leicestershire. (English Heritage)
Apethorpe Palace, Northamptonshire (English Heritage)
Hill Hall, Essex. (English Heritage)

Patricia Ayling

Portland Castle, Dorset. (English Heritage)

Acknowledgements

First and foremost, to my husband Len, who has painstakingly read all my drafts (and there have been many over several years).

Also to my independent editor, Jack Bates, whose initial red pen obliterations and marking horrified me. I did more pruning than I would for a field full of roses.

My friend and avid reader, Sam Hopwood, who like Jack, gave me excellent feedback and is a stickler for grammar!

Another friend and reader, Margaret Dawson, encouraged me at a low point by reading it all in one day, because she couldn't put it down and last, but not least, my grandson Oliver, who is thirteen and gave me sound advice re the story's structure and content.

When attempting to self-publish, my dismal lack of expertise was clearly evident (and heard by those in close proximity).

If it were not for the services and feedback of Anne Grange, a published author herself – 'Outside Inside' and 'Distortion' are her novels, The Curse of Becton Manor would still be collecting dust on the hard drive!

Although I was so grateful Anne's support, I periodically submitted my story to agents and publishers in the hope of securing a publishing deal.

In April 2020, I submitted my work to 'Burning Chair' a publisher based in the UK. Within a few weeks they requested the full manuscript, but I was afraid to get excited.

The team however loved it. Simon fine tooth combed it, then Pete did the copy edit. It needed more work. I thought 'Oh no, not again' but I am so appreciative of everyone's critique, feedback, thoroughness and honesty.

The story has improved due to all their support. and the work on the front cover has resulted in a well presented novel, thank you.

About the Author

Patricia Ayling is married with five grown up children, several grandchildren and a giddy Labrador. She lives on the border of South Yorkshire and North Derbyshire.

The inspiration for this novel stems from stories of strange incidents in her grandparents' farmhouse in Wiltshire. She also enjoyed researching the last years of the Elizabethan era, including visits to Chatsworth House and Hardwick Hall. The combined interests led to the writing of *The Curse of Becton Manor*, which was completed while she lived in Cyprus.

She is fascinated by what makes people tick and enjoys writing gritty and pacey plots with strong characters.

About Burning Chair

Burning Chair is an independent publishing company based in the UK, but covering readers and authors around the globe. We are passionate about both writing and reading books and, at our core, we just want to get great books out to the world.

Our aim is to offer something exciting; something innovative; something that puts the author and their book first. From first class editing to cutting edge marketing and promotion, we provide the care and attention that makes sure every book fulfils its potential.

We are:
- Different
- Passionate
- Nimble and cutting edge
- Invested in our authors' success

If you're an author and would like to know more about our submissions requirements and receive our free guide to book publishing, visit:

www.burningchairpublishing.com

If you're a reader and are interested in hearing more about our books, being the first to hear about our new releases or great offers, or becoming a beta reader for us, again please visit:

www.burningchairpublishing.com

Other Books by Burning Chair Publishing

Near Death, by Richard Wall

Blue Bird, by Trish Finnegan

The Tom Novak series, by Neil Lancaster
    Going Dark
    Going Rogue
    Going Back

10:59, by N R Baker

Love Is Dead(ly), by Gene Kendall

A Life Eternal, by Richard Ayre

Haven Wakes, by Fi Phillips

Beyond, by Georgia Springate

Burning, An Anthology of Short Thrillers, edited by Simon Finnie and Peter Oxley

The Infernal Aether series, by Peter Oxley
    The Infernal Aether
    A Christmas Aether
    The Demon Inside
    Beyond the Aether
    The Old Lady of the Skies: 1: Plague

The Wedding Speech Manual: The Complete Guide to Preparing, Writing and Performing Your Wedding Speech, by Peter Oxley

www.burningchairpublishing.com

Printed in Great Britain
by Amazon

84135705R00163